WINTER'S
CHILD

Deborah Knott novels:

WINTER'S CHILD
RITUALS OF THE SEASON
HIGH COUNTRY FALL
SLOW DOLLAR
UNCOMMON CLAY
STORM TRACK
HOME FIRES
KILLER MARKET
UP JUMPS THE DEVIL
SHOOTING AT LOONS
SOUTHERN DISCOMFORT
BOOTLEGGER'S DAUGHTER

Sigrid Harald novels:

FUGITIVE COLORS
PAST IMPERFECT
CORPUS CHRISTMAS
BABY DOLL GAMES
THE RIGHT JACK
DEATH IN BLUE FOLDERS
DEATH OF A BUTTERFLY
ONE COFFEE WITH

Non-series:

LAST LESSONS OF SUMMER
BLOODY KIN
SUITABLE FOR HANGING
SHOVELING SMOKE

MARGARET MARON

WINTER'S CHILD

WARNER BOOKS

NEW YORK   BOSTON

Copyright © 2006 by Margaret Maron
Excerpt from *Hard Row* copyright © 2007 by Margaret Maron
All rights reserved. Except as permitted under the U.S. Copyright Act of 1976, no part of this publication may be reproduced, distributed, or transmitted in any form or by any means, or stored in a database or retrieval system, without the prior written permission of the publisher.

Enquiry into Plants and Minor Works on Odours and Weather Signs by Theophrastus. Translation by Sir Arthur Hort. Loeb Classical Library, 1916.

Meteorology: A Text-book on the Weather, the Causes of Its Changes, and Weather Forecasting, for the Student and General Reader by Willis Isbister Milham. Macmillan Company, 1918.

Warner Books and the "W" logo are trademarks of Time Warner Inc. or an affiliated company. Used under license by Hachette Book Group USA, which is not affiliated with Time Warner Inc.

Cover design by Diane Luger
Cover art by Shasti O'Leary Soudant

Warner Books
Hachette Book Group USA
237 Park Avenue
New York, NY 10169
Visit our Web site at www.HachetteBookGroupUSA.com

Printed in the United States of America

Originally published in hardcover by Mysterious Press
First Paperback Printing: August 2007

10 9 8 7 6 5 4 3 2 1

For Marilyn, Linda, Nancy, Lia, Judy, and Sue—
y'all know who and y'all know why
(also the when, what, where, and how).

It might seem that the turbulent squall cloud is very vigorous compared with the gentle air currents which build it, but it must be remembered that the squall cloud is near the axis of the whirl.

—Willis Isbister Milham

DEBORAH KNOTT'S FAMILY TREE

Annie Ruth Langdon (1)

(stillborn son)

(1) Robert — m. — 1) Ina Faye
2) Doris > children (including Betsy) > grandchildren

(2) Franklin — m. — Mae > children > grandchildren

(3) Andrew — m. — 1) Carol > Olivia > Braz & Val
2) Lois
3) April > A.K. & Ruth

(4) Herman* — m. — Nadine > *Reese, *Denise, Edward, Annie Sue

(5) Haywood* — m. — Isabel > at least 3, including Valerie, Stephen, Jane Ann > g'children

(6) Benjamin — m.

(7) Seth — m. — Minnie > at least 3, including Jessica

(8) Jack — m.

(9) Will — m. — 1) Patricia ("Trish")
2) Kathleen
3) Amy > at least 2 children

Kezzie Knott

m. ——

m. ——

(2) Susan Stephenson

(10) Adam* — m. — Karen > 2 sons

(11) Zach* — m. — Barbara > Lee, Emma

(12) Deborah — m. — Dwight Bryant > stepson Cal

*Twins

CHAPTER
1

*The signs of rain, wind, storm, and fair weather
we have described so far as was attainable,
partly from our own observation, partly from
the information of persons of credit.*

—*Theophrastus*

The call came through to the Colleton County Sheriff's
Department just after sunset on a chilly Thursday evening
in mid-January. A pickup truck had crashed on a back
road near Possum Creek.

From the sound of her voice the caller was an older
woman and more than a little upset. "I think he's dead.
There's so much blood, and he's not moving."

The dispatcher made soothing noises and promised
that help would be there very shortly. "Where are you
now, ma'am?"

"Rideout Road, off Old Forty-Eight. I'm not sure of
the number."

The dispatcher heard her speak to someone, then a

second woman came on the line. "Mrs. Victor Johnson here," she said and gave the house number as a man's excited voice could be heard in the background. "My husband just came back from looking. He says it's J.D. Rouse."

"We'll have someone there in just a few minutes," said the dispatcher and put out calls to the nearest patrol unit and to the rescue service.

———

Dwight Bryant, chief deputy and head of the department's detective division, was halfway home and had just turned on his headlights when he heard the calls. He mentally shook his head. J.D. Rouse dead from a vehicular accident? Rouse had been picked up for DWI at least once that Dwight knew of, so perhaps it wasn't totally surprising that he'd crashed his truck.

On the other hand, if he'd ever been asked how he thought Rouse might meet his Maker, he would have said, "Barroom brawl. Shot by someone's disgruntled husband. Hell, maybe even stabbed with a butcher knife by his own wife the night she finally got tired of him knocking her around—assuming he had a wife. And assuming he'd treat her the same as he seemed to treat anyone weaker than himself."

Rideout Road was less than three miles from home. He switched on the blue lights and siren behind the grille of his truck and floored the gas pedal. It wouldn't be out of his way to swing by, he thought, as homebound traffic moved aside for him. His wife—and it was still a thing of wonder that Deborah had really married him—had a late meeting so she wouldn't be there for a couple of hours yet.

By the time he arrived, it was almost full dark, but the night was lit up by a patrol unit's flashing blue lights. A thick stand of scrub pines lined one side of the road, the other side was an open pasture that adjoined a farmyard. There, too, a thin row of pines and cedars had grown up along the right-of-way. Despite the rapidly dropping temperature, three or four cars had stopped opposite the wreck and several people had gotten out to watch and exclaim, their warm breaths blowing little clouds of steam with every word.

A bundled-up deputy was emerging from his patrol car with his torchlight as Dwight pulled in behind him. Dwight zipped his own jacket and put on gloves before stepping out into the bone-chilling wind.

"Hey, Major. You heard the call, too, huh?"

Together they approached the white Ford pickup that lay nose down across the shallow ditch.

"Straight stretch of road," the younger man mused. He flashed his torch back along the pavement. "No skid marks. You reckon he had a heart attack?"

Sam Dalton was a fairly new recruit and Dwight had not yet taken his measure, but he liked it that Dalton did not jump to immediate conclusions without all the facts.

Siren wailing, a rescue truck crested the rise and its emergency lights flashed through the pickup's front windshield. As the two deputies approached the driver's side of the pickup, Dwight paused.

"What does that look like to you?" he asked, nodding toward the back window. The glass had shattered in a telltale spiderweb pattern that radiated out from a small hole just behind the driver's seat.

"Well, damn!" said Dalton. "He was shot?"

A few moments later, the EMT who drove the rescue truck confirmed that J.D. Rouse was dead and yes, he had indeed been shot through the back of the head.

"No exit wound, so the bullet's still in there," she said.

There was an open six-pack on the seat beside the dead man. It held three cold Bud Lights. A fourth can lay on the floor in a pool of beer and blood. Otherwise the interior of the truck was uncluttered. No fast-food boxes or plastic drink cups, but the open ashtray was full of butts and there were burn marks on the vinyl seats as if hot cigarette coals had fallen on them. A smoker, thought Dwight, and a careless one at that. It went with what he knew of Rouse, who had grown up in the same community: a man who grabbed what he wanted with greedy hands and with no regard for what he might be wrecking.

"Looks like he'd just popped the top on his beer when he got hit," said the med tech.

Rouse had worn a fleece-lined denim jacket, jeans, and heavy work boots when he died. The jacket was unzipped to reveal a blue plaid flannel shirt even though it was a cold night and the passenger-side window was open about four inches.

While Dalton secured the area, Dwight called for the crime scene van and a couple of his detectives, then he walked over to the people standing across the road. "Which one of you reported it?"

"That was us," said the older gray-haired man, whom Dwight immediately recognized.

Victor Johnson was a generation older and had lived on this farm all his life, so he had known Dwight's family long enough to speak familiarly, but tonight's circumstance made him more formal.

"Did you see it happen?" asked Dwight.

"No, sir. It was getting on for dark and my wife had just called me to the table when we heard Miz Harper banging at the door. She was the one actually called y'all. Soon as she said a truck'd run off the road, Catherine showed her the phone and I come out here to see about it."

"Was the motor still running?"

"Yessir. I opened the door and reached in under him to cut it off. Knowed it was J.D. soon as I seen the truck. He lives on the other side of Old Forty-Eight and cuts through here all the time. Young man like that?" He shook his head. "And there's that poor wife of his with two or three little ones. Somebody needs to go tell her."

"We'll do that," said Dwight. "This Mrs. Harper. Which one is she?"

"Oh, she ain't here. She was so shook up, she wanted to go on home. I tried to get her to let me drive her, but she had her dog and her wagon with her and I couldn't talk her into leaving the wagon here."

"Harper?" Dwight asked, trying to place the woman. "Eddie Harper's mother?"

"No, I doubt you'd know her," said Johnson. "She's one of the new people."

"She lives just over the rise there," said Mrs. Johnson, stepping forward. "First little white house on the right when you turn into that Holly Ridge development. They moved here from Virginia about ten or twelve years ago. Daughter's remarried now and lives in Raleigh."

The woman paused and beamed at him. "I heard you got married last month yourself."

"Yes, ma'am."

"Kezzie Knott's girl."

"Yes, ma'am," he said and waited for the sly grins that usually accompanied his admission that Sheriff Bo Poole's chief deputy had married the daughter of a man who used to run moonshine from Canada to Florida in his long-ago youth.

There was nothing sly in the older woman's smile. "I knew her mother. One of the nicest people God ever put on this earth. I hope y'all are half as happy together as her and Mr. Kezzie were."

"So far, so good," said Dwight, smiling back at her. "So this Mrs. Harper was walking along the shoulder and saw it happen?"

Husband and wife both nodded vigorously. "She's out two or three times a week picking up trash. Said that just about the time he got even with her, she heard a big bang, like the tire blew out or something, and then the pickup slowed down and ran right off the road and into the ditch."

———

Ten minutes later, Dwight stopped his truck in front of the neat little house at the corner of one of those cheaply built developments that had popped up around the county in the last few years like mildew after a summer rain. No sidewalks and the street was already pockmarked with potholes. The porch light was on and a child's red metal wagon stood near the steps. Its carrying capacity was increased by removable wooden rails and was lined with a large black plastic garbage bag whose sides had been snugged back over the rails. The bag was half full of dirty drink cups, plastic bottles that seemed to have been run over a couple of times, beer cans, scrap paper, yellow Bojangles' boxes, and fast-food bags. A soiled pair of thin leather driving gloves lay on top.

When he rang, a dog barked from within, then the door was opened by a wiry gray-haired woman. She wore gray warm-up pants and a blue Fair Isle sweater and Dwight put her age at somewhere on the other side of sixty.

She shushed the small brown dog, waved aside the ID Dwight tried to show her, and held the door open wide. "Come on in out of the cold, Major—Bryant, did you say? Such an awful thing. Mr. Johnson was right, wasn't he? That man really is dead, isn't he?"

"I'm afraid so, ma'am. Did you know him?"

Mrs. Harper shook her head. "I've seen the truck lots of times, but I never met the driver. Didn't even know his name till Mr. Johnson said it. Probably wouldn't recognize him if he walked through the door."

The house was small—what real estate agents call a "starter home"—and was almost obsessively neat and orderly. Cozy, but nothing out of place. Magazines were stacked according to size on the coffee table, and a family portrait was precisely centered above the couch. Dwight recognized a much younger Mrs. Harper. The child on her lap was probably the married daughter Mrs. Johnson had mentioned. The older man seated next to her was no doubt her father. He wore an Army uniform, as did the younger man who stood in back, almost like an afterthought. Colonel and captain.

"My dad," said Mrs. Harper, when she saw him looking at the picture. "I was an Army brat who went and married one."

"They're not with you now?"

"No. Bill and I split up about a year after that was

painted, and the Colonel died three years ago this month."
Pride and love mingled in her voice as she spoke of her
father. "He was a wonderful man. Would have been
eighty-five if he'd lived."

More family pictures and framed mementos hung in
neat rows along a wall that led down a hallway. "Those
his medals?" Dwight asked. He had similar ones stowed
away somewhere from his own Army days.

Mrs. Harper nodded. "But do come and sit. May I get
you something? Coffee? A nice cup of tea?"

Through the archway to the kitchen, Dwight could see
a teapot and a single mug on the table. "Hot tea would be
great this cold night," he said, taking off his gloves and
stuffing them in his jacket pocket.

He trailed along as Mrs. Harper went out to the kitchen
stove and turned the burner on under a shiny red kettle.
She put a tea bag in a second mug and laid a spoon beside it. The kettle was hot from before and began to whis-
tle almost instantly. "I always find that a good cup of tea
helps settle my nerves," she said.

Even so, she was still so rattled that hot water splashed
onto the Formica tabletop as she filled his cup. "I'm
sorry. It was such a shock. The Colonel used to say—but
he was in battle and war is different, isn't it? I never . . ."

Dwight took the kettle from her shaking hands and set
it back on the stove, then pulled out a chair across the
table from her.

"Could you tell me what happened? Cold as it is, I'm
a little surprised that you were out walking so late with
night coming on. It's not terribly safe."

"I can take care of myself," she said sharply, then immediately softened her sharp words with a smile toward

the dog. "She doesn't look fierce, but she's very protective. But you're right. It was later than usual. I always mean to go early but I'm not a morning person and, I don't know, one thing and another, I just seem to piddle around till it's usually four o'clock before Dixie and I set out."

The little dog cocked an ear at hearing its name.

"The Johnsons say you were picking up trash along the roadside?"

Mrs. Harper smiled and nodded. "I adopted Rideout Road two years ago to honor my father. Maybe you saw the sign at the crossroads? Colonel James T. Frampton?"

As part of its anti-littering campaign, North Carolina allows individuals or corporations to "adopt" a road or a two-mile stretch of highway and will put up a sign to that effect if the volunteers agree to clean their stretch at least four times a year.

"My wife's family has the road that cuts through their farms," Dwight said, "but I don't think they're out picking up litter every week. And for sure not when the weather's this cold."

Mrs. Harper shrugged her rounded shoulders. "It's not bad once you get to moving good. I just can't bear to see trash build up on a road dedicated to the Colonel. Besides, it's good exercise for Dixie and me and neither of us is getting any younger, I'm afraid."

This time, the corgi put a paw on her mistress's trousered leg and she smiled down indulgently. "With all the excitement, I forgot all about your treat, didn't I, girl?"

Dwight waited while she took a Milk-Bone from the

cut-glass candy dish in the center of the table and gave it to the dog.

"Tell me about this evening," he said.

"There's really not much to tell." She lifted the mug to her pale lips, then set it down again. Despite her obvious distress, though, she was able to convey a good sense of the circumstances. "It's so cold that the wind made my eyes water. I had picked up what little there was on the eastbound side and we were on our way back down the westbound side. It was too early for what you'd call rush hour out here and the road doesn't get all that much traffic anyhow. There's only fourteen houses till you get to this subdivision, and most of the people who live here and work in Raleigh usually take Old Forty-Eight. It's a little more direct, although enough do use Rideout. Maybe because it's still country along here? Used to be an older man who would park out of sight of any houses and have himself a couple of beers before going home and he'd just dump the evidence on the shoulder. When I called him on it, he apologized and started getting out and hiding his empties in the trunk. And another time—oh, but why am I going on like this? You don't want to hear about litterbugs. You want to know about tonight."

Dwight smiled encouragingly, knowing how some people have to take a running start to launch into the horror of what they have witnessed.

"Anyhow, I was fishing a McDonald's bag out of the ditch when I heard the truck coming. About the time it got even with me, I heard a loud bang. Like a backfire or something. And then the truck just rolled on off the road. I thought maybe it'd blown a tire."

She hesitated and looked at him. "I was wrong,

though, wasn't I? I hear enough hunters, and the Colonel was in the infantry. It was a gunshot, wasn't it?"

"Yes, ma'am," said Dwight. "I'm afraid so."

Her hand shook as she tried to bring the mug to her lips again.

"Could you tell where the shot came from?" he asked. "Which side of the road?"

"Which side?" She considered for a long moment, then shook her head. "I'm sorry, Major Bryant. It happened so fast. The truck. The bang. The crash. All I know is that it came from behind me somewhere, but whether it was from the woods or the Johnson farm, I just can't say."

———

J.D. Rouse's place of residence was a whole different experience from Mrs. Harper's tidy home.

Three generations ago, this had been a modest farm, but dividing the land among six children, none of whom wanted to farm, had reduced the current generation's holdings to less than two acres. A typical eastern Carolina one-story clapboard farmhouse in bad need of paint stood amid mature oaks and pecan trees at the front of the lot. Dwight seemed to recall that the house was now inhabited by Rouse's widowed mother and older sister. Behind it lay a dilapidated hay barn, and farther down the rutted driveway was a shabby double-wide that had been parked out in what was once a tobacco field. The mobile home was sheltered by a single pine tree that had no doubt planted itself, since his headlights revealed no other trees or shrubs in the yard to indicate an interest in landscaping.

Weather-stained and sun-faded plastic toys littered the yard along with abandoned buckets, and his lights picked up a vacant dog pen and the rusted frame of a child's swing set. The original swings were long gone, replaced with a single tire suspended by a rope. It swayed a little in the icy wind. An old Toyota sedan sat on concrete blocks off to the side, and more blocks served as makeshift steps. When he knocked on the metal door, it rattled in its frame like ice cubes in an empty glass. The place was dark inside and no one responded. He went back to his truck and tapped the horn.

Nothing.

As he started back down the rutted drive, he saw that the back-porch light had come on at the old Rouse home and a heavyset woman was standing in the open doorway, so he turned into the yard beside the back door and got out to speak to her.

It had been years since they had been in school together and he was not sure whether or not this was J.D. Rouse's sister. The Marsha Rouse he remembered had been beanpole skinny, with long brown hair. This woman was carrying at least sixty extra pounds and her short hair was bright orange. She wore baggy gray knit pants and a thick black sweater over a bright purple turtleneck, and she hunched into her clothes with her arms folded across her ample chest as if to stay warm.

If she recognized him here in the darkness, it was not evident by the suspicious tone in her voice as he approached. "You looking for J.D.? He ain't home yet."

"Marsha?" he asked.

She peered at him more closely as he stepped into the light. "Dwight? Dwight Bryant? Lord, it must be a hundred years since I seen you. What brings you out here? J.D. in trouble again?"

"I was hoping to speak to his wife, but she doesn't seem to be at home."

"Naw, she's left him. Packed up the girls this morning and went to her brother's. Is that what you're here about? She take out papers on him this time?"

"This time?" he asked.

She shrugged. "J.D.'s got a temper. Always did. And he can have a mean streak when he gets to drinking too much. Is that why you want to see him?"

Dwight hesitated. A victim's next of kin was usually the first one to be notified, but Marsha was his sister, while his wife was who knows where.

"I'm sorry to have to tell you this, Marsha, but J.D.'s dead."

"What?"

"Somebody shot him about an hour ago."

"Shot him? Oh my God! Who?"

"We don't know yet. He was in his truck on Rideout Road when a bullet came through the back window. We don't even know if it was an accident or deliberate."

An elderly woman in a blue cardigan over a print housedress appeared in the doorway behind Rouse's sister. She was pushing an aluminum walker and shuffled along in thick woolly bedroom slippers. "Marsha? Who you talking to? And how come you're standing out in that cold with the door wide open? You won't raised in no barn."

"Go back inside, Mama," Marsha said harshly. "I'll be there in a minute."

She pulled the door closed and shook her head at Dwight. "This is going to pure out kill her. She thinks J.D. hung the moon."

"You don't sound like you think he did," said Dwight.

"Easy enough to be the favorite if you bring her a Butterfinger every week and sweet-talk her for two minutes and then don't lift your finger to do a damn thing to help out the rest of the time. Nita does more for her than he ever does and she's a Mexican."

"Nita?"

"J.D.'s wife."

"J.D. have anybody gunning for him that you know of?"

"Nita's brother maybe? He cussed J.D. out in Mexican and said he'd put a beating on him if he ever hit Nita or the kids again. But that was just talk. He's not even tall as me. J.D. punched him in the face and that was two months ago. Mexicans, they got hot tempers, too, and I don't know as he'd wait two months and then come after him with a gun, do you? Less'n Nita got him riled up today?"

Dwight sighed and asked for directions to Nita Rouse's brother's house.

"What about J.D., Dwight? What'll I tell Mama when she wants to know where he is?"

Dwight explained the need for an autopsy before the body could be released for burial and promised that someone would notify the family.

———

Back at the site of the wreck, more people on their way home had stopped to gawk and ask questions. The crime scene van was there now and Percy Denning had set up floodlights to facilitate taking pictures that might one day bolster the State's case against the shooter. Assuming they could find him.

Or her, thought Dwight with a wry tip of his hat to his

wife. Not that he needed Deborah's opinionated reminder that women are just as capable of murder as men.

He watched as Rouse's body was moved to the rescue truck to be transported to the medical examiner in Chapel Hill.

Among his officers working the scene was Deputy Mayleen Richards and he motioned to her. "You speak Spanish, don't you?"

Tall and sturdily built with a face full of freckles inherited from her redheaded father, the younger woman nodded. "A little. I've been taking lessons out at Colleton Community."

"Way the state's going, I probably ought to join you," he said. "How 'bout you come with me to tell his wife she's a widow now? I understand she's Mexican."

"Sure," said Richards, grateful that darkness hid the hot flush she had felt in her cheeks when he spoke of joining her in Spanish class.

She lifted her head to the cold north wind, grateful for its bite, and started toward the patrol unit she and Jamison had driven out from Dobbs, but her boss gestured toward his truck. "Ride with me and I'll tell you what we have so far."

With a flaming red face, Richards did as she was told.

Stop it, she told herself as she opened the passenger door of the truck. *He's married now. To the woman everybody says he's loved for years. She's a judge. She's smart and she's beautiful. The only thing he cares about you is whether you do the job right.*

Nevertheless, as he turned the key in the ignition, she could not suppress the surge of happiness she felt sitting there beside him.

CHAPTER
2

He greeted me courteously, and after he had spoke of the weather and the promise of the sky, he mentioned, incidentally, that he was going to Paris.

—*Robert Neilson Stephens*

After court adjourned that chilly Thursday evening, I killed time till my meeting with a quick visit to my friend Portland Brewer, who was still on maternity leave from the law practice she shares with her husband, Avery.

Carolyn Deborah Brewer is about eighteen hours younger than my nearly one-month marriage to Dwight Bryant, and I was still enchanted with both of them. She's twenty-one inches long, has fuzzy little black curls all over her tiny head, and smells of baby powder. He's six-three, has a head of thick brown hair, and smells of Old Spice. I love kissing both, but only one kisses back, and as soon as my meeting adjourned a little after eight, I phoned to let that one know I was on my way.

"I was just about to call you," he said. "I'm running late, too. Want me to pick up something for supper?"

"We still have half of that roast chicken and some gravy from yesterday," I reminded him. "Hot sandwiches and a green salad?"

"Sounds good to me. I'll be there as soon as I drop Richards off and see if Denning has anything else for us right now."

I rang off without asking questions. Denning? That meant a crime scene. And if he had Richards with him, that meant at least one other detective on the scene with Denning.

Which all added up to something serious.

I'm as curious as the next person—"Curious?" say my brothers. "Try nosy."—but a cell phone is not the best place to ask questions. If the incident was something Dwight could tell me about, he would be more open face-to-face over a hot meal.

I'm a district court judge, he's chief deputy of the Colleton County Sheriff's Department, which generates a large proportion of the cases that get tried in our judicial district. We had forged a separation of powers treaty shortly after our engagement back in October—he doesn't talk about things that have a chance of showing up in my courtroom, I don't ask questions till after they are disposed of, and everyone at the courthouse knows not to schedule me for any district court cases where he has to testify. Fortunately, most of Dwight's work concerns major felonies that are automatically tried in superior court, so we actually have more freedom of communication than we had originally expected.

We got home about the same time, and as we put together a supper of leftovers, he told me about the killing. I was surprised, but not really shocked to hear that J.D.

Rouse had been shot. He was a couple of years ahead of me in school and his reputation was already unsavory back then. As a teenager, I may have flirted around with a lot of pot-smoking, beer-drinking boys—the wild boys who drove too fast, sassed the teachers, and cared more about carburetors and carom shots than physics and philosophy, but they were basically good-hearted slackers, loyal to their friends.

Wild is one thing, mean is a whole 'nother ball game.

J.D. was one of those guys who would get a pal drunk and then use him for a urinal. He was a bully and a sexual predator who loved to brag about the girls he'd gone down on, but he had a quick tongue that his buddies found funny when it was turned on someone else and he was good-looking enough that the mirror didn't crack every time he combed his hair.

When I wouldn't go out with him, he tried to hassle me, but I just stared him down and he suddenly remembered whose daughter I was. With several older brothers still living at home and a father who had a reputation for taking care of those who crossed him, my firepower was a lot stronger than his. I think he managed to scrape through high school, and someone said he joined the Army. That was the last time I gave him a thought till he turned up on a speeding charge in my courtroom a couple of years ago. It was not old home week but I did grant the prayer for judgment continued he asked for.

He still wasn't high on my radar screen until this past Thanksgiving when he was charged for beating up on his wife. Despite the bruises on her face and the testimony of the officer who had responded to the 911 call, the woman, a pretty young Mexican with almost no English, refused to testify against him. There was a time when a battered woman could be swayed by her man's sweet talk and "take up the charges," which meant that she would be fined court costs for her "frivolous prosecution" while he walked free.

No more. If an officer charges a man with assault on a female, that man *will* stand trial, and if convicted, faces a maximum sentence of 150 days in jail plus a hefty fine.

The arresting officer testified that there were two little girls in the home and that Rouse appeared to be their only support. In broken English, his wife begged me not to send him to jail, that it was all a misunderstanding.

You never know if a stern sentence and sizable fine will get someone's attention or whether it'll simply stress him out so that he hammers on his family even more. Because this was Rouse's first documented offense, I low-balled it and gave him thirty days suspended for a year, fined him a hundred dollars and court costs (another hundred), and required him to complete an anger management program at the mental health clinic there in Dobbs.

"Big waste of time," I told Dwight. "A person has to want to change for the program to do any good and I figured J.D. was going to have to piss off somebody a whole lot meaner than himself for that to happen." I put the skin and bones of the leftover roast chicken in a pot with celery and onions to boil up for stock, and shredded the rest of the meat. "I wouldn't be a bit surprised to hear his shooting was no accident."

"Be awfully coincidental for a hunter's stray bullet," Dwight said as he put bread into the four-slice toaster someone had given us as a wedding present. "One slice or two?"

"One," I said virtuously.

"I'll get people out walking along the woods and the pasture first thing tomorrow, but we'll have to wait for the ME to tell us if the track of the bullet veers to the left or right enough to indicate which side of the road the shot came from. I'm betting on the woods."

"Because that woman picking up litter didn't see him?"

"And he must not've seen her. Or else didn't care because he was so well hidden." He shook his head pessimistically. "Damn good shooting if it was intentional. Back of the head. Twilight. Moving target."

I added the shredded chicken to the rich gravy I had heated in one of Mother's old black iron skillets while Dwight told me that J.D.'s sister said that he was a roofer with one of the local contractors and that they usually knocked off about the same time every evening so someone who knew his habits could have been lying in wait.

"It's almost like last month, isn't it?" I said, recalling the death of a colleague shortly before our wedding. "Only this time, the shooter wasn't driving alongside, talking through their open windows. Not on that two-lane road."

Dwight frowned. "Actually, *his* window was open, too. Not all the way." He measured four or five inches with his hands to illustrate.

"Did your witness see another vehicle?"

Friends or neighbors who meet on backcountry roads often stop and talk until the appearance of another car or pickup makes them move on.

Dwight shook his head. "Anyhow, it was his right window that was open," he said, following my line of thought.

"Was he a smoker?"

"Yeah. Cigarettes in his shirt pocket. Stubs in the ashtray. Burn marks on the seat."

"There you go, then." Except that even as I said it, I thought back to my own brief fling with cigarettes. It was always my left window that I kept cracked so I could flick the ashes out and blow the smoke away, not the right one.

I started smoking about the time I got my driver's license. It seemed to go with my sporty little white T-Bird. I quit, cold turkey, two years later when Mother was dying from lung cancer. It was part of my attempt to bargain with God: *Please let her live and I'll never light another cigarette, never drive over fifty-five, never get in the backseat with another boy, never skip church again, please?*

Giving up cigarettes was the only part of the vow that I stuck with.

But then God didn't keep His side of the bargain either.

———

The toaster dinged and the fragrance of nicely browned bread mingled with the aroma of bubbling chicken gravy.

But thinking of bargains and litter reminded me. "If it warms up some, Minnie and Doris want us all out Saturday morning to clean up our own stretch of road. It's getting pretty messy."

"I'd love to help y'all," Dwight said with a grin, "but Rouse's killing will probably eat up most of my free time unless we clear it fast."

"You think he was shot by someone in his wife's family?"

"Well, he did beat her up pretty bad this time," Dwight told me as he ladled hot chicken over his toast and helped himself to salad. "Her brother took her to the emergency room last night and she and the kids are staying with him right now."

"How'd she take the news?"

"Started crying as soon as we told her. Hard to say if she was crying for herself or the kids." He added some bread-and-butter pickles to his plate and passed the jar to me. "The brother and sister-in-law weren't shedding any tears, though. Richards couldn't understand everything they said, but the gist seemed to be that it couldn't have happened to a more deserving dog. They started right in planning the wife's new life, how she would move in with them and take care of all the children while her sister-in-law goes to work in the brother's lawn care business."

"The brother have an alibi?" I asked, nibbling at a slice of pickle myself. Their crisp sweetness was made for hot chicken sandwiches.

"Said he was on the job till full dark. Richards will check it out tomorrow."

"Tomorrow?" That reminded me. "Portland asked if we could babysit tomorrow night so she and Avery can go to a movie. It'll be the first time they've both left the baby."

"And they're going to trust us?"

"Who better? You've practiced on Cal and I've been babysitting nieces and nephews since I was twelve. Besides, they figure that if there's an emergency, you could get help faster than anybody else in the county."

"On one condition. Avery got a boxed set of early Marx Brothers movies for Christmas."

I groaned. He knows I hate slapstick as much as he hates chick flicks, yet he keeps trying to get me to sit through endless reruns of Laurel and Hardy or *Fawlty Towers*.

"Did he tell you that Portland's mother gave her the original *Love Affair*?" I asked sweetly. "The 1939 version with Charles Boyer and Irene Dunne?"

"They shot that damn thing twice?"

"Four times, if you count *Sleepless in Seattle*," I said.

"I'll make you a deal. If you can watch *Duck Soup* without laughing, I'll watch Irene Dunne fall under a taxi. Hell, I'll even get you your own box of Kleenex."

———

We were clearing the table and loading the dishwasher when Dwight's cell phone rang. He frowned at the number displayed on the little screen.

"Shaysville," he muttered.

I glanced at the clock. Shaysville, Virginia? Nine-fifteen on a school night? It could be only Jonna, his ex-wife and mother of his eight-year-old son, Cal.

Dwight's voice was carefully neutral when he answered, but it immediately turned warm. "Hey, buddy," he said. "What's up? And how come you're still up?"

He listened intently and I saw a frown begin. "Where's your mom, son? . . . Did she say when she'd be back? . . . Is Nana there? . . . Okay, but— . . . Tomorrow? Sorry, buddy, but— . . . No, I'm just saying that if you'd told me earlier, maybe we could have worked something out." There was another long pause, then his shoulders stiffened in resolution and his voice became reassuring. "No, it's fine. I can do it. How are the roads? It snowed up there last night, didn't it? . . . What's your teacher's name again? . . . Ten o'clock? . . . I'll be there. I promise. Now you scoot on into bed, you hear?"

He laid the phone down with a sigh.

"Something wrong?" I asked.

"Not really. Jonna's out somewhere and her mother came over to sit with Cal, but she fell asleep on the couch so he took advantage of the situation to stay up later than usual and to call me even though Jonna told him not to."

"Not to call you?" I started to get indignant on his behalf.

"He wants me to come to his school tomorrow morning. Says he promised his teacher I'd be there. Jonna told him he couldn't expect me to come running up without any notice, but—" He shook his head ruefully.

"But he knows his dad," I said. "I'll set the clock for four-thirty, okay?"

"Better make it four," Dwight said.

CHAPTER
3

Trees which have been frost-bitten, when they are not completely destroyed, soon shoot again, so that they immediately bear fruit.

—*Theophrastus*

FRIDAY, 21 JANUARY

Even though they had gone to bed at ten-thirty, it had been a heavy week and Dwight felt as if he had barely closed his eyes when the alarm rang at four the next morning. He cut it off at the first sharp trill, but Deborah gave a drowsy groan as he pushed himself out from under the heavy covers. They both preferred a cold room for sleeping and the icy floor was a jolt to his bare feet. The bathroom was warm, though, and the hot shower left him feeling he could face a day that would probably include facing his ex-wife. He had told Deborah the night before that there was no need for her to get up, but when he came back into the bedroom to dress in a dark red wool shirt, black slacks, and a red-and-gray-striped tie, their bed was empty and the aroma of freshly brewed coffee drifted down the hall from the kitchen.

He was tying his shoelaces when she returned with a steaming mug. "You didn't have to do that."

"I know." She used her own mug to cover another yawn. Standing there in an old blue sweatshirt with tangled hair tucked back behind her ears, she was sleepy-eyed and so utterly desirable that without the long drive in front of him, he would have pulled her back beneath the covers. Instead, he took the Thermos of coffee she had filled to help him through the drive, put on his black leather jacket, and promised to be back that night before Portland and Avery got home from their movie.

———

By the time Dwight reached Greensboro, there were patches of snow in the shady spots, and after he crossed the state line into Virginia, more of the landscape was blanketed with Wednesday night's four-inch snowfall. Plows and scrapers had left thick banks of snow alongside the highway, but the January sun shone brightly in a cold blue sky and the road itself was dry. Stifling a yawn, he turned the heater off so that the chill would help keep him alert.

When he tired of NPR's bleak recital of world news, he fumbled through a handful of CDs Deborah had given him for Christmas. One three-disk set held more than seventy Johnny Cash songs, but he'd already listened to the whole set twice, so he popped an Alabama collection into the player instead. As the gentle harmonies of "Feels So Right" filled the truck, he found himself contrasting the two women he had married.

At thirteen, Deborah had been a headstrong kid,

already full of the sass and vinegar she would possess as a woman, and the six years between them seemed so insurmountable that he had joined the Army to avoid temptation. Yet every time he came home on leave and hooked up with her brothers, there she was, more tempting than ever. He put in for special training and was reassigned to Germany, where he thought he was over his infatuation. He told himself it had been a matter of forbidden fruit, an aberration; and when he met Jonna Shay, who was visiting an Army friend in Wiesbaden, he was taken in by her soft Southern voice, her beautiful face, and her slightly patrician air.

"But she didn't fall into your bed right away, did she?" his mother had said the one time he discussed it with her after the divorce. "And there you were, ripe for marriage. Any reasonably compatible woman will do when a man's ready."

And yes, he'd been ready. And no, it wasn't all bad. She had thought he could be molded into an officer and a gentleman, and he was willing to try. He took enough college equivalences to almost qualify for officer training, and with some strong recommendations from his commanding officers and a few bent rules, he made it into OCS through the back door. It was only later, when he was commissioned and his workload eased off a little, that he fully comprehended just how much Jonna felt she had lowered herself by marrying an enlisted man.

After her stint as Mrs. Sergeant Bryant, she was delighted to be Mrs. Lieutenant Bryant, to lunch regularly at the officers' club, and to play bridge with the wives of majors and colonels. In the Army's rigid caste system, enlisted and commissioned seldom socialize, but when she used that as an excuse not to hold a farewell cookout when the friend who had introduced them was being transferred, he realized that she had quietly dropped every enlisted friend still assigned to the base.

Well before they were posted to the D.C. area, he knew the marriage was a mistake. A quick visit home for his mother's birthday only confirmed the seriousness of that mistake. One glimpse of Deborah, newly admitted to the bar, lusty and vital and more desirable than ever, and he knew that what he had felt was not youthful infatuation, that he really did love her. Would love her forever. But she was involved with a state representative at the time and he was married, which meant that she was doubly off-limits. He had made his bed and he would keep sleeping there even though he found no joy in it. He spent long hours at his job with Army intelligence while Jonna kept a serene house and played bridge twice a week. There were no fights, no friction. From the outside, it looked like a good marriage.

Then the political climate changed. A couple of incidents grated on him so strongly that he abruptly resigned his commission and joined the D.C. police. Jonna was quietly furious. Not only did she lose her O Club privileges, she felt as if he had deliberately put her back on the enlisted side of the fence.

After that, they seemed to be simply going through the motions. It surprised the hell out of him when he learned that she had quit taking her birth control pills; but he was willing to try harder for the sake of the baby she had conceived.

With Cal's birth, she quit pretending to like sex, and when she asked for a divorce, he did not fight it.

Nor did he try to stop her when she took Cal and moved

back to the small town in western Virginia that had been named for her early nineteenth-century ancestor, even though the distance made it harder for him to see his son as often as he wanted. Shaysville, on the edge of the Great Smokies, was whitebread America—small enough that most of its middle-class citizens felt they knew everything worth knowing about one another, yet big enough to support a shopping center and a couple of furniture factories. Meth labs were gaining a toehold up in the hollows, but so far there were no gangs, and crime was pretty much limited to petty larceny and occasional drunken brawls.

Jonna's sister, Pamela—"my nutty sister Pam" was how Jonna always prefaced remarks about her—was married and lived in Tennessee and Dwight had never met her; but Mrs. Shay, their elderly mother, was there to babysit and help out in emergencies.

Shay was still a big name in the furniture industry and the factory had not yet moved offshore, but Shays no longer owned it. Shays no longer owned sawmills or lumberyards either. Jonna's father had been the last male Shay, and he died while Jonna and her sister were mere infants, leaving behind a wife who could read French romances, could instruct a servant how to make quiche, and knew the difference between a takeout double and a double for penalties, but Mrs. Shay "enjoyed poor health," as the saying goes, and her husband had carefully shielded her from "boring old business talk." Jonna thought her mother had received a tidy fortune when she sold the last remnants of the family businesses, even though they had soon moved to a smaller house and the live-in housekeeper became daily, then weekly help.

Nevertheless, the Shay name remained high in the

town's social pecking order, and Shaysville was not the worst place for his son to grow up.

After the divorce became final, he realized that the distance between Washington and Shaysville was about the same as the distance between Shaysville and Colleton County, and there was Sheriff Bowman Poole looking for a good right-hand man.

"... *take me down and love me all night long* ..."

When the words of that song floated through the truck's cab, memories of Jonna's cool propriety were crowded out by images of Deborah's impulsive warmth and propriety be damned.

As if conjured up by those images, his phone rang and her number appeared on its screen.

"Where are you?" she asked. "Still in North Carolina? Just passing Durham?"

He grinned. Her foot was always on the accelerator and she loved to needle him about cruise control and slow driving. "Actually, I'm a little less than an hour from Shaysville. Where are you?"

"In Dobbs. At the courthouse. Getting ready to go do some justice."

"Did you get any sleep after I left?" he asked, muffling a yawn.

"I did. How are you holding up?"

"Not too bad."

They talked a moment or two longer, then she rang off and he called his boss to explain where he was and why he was taking a day of personal leave. "I should be back before dark," he said, and filled the sheriff in on last night's homicide.

"Yeah," said Bo Poole. "Richards was just telling me."

"Let me talk to her a minute," Dwight said, and when Richards came on the line, he told her that she was now his lead detective on the Rouse investigation. "It means you'll have to call over to Chapel Hill and attend the autopsy," he warned.

She took the assignment in stride. "And then I'll check out the brother-in-law's whereabouts, see if we can find anyone else with motive."

This was their only active homicide at the moment, and before ending the conversation he asked her to pass on some instructions on other pending felony cases. "I'll be back this evening, but you can call me if there are problems."

"Yessir."

———

Shaysville's elementary school lay on the west side of town and was close enough to the house Jonna had bought with her share of the divorce settlement that Cal could ride his bike to school in good weather. It was a one-level brick sprawl with a couple of mobile classrooms parked alongside the main building.

He was still not exactly clear on why his son wanted him here this morning—all Cal had said was, "And could you please wear your gun and stuff?"—but before he left town today, he planned to find out if Jonna was making a habit of leaving Cal alone with her mother at night. Mrs. Shay was in her seventies now and clearly too old to keep tabs on an active eight-year-old if she fell asleep before he did.

The parking lot had big piles of snow at either end and there were patches of ice where the holly hedges cast their shadows. Dwight parked his truck in one of the visitor's slots a few minutes before ten, and he did not know if he was pleased or dismayed that the only security on view was a gray-haired secretary at the front desk who smiled and said, "May I help you?"

"I'm Cal Bryant's dad. Here to see Miss Jackson. I believe she's expecting me."

"Which Jackson? Chris or Jean?"

Dwight shrugged. "Whichever teaches third grade?"

"That would be Jean Jackson. If you'll follow me?"

She led him through a maze of hallways decorated with colorful posters and student drawings to a door marked "Miss Jean Jackson's Third Grade," stuck her head inside, and said cheerfully, "Company, Miss Jackson."

Halfway down the third row of desk chairs, he spotted his son. The instant Cal recognized him, his little face lit up with such happiness that Dwight immediately forgot how tired he was.

A girl dressed as Snow White stood in front of a map of the United States with a pointer and she stopped talking to stare at Dwight.

The pleasant-faced teacher who came over to greet him wore gray slacks and a blue sweater that sported white snowflakes and a border of snowmen. She told the little girl, "Wait just a minute, Ellie. Major Bryant? If you'll take this chair, we'll be ready for you after Ellie finishes. Go ahead, Ellie."

Dwight sat as he was directed and gave his attention to the girl, who carefully pointed to Florida and explained how she and her parents and her two sisters had driven all the way down to Disney World from Shaysville over the

Christmas holidays. She traced the route with her pointer and named each state in turn, then held up some of the souvenirs she had bought with her allowance.

"Thank you, Ellie," said the teacher. "Cal? You want to be next?"

The boy nodded shyly and walked over to Dwight, took him by the hand, and led him to the front of the room.

"My name is Calvin Shay Bryant and this is my father. His name is Major Dwight Avery Bryant. He's the chief deputy for the sheriff of Colleton County down in North Carolina. Show 'em your badge, Dad."

Before Dwight could move, Cal flipped back the left side of his jacket to show the badge on his belt.

"Show 'em your gun, Dad." He pulled back the right side of Dwight's jacket to reveal the gun holstered there.

"Show 'em your handcuffs, Dad." He gave Dwight a half-turn and flipped up his jacket. "That's what he uses when he arrests somebody."

Another half-turn and "Show 'em your Kubaton, Dad."

Dwight kept his face perfectly straight as his son twirled him around, pointing out each piece of equipment and explaining what it was for. When Cal finished, he turned to his teacher. "My name is Calvin Shay Bryant and this is my show-and-tell." His brown eyes shone as he looked up at Dwight.

"Thanks, Dad," he said and returned to his seat.

Miss Jackson said, "Jeremy, you're up next, so be thinking what you want to say."

She held open the door for Dwight and followed him out into the hall. "What a nice surprise it was when Cal told me this morning that you were coming today, Major Bryant. I know this meant a lot to him."

Puzzled, Dwight said, "He didn't mention me till this morning?"

"Oh, he talks about you all the time, Major, but not that you were going to be his show-and-tell." She smiled and easy laugh lines crinkled around her hazel eyes. "This is a first for us. We never had a parent as our topic before."

"Any chance I could speak to him a minute?" Dwight asked.

"Sure. I'll send him right out and if you'd like to have lunch with him, we go to the cafeteria at eleven-forty-five."

At eight, Cal was still young enough to lack self-consciousness about showing affection, and Dwight felt a primal surge of love as his son launched himself straight up into his arms for an off-the-floor hug.

With his arms laced around Dwight's neck, he leaned back and grinned happily. "That was so cool, Dad! Did you see Jeremy's eyes when he saw your gun? All he has is that same dumb snake he brought for show-and-tell last year."

Dwight set him back on the floor and squatted down beside him. Every time he saw Cal, the boy seemed to have grown another inch and to have matured more in his speech and comprehension. He decided not to ask about the discrepancy between what Cal had said last night and what Miss Jackson had just told him, but damned if he wasn't going to ask Jonna to let him have Cal for the whole summer. If she balked this year, he was ready to take her back to court and get the custody agreement amended. No way was he going to let himself be side-lined from his son's childhood.

"You're not going back right now, are you?" Cal asked.

"Miss Jackson said I could have lunch with you," Dwight said reassuringly. "So you'd better get in there and see if that snake's learned any new tricks since last year."

Cal giggled. "Snakes don't do tricks," he said, but he gave Dwight another hug and scampered back to his classroom.

———

To kill the next hour, Dwight drove over to the local police station. The Shaysville chief was an old Army buddy from D.C. and Dwight liked to touch base whenever he was in town.

"Hey, bo! Long time, no see," said Paul Radcliff when Dwight appeared in the doorway of his office. Like Dwight, he was dressed in casual civvies. He was almost as tall as Dwight, but his hair was completely white and his belly strained against his gray wool shirt.

"How's it going?" Dwight said.

"Slow as molasses. The only arrests we've made all week were two D-and-Ds and a woman who got in a fight with her sister over a lottery ticket. How 'bout you? Jimmy says you gave Cal a new stepmother for Christmas."

Radcliff's youngest was on the same Pop Warner team as Cal.

"A judge was what I heard. That right?"

Dwight admitted that it was.

"Got a picture?"

He obligingly pulled out a snapshot Deborah's niece had taken of them at the wedding.

"Another looker," Paul said with an admiring shake of his head. "And this one even sounds smart. I don't know how you keep fooling them."

They talked trash for a while, then Radcliff said, "Sandy's making her cold-weather chili for lunch. Why don't you come home with me? She'd love to see you."

"Thanks, Paul, but Cal's teacher said I could eat lunch with them." He glanced at his watch. "Speaking of which, I'd better get back over to the school. See you at Easter."

———

Weird, thought Dwight, the way all school cafeterias smell the same. Like the ones of his boyhood, this one smelled of overcooked broccoli with a substratum of sweet rolls or fruit cobbler even though today's vegetables were a choice of lima beans or carrots and the dessert was chocolate pudding. He sat at a table with Cal and his classmates and answered the questions the children posed. But his son seemed a little subdued and only picked at his food.

When Miss Jackson stood, signaling the end of their lunch period, Cal hung back and Dwight said, "Okay then, buddy. I'll try to get up again as soon as I can and we'll—"

"Can I go back with you?" Cal blurted. "Today? For the weekend?"

"Today? But your mother—"

"She won't care. Please, Dad."

"What's going on here, Cal?"

The boy shook his head. "Nothing. I just want to go home with you. See Grandma and Miss Deborah."

"You know she did say you could drop the Miss and

just call her Deborah now," Dwight said, stalling for time to consider what lay behind Cal's urgency.

"I know. I keep forgetting. I'm sorry."

"Son, it's nothing to be sorry about. Tell you what. I'll go talk to your mother. If she says it's okay, then sure."

The boy's relief was so evident that it only increased Dwight's concern, but he let Cal rejoin his class and glanced down at his watch. Deborah should be on her own lunch break about now and he touched her speed dial number.

She answered on the first ring. "So tell me. What was so urgent that Cal wanted you there this morning?"

"Show-and-tell," he said dryly.

"Show-and-tell what?"

"Me."

He waited till she quit laughing and said, "He wants to come home with me for the weekend. That okay with you?"

"You know it is. I'll call Kate and see if Mary Pat and Jake want to do a sleepover tomorrow night."

"He'd like that," said Dwight.

A few years earlier, his brother Rob had married Kate Honeycutt, a widow with a newborn son and the guardianship of a young cousin who was only six months older than Cal. They were expecting their first child together any day now. Although Deborah and Cal were slowly reforging the comfortable relationship that had existed before the engagement, having the other children around helped ease the residual stiffness between them.

"Maybe you should wait till I can get up with Jonna and clear it with her first. I'll call you back as soon as I see her, okay?"

"Whatever. This is going to put you home awfully late, though, isn't it?"

"I promise I'll keep it three miles over the speed limit the whole way."

"Really?"

"Really."

"Wow! That means you'll be pulling in the driveway any minute now."

He laughed and her voice was warm in his ear.

"Love you," she said softly.

"Hold that thought," he said. "I may even set the cruise control for four miles over the limit."

———

Although Jonna had never worked for money until after the divorce, she now held a part-time job at a historic house that had been built by one of her ancestors, but her schedule was too erratic for Dwight to keep up with.

He called her home phone and got the answering machine. No luck with her cell phone number either. According to her server, "The customer you have called is not available at this time. Please try your call later," which probably meant she had switched it off.

He frowned at that. Why would she turn it off when Cal might need to call her?

Next he tried the number at the Morrow House. A recording informed him that winter hours were only on the weekend or by appointment. "Please call between the hours of ten and four on Saturday or one to five on Sunday. Thank you."

Rather than keep punching in numbers on the keypad,

Dwight drove the short distance to the house. No sign of Jonna's car, and she did not answer the door when he rang.

Her mother's house was but a few blocks closer to the center of town, so he tried there next.

There were footprints through the snow that still covered the front walk and the steps were so icy as he walked up on the front porch that he grabbed for the railing to keep his balance. He had to ring several times before Mrs. Shay answered the door. She seemed sightly disoriented and frowned as she looked up at him as if he were a complete stranger, which, considering how seldom they had seen each other, was not that far from the truth.

"Yes?"

"I'm Dwight, Mrs. Shay. Cal's dad. Is Jonna here?"

"Here?" Mrs. Shay looked around in bewilderment. "I don't think so." Then her face cleared. "Dwight? Oh my goodness, come in out of this cold. What are you doing up here? Nothing's wrong with Cal, is there?"

"No, ma'am, he's fine. I just had lunch with him at the school, but I'm trying to find Jonna and she doesn't seem to be answering her phone."

"I know, dear. That's been worrying me, too. She hasn't called since yesterday morning and that's just not like her. She always calls me every morning, but not today. And the young man who usually shovels my snow hasn't come either. I've had a terrible time getting in and out."

"Was everything all right when she got home last night?"

"Was she out last night?"

"Of course she was. You sat with Cal."

His former mother-in-law was shaking her head. "No, I played bridge with my Thursday night group last night."

"But Cal said you were there. He called me. He said you had fallen asleep."

Mrs. Shay frowned. "Now why on earth would he tell you a story like that?"

CHAPTER
4

At one time through love all things come to-
gether into one, at another time through strife's
hatred they are borne each of them apart.

—Empedocles

FRIDAY AFTERNOON, 21 JANUARY

Angry that Jonna would have left Cal alone even for a
couple of hours, Dwight drove back to her house. This
was an older established neighborhood of tidy, single-
family homes sheltered by tall oaks and maples. More
trees lined the strip of grass between sidewalk and pavement. Their branches were bare now, but in the summer
they met overhead to provide a welcome shade. It was
like driving through a green tunnel.

Today, the street had been plowed and low banks of
snow pushed up against the tree trunks. The sidewalks
themselves were clear and cars were parked along the
sunny side, but not one of them was Jonna's. Her drive
was unshoveled except where it crossed the sidewalk to

the street, and he could see that her Honda had stood
there during Wednesday night's snowfall because of the
car-shaped bare spot on the concrete. Her front walk and
step were clear of snow, though. Again, he went up on the
porch to ring and then pound on the door.

This time, from far inside, he heard the bark of Cal's
dog Bandit, so named for the comical patch of brown fur
over his eyes. The smooth-haired terrier was kept caged
during the day whenever they were out.

Dwight walked around to the side entrance and saw
that a narrow footpath had been shoveled out to the car.
He opened the gate and stepped inside. Paw prints
tracked across the snowy yard to where Bandit had gone
to do his business among the bushes at the rear of the
yard. More paw prints mingled with those of Cal's boots
around the base of a half-finished snowman.

Dwight peered through the door window, and Bandit danced up and down in the big wire crate, whining
hopefully.

"Sorry, guy," Dwight muttered and turned to see a suspicious face looking at him from a side window in the
house next door.

He and Jonna mostly limited their infrequent conver-
sations to Cal, and if she had ever mentioned her neighbor's name, he could not recall it; but he went up to the
hedge that divided the two driveways and gestured for the
older man to open his window, which he grudgingly did,
if only for a narrow crack.

"Yeah?"

"I'm looking for Jonna Bryant. I'm Cal's dad."

"Yeah?"

"Could you tell me when she left?"

The man pursed his lips and glared at Dwight. "I don't make it my business to keep tabs on my neighbors."

"I appreciate that, sir, but—"

"And I don't stand around with my windows wide open in the middle of January either."

"But—"

"Sorry. I can't help you."

And with that, the old man pulled the window firmly shut and pushed down the latch for good measure.

———

It took a couple of false starts, but Shaysville was not that big, and eventually Dwight fumbled his way over to the Morrow House. Indeed, as he zeroed in on it, he recognized earlier landmarks and realized that it was only a block or two from Mrs. Shay's house. That must be convenient for Cal and Jonna both, he thought. He felt optimistic when he saw that the walks had been freshly shoveled and that the nearest slot in the half-empty parking lot held a black four-door sedan.

The main entrance of the old stone mansion was locked, but after much determined pounding, an elderly man in a shirt, tie, and gray tweed jacket emerged from somewhere behind the central staircase of the grand foyer. He was tall and thin, with white hair, and he shook his finger reprovingly at Dwight as he approached to speak through the door. "I'm sorry, but we're closed on weekdays."

"I know," said Dwight. "I'm looking for Jonna Bryant."

"She's not here today."

"Do you have any idea where she could be? I'm Cal's dad and I really need to talk to her."

The man hesitated, then opened the door.

Dwight started to unzip his jacket before realizing that the entrance hall was only marginally warmer than outside. At least he was out of the wind, though.

"Oh, my," said the man, who had caught a glimpse of Dwight's gun beneath his jacket. "You're a police officer, aren't you? Isn't that what Jonna said?" His Ben Franklin glasses had slipped down on his narrow nose and he pushed them up with his index finger.

Dwight nodded. "Have you talked with her today?"

The man shook his head and his glasses slowly began to edge back down his nose. Dwight realized that those nerdy glasses, stooped build, and head of silver-blond hair had caused him to overestimate the man's age by at least twenty years. He was probably not much over forty.

"I'm Frederick Mayhew," he said, offering a hand that felt boneless when Dwight shook it. "I'm the director of the Morrow House here."

"Dwight Bryant. From down near Raleigh."

"Yes, Jonna's mentioned you."

"She didn't happen to mention where she'd be today, did she?"

Mayhew adjusted his glasses and shook his head. "Actually, she was supposed to be here today. At least I think she was. No, I'm pretty sure that's right. I called her around ten to see if I'd misunderstood this week's schedule—we're quite informal here during the winter and only work three days a week. Saturday and Sunday, of course, and then either Friday or Monday so we can turn the heat down the rest of the time and save money. Isn't it absolutely wicked how much heating oil costs these days? Anyhow, I thought we'd agreed on Friday this week, but occasionally I get it muddled and I'll come in on a Friday only to find that we'd agreed on Monday."

"Was she there when you called?" Dwight asked, trying to get Mayhew back on track.

"No, just her answering machine."

"Does she usually call if she's not coming in when she's supposed to?"

"Oh, absolutely. She's thoroughly reliable and conscientious. We—the board and I—we feel very lucky to have her. And of course she's a Shay, so she knows the Morrow House intimately."

He picked up on Dwight's blank look and frowned. "Her mother was a Morrow. Didn't you know?"

"I guess it never really registered." For a moment, Dwight felt as if he ought to apologize for his lapse.

"Oh, well, you're not from here, are you? So it wouldn't mean as much to you, would it?"

Mayhew's tone was one of gentle commiseration for Dwight's misfortune at being born elsewhere.

"The Morrows arrived here shortly after the first Shays founded the town in 1820," he said, sliding into what must be a familiar lecture. "They had been merchants and traders in Philadelphia, but down here they were mainly lawyers, judges, and politicians. Judge Peter Morrow, who built this house, was a United States representative at the time of the Civil War. Afterwards, he became even more important as a judge during Reconstruction. It's his youngest daughter that haunts the Rose Bedroom."

"You have a ghost?" Dwight asked, momentarily diverted.

"Oh, yes," Mayhew said proudly. "She died of a broken heart when her lover was killed at Shiloh. Now, Peter's grandson lost the family fortune during the great stock market crash. Took a lot of Shay money with him, I'm afraid, which precipitated his death in 1931."

"That's very interesting," Dwight said, "but Jonna—"

"Yes, of course," said Mayhew. "I do ramble on, don't I? Now what was it you wanted to know about Jonna?"

"When you last spoke to her?" Dwight said patiently.

"Let me see . . . Sunday? Yes, I'm almost positive it was Sunday."

"If you speak to her again, would you tell her to call me?"

Dwight scribbled his cell number on a slip of paper and Mayhew placed it in his wallet with solemn care.

By now, it was almost two, so Dwight drove back to the school and stuck his head inside Cal's classroom.

Miss Jackson looked up from the storybook she was reading aloud to the class and gave a smiling nod to Cal, who immediately shrugged his backpack on over his heavy jacket and joined Dwight in the hall.

"Don't you have a hat?" Dwight asked. "Or gloves?"

"I forgot them this morning," Cal said. The bitter January wind whipped their faces red when they walked outside and over to the bike racks.

Dwight waited for him to unlock the chain on his bike, then hoisted it on his shoulder.

"Cold as it is, I'm surprised Mother let you ride off without them."

Normally, Dwight never spoke critically of Jonna to Cal, not wanting to try the child's loyalties, but there was that bombshell from Mrs. Shay. As they walked over to visitor parking, he said, "Nana told me that she didn't sit with you while your mother was out last night."

Cal's stricken look was all he needed. Dwight put the bike in the back of his truck and stooped to sit on his haunches at eye level with his son.

"This is serious, buddy. Why did you tell me Nana was with you last night?"

Cal's eyes dropped. "Because I knew you'd be mad if I said I was home by myself."

The final bell must have rung, because children began to stream from the building, some fighting against the strong gusts as they hurried for the buses, others pushed along toward the bicycle racks.

Dwight unlocked the truck, helped Cal take off his backpack and fasten the seat belt, then went around and got in the driver's side. He put the key in the ignition and started the engine so as to warm up the frigid cab. The wind had turned Cal's ears as red as his cheeks, and he held his small hands over the vent to let them thaw as he looked apprehensively at his father's stony face.

A cold fury was building in Dwight's head, but he tried to keep his tone mild. "Was she still gone when you got up this morning?"

Cal nodded mutely.

"Well, what did she say when she left last night?"

Cal's lip quivered and his eyes began to fill with tears. "She wasn't there last night."

"Not at all? Not when you got home from school?"

"No, sir," he whispered, half fearfully.

"Son, I'm not mad at you. I'm just trying to understand."

Tears spilled down Cal's cheeks.

"Hey, it's going to be okay," Dwight said.

He unsnapped the seat belt and pulled the child close and let him cry out all his fear and bewilderment. Between sobs, Cal told Dwight that he had not seen Jonna since she dropped him off at school the morning before.

Thursday morning.

And this was Friday.

"I didn't tell the truth last night because I was scared you'd get mad if I told you Mother wasn't here. I tried to call Nana, but she wasn't home either."

"You did right to call me, and you don't ever have to be afraid to tell me anything."

"But Mother said—"

He broke off.

"Mother said what?"

"That I wasn't going to see you as much now that you married Miss Deborah. She said you'd probably have new babies and forget about me."

Once again, his brown eyes filled, and Dwight took that small face between his big hands. "Look at me, Cal. Have I ever lied to you?"

"No, sir."

"I never have. I never will. So listen up. You're my son. You'll always be my son and I'll always love you. I could have a dozen more children and none of them would ever take your place or make me love you less. You got that?"

The boy gave a tremulous smile. "Yessir."

"Good. Now tell me everything you can remember about yesterday."

From Cal's viewpoint, Thursday had begun as a normal day. Jonna had already shoveled the front steps and walk by the time he got up and they both ate bacon and pecan waffles for breakfast. Afterwards, she had driven him to school since Wednesday night's snowfall had left the sidewalks too blocked for his bike. That was the last time he had seen her.

"Did she seem worried or upset?"

Again Cal shook his head.

"Okay, buddy, here's what we're going do," Dwight said decisively. "First we're going to go talk to Jimmy Radcliff's dad. See if he knows anything. Maybe she slid off the road in the snow and forgot to charge her cell phone before she went out. Then we're going to pack your suitcase and you're coming home with me today."

Cal gave him a relieved hug, settled back in his seat, and clicked his seat belt. "Could Bandit come, too?"

"The more the merrier," he said and wondered how Deborah felt about house dogs. Mr. Kezzie gave two of his hounds the run of his house and he had never heard her speak against it. Their own house might be different, though.

———

At the police station, Dwight left Cal happily chattering with the desk sergeant who refereed their Pop Warner games while he went into the chief's office.

"Jonna's gone missing?" Paul Radcliff asked in disbelief when Dwight explained why he was back.

Dwight shrugged. "Cal says he hasn't seen her since she drove him to school yesterday morning. Mrs. Shay hasn't heard from her, and her boss out at the Morrow House says she didn't come in today the way she was supposed to."

"Still and all—"

"Look, Paul. Jonna and I may have our differences, but

she's a good mother. Cal says she's never left him alone before and you know how protective she is. Overprotective at times."

"Yeah. Jimmy said she almost didn't sign the permission slip for him to play football. She thought it was too rough."

"No way would she go off and leave him alone this long."

"Okay. I'll notify the highway patrol to be on the lookout for her car. A blue Honda, right?"

"So far as I know." He stepped to the doorway and called to Cal. "Your mom still have that blue Accord?"

Cal nodded. He looked so anxious again that Dwight gestured for him to come join them and he laid a reassuring hand on Cal's shoulder. "Don't worry, son. Chief Radcliff's going to find her for us."

"Sure thing," Radcliff said. "Bet you a nickel she had a flat tire on one of those snowy back roads that didn't get plowed yet. We'll check 'em all out. I've got your dad's cell number and I'll call as soon as we find her."

———

Back at the house, Cal looked all around to make sure no one was watching—"Mother says to keep it secret"— then retrieved a spare house key from beneath a rock beside the front porch steps and carefully replaced it as soon as he had unlocked the door.

The house felt cool, and when Dwight automatically checked the thermostat in the hall, he found it set at sixty-five degrees.

"We turn it down during the day if we're both gone," Cal said. "Saves on heating oil." He hurried past Dwight, through the kitchen, and out to the utility room to the dog's crate. "I better let Bandit out for a few minutes."

More cold air swept in when he opened the door. The little dog bounded outside and immediately headed for the bushes along the back fence.

Upstairs, Cal pulled his suitcase, a bright red roller-board, from the closet and rummaged through his dresser for the clothes he wanted to put in it.

"Pajamas, underwear, and socks," said Dwight, opening drawers. "Your heavy blue sweater and maybe your sneakers, too, since we didn't get any snow down there."

"I'll go let Bandit in and pack up some food for him," said Cal.

While his son went down to take care of the dog, Dwight packed the things he thought Cal would need. "And don't forget your backpack if you have homework," he called down the stairs.

As he zipped shut the red bag, he remembered toothbrush and toothpaste and went to find them in the bathroom next door.

He had no intention of snooping, but the door to Jonna's bedroom was open and he saw an unfamiliar picture of her with Cal that must have been taken around Christmastime because they both wore red sweaters and Jonna held a sprig of red-berried holly.

He pushed the door wider to take a closer look at Cal's snaggletoothed grin and saw that Jonna's bed, a chaste double bed, was neatly made with nothing out of place. Still the perfect housekeeper—unlike Deborah, who thought it was a waste of good time to do more than pull up the covers on a bed you were going to crawl back into that same night.

Not that Deborah was a slob; merely that she never worried about a little disorder. Their house was for living, not a place to be kept pristine enough to show to prospective buyers at a moment's notice.

A second framed picture was a family snapshot of Jonna, her older sister Pamela, and their parents that had been taken when the girls were still quite young. Dwight had almost forgotten it and he looked closely at the man who had accidentally shot himself before Jonna's second birthday.

Cal's grandfather. There seemed to be nothing physical of Mr. Shay in either daughter. The way Jonna looked now, she could almost have posed for this old picture of her mother. Dwight set it back on the dresser, obscurely pleased that Cal took after his side of the family.

He looked around again. There was very little of the personal about this room beyond those two photographs. Everything else was tidied away into closed drawers and closets. It could be an ad for a furniture store. Again, he thought of the snapshots that cluttered the wide ledge of the headboard on the bed that he and Deborah shared. It was a jumble of brothers and nieces and nephews, of Cal and him laughing in the rain, of her mother and Mr. Kezzie on a long-ago summer day, of Mr. Kezzie and his own mother dancing at his and Deborah's wedding less than a month ago.

He was pulled from those thoughts by the barking dog. Stuffing Cal's toothbrush and comb into a side pocket of the rollerboard, Dwight went downstairs.

"Better let Bandit in," he called. "He sounds cold."

Cal didn't answer.

"Hey, Cal, a little speed here, buddy. I promised Deborah we'd be home before bedtime."

He set the suitcase down in the living room beside Cal's backpack and went to see what was keeping the boy.

He was not in the kitchen, and Dwight followed the barks of the dog through the utility room to the side door. The instant he opened it, the terrier darted inside, shivering from the icy wind.

"Cal?"

Dwight stepped out into the snow-covered yard. There was no sign of his son. Was he still in the house?

"Cal?"

The little dog looked up at him anxiously.

Dwight went back outside and called again, roaring Cal's name.

Beyond the snowcapped hedge, he saw the same unfriendly neighbor appear in the window. This time, the man opened the window without being asked and called, "If you're looking for that boy, he just left with his mother."

CHAPTER
5

If I cannot bend Heaven, I shall move Hell.

—Virgil

FRIDAY AFTERNOON, 21 JANUARY

"How many times do I have to tell it?" Leonard Carlton asked testily, his white hair standing up in tufts where he'd plunged his fingers in exasperation.

"As many times as it takes," Paul Radcliff said, exercising his authority as Shaysville chief of police. "You told Major Bryant. Now tell me."

"There's nothing much to tell. The kid opened the door and let the dog out. A few minutes later, he walked out, too. Mrs. Bryant came out right behind him and took his hand. He didn't want to go at first, but she said something to him and they both came through the side gate, closed it so the dog couldn't get out, then walked down the drive to the street pretty fast and turned the corner, and that was it till he came out."

"By 'he,' you mean Major Bryant?"

"The kid's dad? Yeah."

"Did they get in a car?"

Jonna's elderly neighbor gave an indifferent shrug, and it took all of Dwight's self-control not to pick up the sour little man by the scruff of his skinny neck and shake him till he turned loose something that would lead them to Cal.

Instead, he leaned against the doorjamb and looked through Carlton's window, past the hedges, to the side door of Jonna's house, where Paul, as a favor to him, had his people processing the door, the yard, the gate, and the drive where Cal and Jonna were last seen a bare two hours ago.

Virginia's blue sky had gone a dirty gray and the air felt as if more snow was on the way, snow that could blanket all traces of his son.

What the hell was going on here? he wondered. Why would Jonna sneak around her own house and take Cal without saying a word to him?

"How come you say that he didn't want to go with her?" Radcliff asked.

"Just at first," said Carlton. "When she took hold of his hand, it looked to me like he was trying to pull away and go back in the house. But whatever she said, he quit arguing and it was almost like he was the one pulling her down the drive."

"You said you didn't see them after they turned the corner, but could they have left in a car? Did you hear one drive off?"

"Cars are back and forth all day. Can't say as I'd've noticed. But they did turn to go in front of their house, like they were going over toward Main Street."

"When did you last notice Mrs. Bryant's car here in the drive?"

"Yesterday morning. I saw her drive off with the boy, but that's the last time."

"Can you describe how she was dressed?"

Leonard Carlton squinted his faded blue eyes as if trying to picture again what he had seen. "One of those puffy blue parkas. She had the hood up and it had black fur around the edges." His wrinkled hand traced a circle around his face. "The sun was real bright on the snow and she had on a pair of those . . . what do you call 'em? Wraparound sunglasses?"

"Was the parka dark blue or light blue?"

"More like navy, I'd say."

"Pants or a skirt?"

"Some sort of black pants and black shoes or boots. I didn't notice which."

Radcliff raised an inquiring eyebrow to Dwight. "You got any more questions now?"

Dwight shook his head and Radcliff thanked the old man for his patience. For the first time, Jonna's neighbor thawed a little. "Hope you get up with your boy, Bryant."

———

"Sorry, Major," said one of Radcliff's officers when they had crossed the snow back to the other house. Dwight had provided them with pictures of Cal from his wallet. "We canvassed the street two blocks in both directions. No one saw your son leave. 'Course now, there were a few places where nobody answered the door. If she doesn't turn up, we'll come back and ask the ones we missed."

"We did take good close-ups of their shoe prints in the snow, though," said a second officer. "And good prints from your wife's hand on the doorknob, too."

"Ex-wife," Dwight said automatically, and for the first time since Cal's chilling disappearance, he thought of Deborah, who must surely assume that he and Cal were halfway home to Colleton County by now.

Four o'clock.

She would still be in court with her phone turned off. All the same, he hit his speed dial and left a message for her to call him back.

The first officer reported that a neighbor two doors down saw Jonna come home shortly before eight-thirty as he was leaving for work yesterday morning. She had parked her blue Accord on the street in front of her house and had given him a wave as she went up the front walk.

"We've alerted both the sheriff's department and the highway patrol about the car," Radcliff told him.

"What about an Amber Alert?"

His friend glanced away uneasily.

"Christ, Paul! You know the sooner that's out, the more effective."

"In a true kidnapping, yes, but Jonna *is* the custodial parent, Dwight. I know you're worried, but face it, pal. She's done nothing illegal."

Dwight balled his fists in frustration. "You don't call sneaking my son out from under my nose illegal?"

Radcliff just looked at him. "You know the criteria for a Code Amber. Do you honestly believe Cal's in imminent danger of serious bodily injury?"

Dwight groaned. "Okay, okay, so I'm acting like a civilian. But this is Cal, Paul. What if it was one of your kids?"

"I'd be ready to wring Sandy's neck," Radcliff agreed. "All the same . . ."

"All the same, something's wrong here," Dwight insisted. "Except for a couple of neighbors, nobody's seen Jonna since early yesterday morning. She leaves Cal alone overnight. She misses work. She doesn't call her mother—that's not her normal behavior."

"No, probably not," his friend agreed. "And you can punch me in the nose if you want, but you know I've got to ask. Have you done anything to make Jonna afraid of you? Afraid for Cal?"

Dwight's jaws clenched so tightly that he could barely get the word through his teeth. "No."

Radcliff waited for him to elaborate, then shrugged. "Listen, pal, I've seen you back down a general. You can be pretty damn intimidating when you put your mind to it."

Dwight let out the breath he'd been holding. "I don't hit women and I don't scare little kids. You do what you have to, Paul. Ask the questions you have to. But while you're doing it, I'm going to take this house apart. There has to be something here to tell me why she's gone off with Cal like this."

They agreed to touch base if any leads turned up, then Radcliff returned to his office and Dwight reentered the house.

He let Bandit out of the crate and began in the kitchen with the wall-hung phone and answering machine, whose blinking lights indicated messages.

The first was time-dated 10:17 yesterday morning from Mrs. Shay, who complained in one long, nonstop sentence about her icy steps and walks and how nervous they made her and she wasn't sure how she was going to get out for bridge that night and why didn't Jonna call?

That was followed at 11:48 by a woman who was unsure of where a reunion committee was meeting.

Today's messages started with Mrs. Shay peevishly asking why Jonna did not call and a message from Mayhew at the Morrow House.

There were dirty dishes in the dishwasher and a sticky cereal bowl in the sink where Cal had fixed himself a bowl of cereal this morning. Except for a stray cornflake and a smear of peanut butter on the table, the kitchen was otherwise spotless, which meant that she had cleaned up after yesterday's bacon and waffles. Nothing jumped out at him to show that Thursday had been anything other than a routine morning.

Ditto for the dining room and living room, formal spaces with nine-foot-high cove ceilings and damask drapes that had hung in the house in which Jonna had been born, the house Mrs. Shay had to leave after her husband's early death reduced the family's finances. A large gilt-framed portrait of Jonna's Shay great-grandparents hung over the mantel and a much smaller portrait of a solemn-faced husband and wife hung in the dining room. As Dwight recalled, that one had been a wedding gift from Mrs. Shay. Were they the famous Morrows? He had forgotten the details of how the couple were related to Jonna, but he did remember that when it arrived in Germany she had been quite pleased that her mother had sent it to her rather than giving it to her sister. She had hung it with artful casualness where it was sure to be noticed by visitors to their house—a subtle indication of status among the other military wives.

There was a desk in Jonna's bedroom and one drawer contained hanging files. At the front were folders that related to her work at the Morrow House. One folder held a thick sheaf of papers that appeared to be a copy of an inventory of the furnishings of Morrow House that someone had typed up in 1976, according to the heading on the first page. There were interlineations and notations in Jonna's careful hand of certain items that had been donated to the house since then, as well as a few question marks beside some of the items.

Next came her current financial records. Upon their divorce, her share of their Arlington house had almost paid for this house, and her mortgage payments were absurdly low. She seemed to be living modestly and within her means, which included a few shares of a utility company, the child support he paid for Cal, her part-time salary at the Morrow House, and a small monthly allowance from Mrs. Shay. No apparent savings, but no debt either. Well, she had always been a good manager, never exceeding their budget. Money was something they had never fought about. One of many things they had never fought about, he reminded himself. Except for the occasional cutting remark, Jonna did not fight. Any attempt slid right off her smooth and polished surface.

Personal papers came next—her birth certificate and expired passport, Cal's birth certificate and medical records, a CV that she seemed to have drafted for a job that she never took, and, most surprisingly, a snapshot of himself the day he was commissioned.

The final group of folders held paperwork generated by their divorce settlement and another surprise: an account of his and Deborah's wedding that had been cut out of the Dobbs *Ledger*. Now, who would have sent her that? Or had Cal brought it home with him? The clipping was stapled to a computer printout of the salary range for North Carolina district court judges. Natural, he supposed, for Jonna to be curious about Deborah.

If there were any men in his ex-wife's life, there was nothing in her bedside table or bathroom to indicate it. No birth control pills, no man's razor.

As he and Bandit headed back downstairs, his phone rang.

"Are you back in North Carolina yet?" Deborah asked. "Did she let Cal come home with you?"

"No," he said and quickly brought her up to speed on what Jonna had done instead.

Deborah was instantly shocked and angry on his behalf, especially when he told her what Radcliff had asked. "That's awful! How could she leave Cal alone all night? And how could she do this to you? Let me know the minute they show up, okay? I'll be at Portland's—she and Avery are really looking forward to their first night out— but I'll leave my phone on."

As Dwight clipped his phone back on his belt, Bandit cocked his head and gave him a look as if to say, "What's next?"

"Damned if I know," he told the little dog. "Too bad you can't talk. And too bad you're not a bloodhound."

On the other hand, he told himself, Bandit did seem to understand a few basic words: *Find your ball. Want to walk?* and *No!* He knew his name; he knew Cal's.

"Where's Cal?" Dwight said. "Find Cal!"

The terrier immediately trotted over to the door and looked back at him with an expectant whine.

Feeling slightly foolish, Dwight got his leash, snapped it on, and opened the door. "Find Cal," he said again, and the little dog headed straight for the gate. Without stopping for his jacket, Dwight followed, and when he opened the gate, Bandit raced down the drive and turned left along the sidewalk.

"Good dog!" he encouraged. "Find Cal!"

At the corner, Bandit sniffed around, then pulled Dwight across the street where he stopped short at a spot beside the curb. Dwight could read their shoe prints in the snow. He saw where Cal must have walked up to the car door and climbed in, then Jonna's boot prints went around and left the curb where she had circled around to the driver's side.

With the two of them shivering from the cold, he again said, "Find Cal!" even though they both knew it was useless.

———

Back at the town police station, Paul Radcliff had only one tiny bit of news. "A neighbor across the street heard about our canvass and called us. She said that Jonna drove away around nine yesterday morning wearing a red jacket and a white toboggan."

"Red jacket? I thought that crank next door said it was a blue parka with a hood."

"She must have changed."

"What about the sheriff's department or the state troopers? They spot her car?"

"Nothing yet."

They were interrupted by a clerk with papers that needed Radcliff's attention.

Outside an icy rain had begun to fall and a deputy entered with reports of a three-car collision on one of the town's main streets, which served to remind Dwight that he, too, had other responsibilities.

While Radcliff attended to business, Dwight called his own office. Mayleen Richards had just walked in from Chapel Hill. J.D. Rouse's autopsy had been bumped back by the murder-suicide of three middle-class teenagers in a neighboring county, so it had been a fairly wasted day. She gave him the gist of the ME's preliminary findings. Rouse had died from a bullet that had entered at the base of his neck and lodged against the upper front of his skull in a fairly straight line. It looked like a .45-caliber slug, but she would get it officially confirmed.

When she finished reporting on the rest of their investigation, Dwight told her that he probably would not be in the next day and asked if Sheriff Poole was around.

"Sorry, sir. I think he's gone for the weekend. Anything I can do for you?"

His troubles with Jonna were nothing that he wanted to share with his subordinates. "That's okay. I'll catch up with him tomorrow."

CHAPTER
6

Fabulous tales are not composed without reason.

—Theophrastus

FRIDAY AFTERNOON, 21 JANUARY

Some of Dwight's deputies spent Friday sifting through the life J.D. Rouse abruptly quit living when someone sent a bullet through his head on Thursday night. Before Mayleen Richards headed over to Chapel Hill for the autopsy, she had asked Jack Jamison and Raeford McLamb to backtrack on Rouse's last day.

"Well, shit!" Red Bixley had said when they caught up with him on the job Friday morning. A pugnacious white man with a face as weathered as an unpainted fence post, he was the owner of a roofing company that was subcontracted to a builder in the northern part of Colleton County. "J.D.'s the fourth worker I've lost this week. I thought I was through climbing up on roofs, but if I don't get lucky this weekend, that's exactly what I'm going to be doing come Monday morning if I hope to meet the schedule."

Six men were up on the multiangled roof of the half-built house behind him, and their hammers beat out an uneven rhythm in the frosty air. Another four men scrambled around on top of the adjacent house as a fifth and sixth man hoisted up a fresh bundle of shingles. Both houses were three stories tall and dormers sprouted from jutting angles with no apparent logic.

When asked what kind of employee Rouse had been, Bixley shrugged. "He carried his share of the load. Didn't bust his ass, but probably did as much as any of the rest."

"Was he liked?" Deputy Jamison persisted. "Did you like him?"

Again the shrug. "Would I have a beer with him? Sure. More than that? No, I can't say as I would. He could have a mean mouth on him, y'know? Not with me, but with some of the others."

"Anybody in particular?"

As if realizing that naming names might leave him five men short instead of the current four, Bixley denied that Rouse had mixed it up with anybody in particular. "Besides," he said, "didn't you say he was shot on his way home? Well, he was always first off the job. In his truck and gone before the last man was down the ladder, so none of my guys could've done it."

"We think he stopped to buy beer on the way," said Jamison. "That would've slowed him down a little."

They became aware that the hammering had slacked off as the workmen high above them strained to hear what was going on.

"We're going to need to speak to your men," McLamb told him. "Who was working with him yesterday?"

Bixley grumbled about getting further behind schedule, but signaled to one of the men hoisting shingles to come over.

Juan Lunas listened impassively when Bixley introduced the two officers and told him why they were there. Like his boss, he denied knowing of any serious animosity between Rouse and the rest, a mix of African Americans, Anglos, and Mexicans.

McLamb tried to push him, but Lunas gave him the same shrug his boss had. "He don' like your people and he don' like mine. He works with us, but he don' like us."

"But his wife is Mexican," said Jamison.

A wry smile flitted across the man's face. "Yeah," he said.

Although they had then questioned the rest of the roofers, no one would admit any serious problems with Rouse. Except for Bixley and Rouse, they rode to work together in twos and threes and could alibi one another. "Besides," said one of the black guys, "by the time the rest of us cranked up, he was out of sight."

———

From the building site, there were two equally short routes back to Rideout Road where the shooting had occurred. They had no luck along the first route, but when they came to the first convenience store along the second route, the owner looked at the picture and said, "Yeah, I remember him."

There was a sour note in his voice.

"You see him yesterday?"

"Naw, it was last week. He don't stop here no more."

"What happened?"

"Ah, guys like him piss me off. Think they own the world and like you're gonna go broke if they quit buying from you. If he's in trouble, you can bet he went looking for it. He comes back here again, I'll bust his nose."

Since the guy was at least six feet tall and built like an oak tree, they could believe he was capable of it.

He was still pretty frosted so he did not have to be urged to tell them why. He said Rouse had begun stopping in about two weeks earlier. "The first few times it was for gas, cigarettes, a loaf of bread, or a handful of Butterfingers, and always a six-pack of Bud Light. The last time—I believe it was Wednesday or Thursday a week ago, there were some people ahead of him in line. He popped the top on a beer and took a swig before he'd even paid for it. I told him nobody was allowed to drink on the premises and he told me to shove it. I was ready to come around the counter but he slammed the money down and was out the door. I might've let it go—people spout off all the time—then one of my customers pointed out the window. Damned if that SOB didn't take his ashtray and dump cigarette butts all over the concrete. Not only that, when he pulled out of my drive, he slung his beer can back out the window just to jerk me off. I see that bastard again, I'll ram a beer can right up his sorry ass."

McLamb looked at Jamison. "So where were you last evening between five-thirty and six o'clock?" asked Jamison.

"Right here," the man said. "Watching the plumber snake out one of my toilets. Why?"

———

At the very next convenience store two miles down the road, the manager remembered running Rouse's credit card the evening before. "A tank of gas, a pack of Marlboros, and a six-pack of Bud Light."

"You sound pretty sure of that."

"He's stopped by almost every day this week," the clerk said. "Tells me he's working that new development on the other side of Old Stage Road."

"Yeah? What else did he tell you?" they asked.

"That's pretty much it. I think he said he's a roofer? What's he done?"

"Got himself shot dead," said McLamb. "You sure he didn't have more to say?"

The man shook his head. "Sorry, he wasn't much of a talker."

———

Rouse's sister and mother were only slightly more helpful when the two deputies questioned them later that day.

"Everybody loves J.D.," said his mother, teary and red-eyed.

"Name two," his sister muttered.

"What? What?" the old woman said, putting her hand to her ear.

"I said, especially you, Ma."

"He's a good boy," she agreed. "Brings me a Butterfinger almost every Friday night."

When McLamb and Jamison questioned the sister out

of earshot of her mother, Marsha Rouse named a couple of men that her brother had fought with.

"We took a closer look at his truck this morning," said McLamb. "Seems like somebody took a car key and scratched something on his door and then tried to scratch it out. New marks, too. You know anything about that?"

She gave a crooked smile. "Happened last weekend. Probably Saturday night. He didn't even notice it till Sunday dinner when Selena—she's only six, but sharp as a hypodermic needle. She was looking out the window and said, 'Aunt Marsha, what does D-I-C-K-H-E-A-D mean?' J.D. was mad as I've ever seen him. He was real particular about that truck of his. First brand-new one he ever had, but he grabbed up Ma's sewing scissors and went out there and scratched some more till you couldn't make out what it said."

"Did he say who he thought did it?"

"No, but it must've happened at the Hub Saturday night."

The Hub was a juke joint on the outskirts of Cotton Grove that catered to a mostly white, mostly male crowd. It was dark and dingy inside and the sawdust and peanut shells on the floor were there not to create ambiance but to soak up spilled beer.

A few regulars were helping to hold up the bar that Friday afternoon, but neither they nor the bartender seemed to know anything about J.D. Rouse's scratched door. They did offer up two more names, though, of men who had invited Rouse to step outside within the last couple of months.

Checking out three of those men would have to wait

till the next morning. As for the fourth, the man the others agreed was most likely to have scratched his opinion of Rouse on the truck door, he was sitting in their own jail at the moment. A trooper had arrested him Wednesday night for driving drunk on a suspended license.

———

Deputy Mayleen Richards returned in the late afternoon as shifts changed and she was telling them the ME's opinion about the path the .45 had taken when Major Bryant called.

He sounded a little distracted when she repeated what she had learned at the autopsy, and his only comment after she reported that Jamison and McLamb had turned up no hard suspects was, "Sometimes knowing who didn't do it is halfway to finding who did. You might want to lean on the wife's brother tomorrow."

"Will you be here?" she asked, trying to sound casual.

"I doubt it. Sheriff Poole around?"

"Sorry, sir, I think he's gone for the weekend. Anything I can do?"

"That's okay. I'll get up with him later."

"Yes, sir," she said, swallowing her disappointment.

CHAPTER
7

Even winter produces flowers, for all that it seems to be unproductive by reason of the cold.

—Theophrastus

When Dwight called to tell me about the rotten trick Jonna had played on him after leaving Cal alone overnight—and what the hell was *that* all about?—I was more annoyed than concerned. Yes, she was Cal's custodial parent. Yes, she had the right to leave her own house and take Cal with her if she wanted to.

But to do it without a word to Dwight?

That was spiteful bitchiness pure and simple, a power play executed for no reason I could see except to rub his nose in the fact that she legally could.

Domestic court is full of vindictive parents who play the children off against their ex-spouses, who try to wedge them apart, who poison those young minds against the non-custodial parent. Male and female both, across the whole economic strata, but I didn't think Jonna was like that.

Not that I've ever met the woman. In fact, the only picture I've even seen of her was in a stack of snapshots Cal took when someone gave him a disposable camera a couple of birthdays ago. Honesty compels me to admit that she is a beautiful woman with blue-violet eyes, dark curly hair, and beautifully arched eyebrows. Happily, the only physical feature Cal seems to have inherited from her is the shape of her eyebrows. I can live with those eyebrows because everything else about Cal seems to be Dwight, from his dark brown eyes to his tall-for-his-age build.

During those years after Dwight came back to Colleton County and started pretending he was just another of my many brothers—"Pay no attention to that man behind the curtain!"—he was a handy arm when I was without an escort, a comforting shoulder to cry on after an affair went sour, an ear for listening while I trashed the men who didn't walk the line or live up to my expectations. Every once in a while, though, I'd feel guilty about the imbalance and I'd ask him about his love life, about Cal, about his defunct marriage.

Cal he would always talk about.

Current entanglements? He didn't kiss and tell.

His first marriage? All he ever said was, "Jonna just didn't want to be married anymore. My fault probably."

And that was it until last month, three or four nights before our wedding, in a week where we'd been given way too many parties and had way too much to drink. Lying together beneath the quilts in the darkness of our new bedroom, I told him about my abortive marriage to a good-for-nothing car jockey and he told me about Jonna's snobbery, how she'd decided on her own to get pregnant, and how she seemed to resent the bond between Cal and him.

"I never loved her half as much as I love you, and I didn't love her at all when we made Cal, but the minute I saw that first sonogram? The day I first held him? I don't know, Deb'rah. It was like she had given me this amazing gift I didn't even know I wanted."

A corrosive rush of jealousy swept over me that she had been there first, that she was the mother of the child he adored, that she would always be special for that reason alone. I could give him a dozen children and I knew he would love them all, but none of those hypothetical children would call up that never-to-be-duplicated primal response of holding his firstborn. This was cold hard reality and nothing could change it.

Ever.

The best I could do was swallow my jealousy and accept it. "Cal really is the best thing that's ever happened to you, isn't he?"

"Till now," he'd agreed, stroking my bare shoulder as we lay entwined.

Happiness bubbled up then and washed away my jealousy. Jonna might have been Dwight's first, but so what? I was going to be his last, and I'd had enough bourbon to be generous with his heart. "You don't have to rank us."

He had laughed then, a low chuckle of drowsy contentment. "I know I don't. That's another reason I love you so much."

So, yes, I was pissed at Jonna when Dwight called me that first time. The second time, when he told me that his friend—his *friend*, for pete's sake!—had asked if there was a reason for Jonna to fear him, I was beyond pissed. I was ready to drive to Shaysville and slap the entitlement right off her smug little face.

"She may not be afraid of *you*, but she'd better damn well be afraid of me. I'll unleash Portland, okay? She's great at getting custody agreements amended or set aside. There's no reason why you shouldn't have custody of Cal now."

"Whoa!" he said. "Slow down, shug. Let's wait and see how this plays out first. There may be something going on that we don't know about."

I hate it when he's logical.

He promised to keep me up to speed and I reluctantly let him go.

That didn't mean I was going to let the whole situation go, though.

———

Portland's been my best friend forever and we've always shared everything—well, most everything—from the time we were two small girls that the adults usually tried to separate because of the mischief we could get into together.

As soon as I got to her house and was settled with a glass of wine, I told her as much as I knew about what was happening in Virginia. While she nursed the baby, we ran through all the scenarios we could think of, including the possibility that Jonna had decided to run off with someone so totally messed up that any court in the country would immediately give Dwight full custody of Cal. By the time we were finished, I was back to being angry. After all, even though Shaysville wasn't as big as Dobbs, Jonna probably knew all the good hiding places.

Little Carolyn Deborah made soft piglike snuffling sounds and my anger eased off as I watched her.

Avery came home, did his daddy thing, and agreed with Portland and me that Jonna's behavior was outrageous, but he was more concerned that I write down the numbers for both their cell phones in large numerals and keep them beside my chair. Portland handed me the baby to finish burping her and Avery gave me his now-this-is-serious-so-pay-attention look that he usually reserves for instructing juries.

"When you put her down in her crib, be sure and lay her on her back," he said, and Portland paused in the doorway to tell me how to warm the bottle of breast milk in the refrigerator should their daughter not be able to hold out the whole three hours they planned to be gone.

"Will you people just go?" I said. "We'll be fine. I promise you she'll still be alive and healthy when you get back."

After a couple of satisfactory burps, the baby gave a big yawn and fell fast asleep. I held her for nearly an hour just to watch her delicate brows arch or knit, as if her dreams alternately astonished or bewildered her.

Eventually, my arm went numb, so I carried her up to her crib and carefully eased her in without waking her. And yes, I did put her on her back. I'm not comfortable sleeping on mine, but this is the current baby-rearing wisdom, and who am I to argue what's comfortable for a one-month-old with a super-cautious tax attorney for a father?

As I settled into the book I'd brought along so I could look intelligent when my book club meets next week, my phone rang and my brother Seth's wife, Minnie, asked if she was interrupting anything.

I explained that I was babysitting for Portland and she

very nicely inquired about my little namesake's progress before she came to the point of her call. "Doris says the Weather Channel's prediction is for that cold front to pass north of us and we're due for sunshine and mid-fifties tomorrow, so we're calling around to see who can help us clean our road. You and Dwight free tomorrow morning?"

"I am, but Dwight's gone up to see Cal and I'm not sure when he's getting back."

"Nothing's wrong, is there?" she asked perceptively.

Minnie's one of my favorite sisters-in-law, and she would be discreet if I asked her, but I wasn't ready to start this story around the family. Instead, I told her how Cal had persuaded Dwight to drive up and be his show-and-tell. She laughed and invited me to come for breakfast. "If we get started by nine, we should be done before noon. Remember to bring a pair of old gloves."

I promised I'd be there.

I roamed the house, poured myself a second glass of wine, and tried to settle back into the book, but it was a pompous tome full of coming-of-age angst, and when my phone rang again I snatched it up eagerly.

"Still no word," Dwight said. He sounded drained and exhausted, and after hearing the nonproductive details of how and why there was no word, I asked him if he'd had any supper.

"Paul brought me home with him," he said.

I heard a woman's voice in the background.

"Sandy says tell you hey. They want you to come up next time so they can meet you."

"Tell her hey back and anytime. Are you spending the night there?"

"No, I'll go back to Jonna's house and crash on the couch in case they come back tonight."

I told him that the family would be picking up road litter the next morning, which reminded me of J.D.'s death. "Did the autopsy tell anything?"

"Nothing useful. I spoke to Richards about an hour ago and she says there wasn't enough deviation to tell which side of the road it came from. The bullet entered almost at the center of the nape of his neck and lodged in his skull just below the hairline of his forehead. The ME thinks he might have been looking down a little, but hell, Deb'rah. He could have had his head turned to either side just as easy. They're checking the alibis of all his known enemies. Sounds like there's a line of 'em."

"I miss you," I said.

"Yeah, me too. Our first night apart."

"Bound to happen sooner or later."

"I guess. But let's not make a habit of it, okay?"

"Okay," I said.

CHAPTER
8

There is time for many words, and there is also a time for sleep.

—Homer

FRIDAY NIGHT, 21 JANUARY

"You sure you don't want to stay over with us tonight?" Sandy Radcliff asked when the last biscuit had been eaten and Dwight had refused the offer of dessert. "Jimmy can bunk in with Nick and you could have his room."

"Thanks, Sandy, but I ought to check on Cal's dog. Besides, if there's any chance at all that Jonna might bring him home tonight . . ."

It was only eight-thirty and Sandy and Paul were good friends, but Dwight was too beat to spend the evening making small talk.

"You go and get a good night's rest," Sandy said. "Things will look better in the morning, right, hon?"

"Sure thing," said Paul. "I'll call if we hear anything."

"Thanks, pal," he said and trudged out through the freezing rain to his truck for the short drive over to Jonna's house, which was still dark and empty when he got there.

The stone with the door key beneath it was frozen to the ground. He pried it up, then nearly slipped going up the ice-glazed steps. All the same, when he had unlocked the front door, he went back into the rain and sleet to replace the key in the weary hope that Cal might find his way back and need it.

Inside, Cal's rollerboard and backpack lay at the foot of the stairs just where they had left them. Only hours ago. It seemed more like a week.

Bandit gave a welcoming bark from his crate in the utility room and Dwight let him out into the backyard for a few minutes, then dumped dog food into an empty bowl. As soon as the terrier finished eating, he trotted through the house and up the stairs to Cal's room. Dwight followed.

The thermostat was still set at sixty-five, and he didn't bother turning it up because he never slept well in a warm room.

He had intended to find pillows and blankets and bed down on the couch, but there was Cal's unmade bed with Bandit curled up at the foot in what must be his usual place, so after using the bathroom, Dwight shucked off his jacket, pants, and shirt, checked that the safety was on before he put his gun under the pillow, then switched off the light and crawled in beneath the comforter.

It felt so good to lie down and stretch out that he let his mind go blank with sheer exhaustion while frozen raindrops beat against the window outside.

He was almost asleep when he remembered the conflicting reports of how Jonna was dressed today. A neighbor down the street had said she was wearing a red jacket and a white toboggan when she left home in midmorning on Thursday. The next-door neighbor said she had on a blue hooded parka when she took Cal this afternoon.

Despite his protesting muscles, he heaved himself out of bed, switched on lights, and went into Jonna's room. There was no red jacket in her closet.

With Bandit at his heels, he went back downstairs and checked out both the front closet and the coat hooks in the utility room.

No red jacket. No blue parka either.

So where had she changed coats? At her work?

Too tired to keep worrying at the puzzle, he went back to Cal's room. Within minutes he was sound asleep.

———

He awoke at first light the next morning from troubled dreams, his T-shirt and the sheet beneath him damp with sweat. Sometime during the night, he had pushed off the comforter, but it was not enough. The room was inexplicably hot and stuffy. He rolled over and saw that the door was closed even though he had left it open. Hot air rushed up through the floor vent beneath the window.

And where was the dog?

Automatically, his hand went to the gun beneath his pillow. With all his senses on full alert, he slid on his pants and eased open the door. The house was silent, but a welcome rush of cooler air swept past him.

"Jonna?" he called. "Cal?"

No answer.

Bandit barked from the foot of the stairs and he hurried down, the gun still in his hand.

The front door stood slightly ajar, which explained why the heating system was working overtime. Chilled by more than the cold north wind whipping through, Dwight clearly remembered locking that door behind him when he came in last night. And something else was wrong. His eyes swept the entry area.

Cal's backpack was still there but his wheeled suitcase was unzipped and the sweater that Dwight had packed for him was now gone.

Jonna must have come back during the night, heard him snoring, and took what she came for without waking him. Surely it was not for a sweater alone?

He walked through the house to see what else she might have taken. He had no idea what clothes she owned, but there did not seem to be any gaps in her closet. All the drawers were still closed and did not appear to have sustained a hasty rummage. After a thorough examination of the house, the only other sign that she had been there was the medicine cabinet in the bathroom. The sliding mirror was half open, and despite his exhaustion, he was almost positive that he would have noticed had it been that way when he splashed water on his face last night. There were empty spaces on the glass shelves inside, but he was clueless as to what those spaces had held.

He picked up a bottle of antihistamine and noted the name of the doctor who had prescribed it. Maybe he would know what Jonna had come back for.

It was only six-thirty, too early to call Paul.

Instead, he finished dressing, fed the dog, and put him in the wire crate before heading back through the house.

Outside, tree branches drooped to the ground under the weight of the ice they carried. Every individual needle of the evergreens and each separate twig of the oaks and maples was encased in crystal. A few limbs had even snapped off. Overhead, the sky was still a dreary gray with no break in the solid cloud cover for the sun to shine through and start melting the ice.

Before locking the front door, he thought to check for the key. It was no longer under the rock.

Now, why would Jonna take that key when she had her own? Unless Cal—? No, it couldn't have been Cal. His son would surely have waked him. But it had to be one of them because Bandit was a barker, and no matter how tired he was, Dwight was certain he would have heard barks had there been any.

When he and Jonna were still married, she used to hang their spare keys on a closet nail. A neat, methodical woman with a place for everything and everything in its place, she had done it in Germany and again in Arlington, so now?

He slid his fingers along the inner jamb of the front closet door and immediately touched the nail. Two keys, and one of them fit the front lock.

He put it on his own keyring, then slowly drove along the ice-slick streets, nearly fishtailing at a stoplight, until he found an open diner. After pancakes, sausage, and three cups of weak coffee, he stopped by a drugstore and picked up shaving gear and other toiletries. He would have liked fresh underwear and a fresh shirt, too, but nothing else was open this early on a Saturday morning. The sand trucks were out, though, and Jonna's street had been sanded by the time he got back to the house.

He showered and shaved and was lavish with the new stick of deodorant. It would have to do till he could get clean clothes.

8:00.

Deborah liked to sleep in on Saturday mornings, but if Minnie was expecting her for breakfast, surely she'd be up by now.

"Just got out of the shower," she said. "I'm standing here drying off. You get any sleep last night?"

He told her what he'd found when he woke up this morning and they kicked it back and forth.

"Something else is going on with her," Deborah said. "There has to be. Have you talked to her girlfriends?"

"I don't know any of her friends."

"Then ask her mother. Ask her boss. Hell, ask Cal's teacher. I don't have to tell you how to do your job. But once you get a couple of names, they'll give you some more, and sooner or later, you'll get to whoever's hiding them."

"You're right," Dwight conceded. "I'm not thinking straight."

"This is why they don't let doctors operate on their own kids."

"Yeah. I need to quit acting like a dad and start acting like a cop."

"You're a good dad." Her voice softened. "And a very good cop."

"Who let his son be taken right from under his nose," he said glumly.

"Don't beat up on yourself, okay? There's no way you could have expected Jonna to do something like this."

After they hung up, Dwight went looking for an

address book and found one beside the kitchen phone. He leafed through it, trying to deduce which names were personal friends who might could offer suggestions or information about his ex-wife.

8:15.

Too early to start calling strangers. Instead, he dialed Paul's number.

"Radcliff here."

"Hey, Paul. Dwight."

"I was just about to call you," his friend said.

"You've got something?" Dwight asked eagerly.

"Not the way you mean. Sorry. I'm at the office reading old background reports. You want to come over?"

"Be right there."

He grabbed up the address book and took it with him on the off chance that Paul could help him sort out the names.

———

At the police station, Paul handed him a mug of strong black coffee and listened attentively while Dwight told him about his nocturnal visitation.

"You know, bo, when Jonna walked away with Cal yesterday, I thought maybe she was just ticked off at you for something. And yeah, I put my people through the motions for you, but it was a slow day and there wasn't much going on here."

He hesitated.

"But now?" Dwight prodded.

"But now I've got to say, whatever Jonna's up to, it doesn't feel normal. My chief clerk grew up here. Her dad was coroner when she was a kid so she knows a lot of the stuff the town tries to keep quiet. She put me onto this." He tapped the open folder that lay on the desk in front of him. "Did you know that Jonna's daddy shot himself?"

Dwight nodded. "Yeah. She told me about it. She was just a baby when it happened, though, and I don't think her mother ever wanted to talk about it much. He was cleaning a gun and didn't know it was loaded, right?"

"That was the official story that got in the paper," said Radcliff. "You might want to read between the lines of these."

Radcliff slid the folder over to Dwight. In addition to the autopsy report, there were several written statements collected by the officers who had worked the incident nearly forty years ago, when the sudden death of one of the town's most prominent businessmen would have been a noteworthy event. Not that there was anything suggestive in the one clipping that detailed the "tragic accident."

The police reports were a different matter. His doctor stated that Eustace Shay had been subject to bouts of depression for years, which probably contributed to his poor business decisions, which led to losing control of Shay Furniture.

According to his secretary's statement, he had been asked to vacate his corner office so that the new president could move in. On that day, he had overseen the packing up of his belongings, and she had stepped out to fetch someone to carry down the heavy boxes while he saw to the last of his personal items. "I had barely closed the door when I heard a gun go off and rushed back in."

That part was supported by other workers in the office. They did not support her assertion that he had been laughing and joking about early retirement and how he was planning to spend his first week of freedom fishing for bass out at the lake. When asked if suicide was a possibility, however, the others had apparently more or less shrugged, while the secretary was adamant that "Mr. Shay would *never* do that to his wife and those sweet baby girls."

Jonna's mother had agreed. Yes, her husband had been upset about business but she certainly did not think he was *that* upset. The gun? A family heirloom that her husband had enjoyed displaying. "I'm sure we never realized it was loaded."

Dwight closed the folder. "Interesting, but I don't—"

"Did you see the gun he used?"

Dwight flipped back through the reports. "An old Colt revolver?"

"Not just any old Colt revolver. It was a silver-plated, engraved presentation piece given to Peter Morrow for using his influence to spare Shaysville the worst of Reconstruction. It's also the same gun Edward Morrow used to kill himself in 1931."

"Huh?"

"My clerk says that her dad and the guy who was police chief back then managed to keep that little fact out of the papers because they didn't want to sensationalize things. As soon as I heard that, I called the Morrow House director at his house."

"Mayhew? Jonna's boss?"

Radcliff nodded. "That's where the gun is now. According to Mayhew, Jonna's mother inherited it from her father and she was real proud of it even though her own granddaddy had shot himself with it. After Mr. Shay's death, she decided it was cursed and wanted to destroy it. Mayhew says it took a lot of talking, but the Historical Society eventually persuaded her to give it to the Morrow House. It's on display out there now, but of course there's nothing on the card to tell that the gun was ever fired."

"Why are you telling me all this?" Dwight asked his friend.

Radcliff's eyes dropped and he hesitated for a moment. "Maybe it doesn't mean anything, Dwight, but my clerk says her dad used to say there was talk that Eustace Shay was a little unstable even before he accidentally-maybe-on-purpose shot himself. His mother was reputed to be a little bit odd herself, used to wander around talking to people who weren't there. And some say Jonna's sister's not all that tightly wired either. 'Course, that may be because she's something of an alcoholic."

Dwight immediately saw where Radcliff was heading and shook his head. "And you're thinking Jonna's come unglued, too?"

His friend shrugged. "Well, she's sure not acting normal, is she?"

Before Dwight could argue that he'd never seen any signs of mental instability in his ex-wife, Radcliff's phone rang. The chief had barely identified himself when Dwight heard a loud excited voice practically screaming through the earpiece.

"Slow down!" Radcliff said. "You're not making sense." He listened intently, then said, "Stay put. We'll be right out."

He pushed himself up from the desk. "You'd better come, too. That was Mayhew. That damn gun and two others have gone missing from their display case."

CHAPTER
9

*The constant statements by the older people, that
the winters were colder or the summers hotter
than now, are due to the tendency to magnify
and remember the unusual while the ordinary is
forgotten.*

—Willis Isbister Milham

The Saturday morning air nipped at my face as I left
home to go pick up road litter with my family, but the sun
had already begun to warm up the day. I wore my oldest
boots, jeans, and two layers of ratty sweatshirts beneath a
light jacket so that I could peel down if the temperature
really did get into the high fifties. It took me a while to
find an old pair of work gloves, but I still made it to Minnie and Seth's before all the sausage biscuits disappeared.

Their kitchen was full of brothers and sisters-in-law
who live out here on the farm as well as those of their
children who are still at home. Daddy sat at the table
beaming. He likes it when the family comes together on
a project.

"Us Knotts, we've been keeping up this road for over a hundred years," he said, waving away the extra biscuit Doris tried to press on him. "My granddaddy was a road captain back 'fore nineteen-hundred."

"What was that?" asked Seth's daughter Jessica.

"Means being in charge of a stretch of road. When my pa was a boy, he used to go help Grampa lay off his mile." He smiled down at young Bert, grandson of Robert, my oldest brother. "How you reckon they measured it, little man?"

"Drove his car down it?"

"Naw, won't no cars out here back then."

The child was old enough to know about odometers but too young to conceive of a world without cars, and his brow furrowed with the concept.

"What they done," said Daddy, "was measure around the rim of his wagon wheel and tie a white rag on it. Pa kept count and when that rag come up five hundred times, that was one mile."

"There couldn't have been plastic bags back then either," said Jess, "so what did they pick up the trash in? Bushel baskets?"

"Won't no trash," said Daddy. "Won't nothing much to throw away 'cause stuff didn't come in paper wrappers like today and they won't no hamburger places anyhow. Folks using this road was all farmers who ate at their own tables and growed most of their food. You'd give your table scraps to the dogs or the pigs and you'd burn your trash in a barrel. What couldn't be burned, you put on your own trash pile back in the woods. You surely didn't go flinging it in your neighbor's front ditch."

"So why'd they need a road captain?" asked A.K., Andrew and April's teenage son.

" 'Cause the road won't nothing but dirt. Soon as Grampa got his section marked, he'd call out all the neighbor men and boys to help. They'd come with their mules and plows and hoes and shovels and they'd work all day cleaning out the ditches so the water would drain. Then they'd smooth out the roadbed and fill in the holes. 'Course it never lasted long. Three or four good hard rains and it was a pigmire again."

"Our road won't paved till I was in high school," Robert chimed in. "Many a winter morning the bus would get stuck and we'd have to slog up the hill from the creek in mud higher'n the laces on our brogans."

"That little hill?" scoffed Jess.

"That was before they graded it down and built the high bridge that's there now," Seth told her. "The road used to run right down to creek level and up again."

"Everybody got enough bags?" asked Minnie, clearing away the last of breakfast. "Quicker we get started, the quicker we'll be finished."

Someone had dumped an old couch in the ravine by the creek, so A.K. and Reese volunteered to start with that. There was a time when Reese was so truck proud you had to wash your hands and wipe your shoes before he'd let you get in the cab. Now it's just an old work-horse, and I rode with them down to where our road begins at Possum Creek. A small green-and-white sign noted that this road had been adopted by the Kezzie Knott family.

While my nephews wrestled the couch up the bank and into the back of the truck, I picked cans and broken beer and wine bottles off the rocks beneath the bridge. We filled two garbage bags out of the creek alone and slung them in beside the couch. Our efforts netted us two pieces of junk mail and a telephone bill with the names and addresses still intact, and those we saved in a smaller bag so that Minnie or Doris could report them to the county zoning department, who would call the offenders with the warning that a second call might mean a thousand-dollar fine and community service.

We found every kind of trash imaginable, from dirty disposable diapers and three hubcaps to a bag of wadded-up Christmas wrapping paper and a strip of chrome that Reese thought had fallen off a friend's motorcycle. While we worked, I told them about the sackful of marijuana someone had found behind a tree on a ditchbank a few counties over.

"Better'n that dead dog I found in a box last summer," said A.K. "Remember?"

They had heard about J.D. Rouse getting shot in front of a woman picking up road litter Thursday evening and wanted to know if Dwight had found the shooter yet.

I was standing down in the ditch when they asked, and I glanced over my right shoulder to where young pines fringed the woods that bordered the road there. My head was barely level with the upper bank.

"Run up yonder in the trees," I told Reese.

"Huh?"

"I just want to get a feel for why the killer shot past somebody. Get far enough back in the pines so that you can see the truck but you're mostly hidden."

"Dwight deputize you or something?" Reese grumbled, but he climbed the bank and did as I'd asked. A minute later, he called, "Here, okay?"

"Can you see the truck?"

"Yeah, but I can't see you."

From my position in the ditch, I couldn't see him either.

"I bet the guy didn't think anybody was anywhere around," said A.K., who'd watched with interest. "If I didn't know Reese was back there, I would never've noticed him till he moved, and this is with the sun shining. Been getting on for dark and he stood still, wouldn't anybody see him."

My theory exactly and, despite Reese's smart-mouthing, one I'd share with Dwight when he got home because I drive past the Johnson farm all the time and know its layout. If the shooter had been in the pasture, he and the Harper woman would have surely seen each other.

I took a fresh bag and they drove on down to the others to pick up some of the filled bags and take a first load to the county dumpsters at Pleasant's Crossroads, about four miles away.

Our road connects Old Forty-Eight to a shortcut that leads to Fuquay and eventually to Chapel Hill, so we get our share of traffic. All the same, it was appalling to see how much trash had been thrown out, most of it from fast-food places. As I picked up yet another paper clamshell from Wendy's and retrieved a bunch of unused napkins with the McDonald's logo, I kept remembering Cedar Gap, the pretty little mountain resort town where I'd held court last fall.

"I thought they were just being prissy to ban all fast-food chains," I told Minnie and Doris when I caught up with them. "Now I see their point. Seems like there's a lot more today than the last time we did this."

"It's that new shopping center," said Doris as she stooped for a cardboard Bojangles' tray. "Fast food's not to blame. It's the trashy people who won't keep a litter bag in their car."

With so many of us working, we finished well before noon and gathered at the barbecue house for lunch, Daddy's treat.

"We don't need to wait so long to do this again," said Doris. "I was getting right ashamed to have our name on that sign."

Now that the job was over, it was easy to agree with her.

———

As we rode back to Seth's for me to pick up my car, a silver Acura zipped around us. Just as it entered the rising curve ahead, we saw a telltale yellow-and-red bag go flying out the window onto the shoulder and bounce down into the ditch.

"What the hell?" cried Reese.

Enraged, he floored the accelerator, flashing his lights and blowing his horn.

"Write down their license number," he yelled, reading it off to us.

"No pencil," said A.K., who was also cursing the driver ahead.

I was equally furious. Less than an hour after we'd cleaned our road and somebody was already trashing it?

"If I catch him, can we make a citizen's arrest?" Reese asked.

"Go for it, Gomer," I said. All I had in my pocket was a lipstick, but I used it to write the number on my hand in case the car got away.

That wasn't necessary, though. Bewildered by the lights and horn, the Acura slowed and pulled to a stop in front of Doris and Robert's drive.

Reese was out of the truck before it quit rolling and I made A.K. put down the window on that side.

"What's wrong?" asked the teenage driver.

"I'll tell you what's wrong, you jerk!" Reese shouted as he approached the car. "What the hell kind of slob are you to dump your fu—fricking garbage out the window?"

I admired his restraint. Angry as he was, he'd realized at the last minute that the driver was a shorthaired girl instead of a guy.

"Huh?" The girl looked past Reese and recognized my other nephew. "A.K.?"

"Sorry, Angie," he said, "but we just spent the whole morning cleaning up the road and the first time we drive back down it, we see you trashing it."

The girl had the grace to look embarrassed. She apologized and offered to go back and pick up the Bojangles' bag.

Mollified but still steamed, Reese pulled his truck forward so that she could turn around and then he sat there with his engine running till he saw her get out of her car and retrieve the bag.

A.K. was also watching in the side-view mirror. "Okay, she's got it, so let's go," he said. He seemed almost as embarrassed by the incident as the girl.

Reese grinned at his discomfort, but drove on down to Seth and Minnie's, where he came to a stop beside my car. "Girlfriend of yours?"

"A friend, not a girlfriend. I mean, a friend who happens to be a girl."

Reese and I were both laughing by then.

"Oh, the hell with both of you!" He jumped out of the truck and headed for his own wheels.

"She was cute," said Reese. "All the same, I bet she thinks twice before she shoves her trash out a window again."

CHAPTER
10

They are honest in their dealings with one another. Wherefore no one keeps watch.

—*Theophrastus*

SATURDAY MORNING, 22 JANUARY

Despite the cold, the director of the Morrow House was pacing the flagstone terrace out front in his shirtsleeves when Dwight and Paul Radcliff arrived, followed by a couple of Radcliff's officers.

"Thank goodness you're here!" said Frederick Mayhew. His teeth were chattering, but whether from anxiety or the frosty air was hard to say. "I simply don't know what to think. Everything was locked and I'm sure the alarm system was set when I left. We've never had a robbery before. Oh, some of the children might pick something up—we did lose a doll bonnet once but the child's mother made her bring it back—but this!"

He opened the door for them so vigorously that it

banged hard against the wrought-iron stop and Dwight almost expected the beveled glass to shatter.

"We keep them in the library," Mayhew told them and led the way through the spacious entrance hall and large front parlor to a smaller room lined with bookcases. "There!"

On a rectangular oak library table that stood in the center of the room sat a glass-topped display case. An empty glass-topped display case.

Indentations in the crushed red velvet marked the places where a small derringer, a dueling pistol, and a long-barreled revolver, each neatly labeled, once lay. The case was closed but not locked, as Mayhew quickly demonstrated, yet there appeared to be no scratches on the lock itself.

"Who else knows how to work the alarm system?" asked Radcliff.

"Just Jonna."

"And when's the last time you saw the gun?"

Mayhew pushed his rimless glasses up on his nose and frowned. His pale blond hair stood up in disordered tufts. "I can't honestly say. Definitely during Christmas week because a troop of Boy Scouts visited, and boys are always interested in firearms."

"The case is normally locked?"

"Oh, absolutely. We couldn't have anyone handling them, tarnishing the silver plating. The temptation to touch is such a human foible, isn't it? Taken together, the three guns are valued at nearly half a million dollars, and the presentation gun is one-of-a-kind. Irreplaceable."

"Half a million!" Radcliff exclaimed. "And you kept them out like this?"

Mayhew gave a fatalistic shrug. "My hands are tied. It's a condition of the donors. They quite naturally like to see their names on the display cards. Besides, they are well documented and the insurance company had them laser-tagged with our own ID code. No one could sell them."

"Who has the key to this case?"

"There are only two. They hang with the rest of the keys on a board in a locked cupboard, and before you ask, both keys are still there."

"Then who has access to that cupboard?" Radcliff asked patiently.

"Well, I do, of course, and Jonna. And there's a spare key that we keep in a vase on the mantel in our office."

"Who knows about the spare?"

"Only Jonna and I."

"What about a cleaning woman?"

"Cleaning *man*," he corrected, shaking his head. "Dix Lunsford may have noticed it when he dusts, but I doubt if he knows what it's for. Besides, he's never in the office alone. Not that we don't trust him, heavens no. He and his wife used to work for Jonna's mother and he's devoted to Jonna. He wouldn't take a straight pin that didn't belong to him."

"Does he have keys to the house itself?"

"Certainly not! There are only five. One for Jonna, one for me, and one for each of the three officers on our board of trustees." He paused and pushed up his glasses and sheepishly admitted that perhaps they knew the alarm code as well.

A gust of cold air announced the opening of the front door.

"I called our chairman. Perhaps that's he now," he said pedantically as he peered over his glasses toward the doorway.

An officer stationed at the door called down the hall, "Futrell's here, Chief."

A youthful-looking plainclothes officer entered the library, carrying a case with the basic tools of an investigation. For anything more complicated, they would have to send for the division's crime scene van, which was centrally manned by the state police.

Radcliff explained what had happened and asked Mayhew, "Did you handle the case?"

"Not this morning," said Mayhew. "Well, I did lift it by the corner there just to see if it was locked. Which it wasn't. But I've certainly touched it in the past. Not since Christmas, though. I'm almost positive not since Christmas. Is there a way to tell how old fingerprints are?"

Futrell stooped and cast an experienced eye over the case. "Wouldn't matter if there was. Looks like it's been wiped clean."

A few minutes later, his brush and powder confirmed that eyeball appraisal.

"Jonna must have taken them," said Mayhew. "They're gone, she's gone, and she had access to the keys. But why? Unless—oh goodness! She's been acting oddly lately. You don't think she took the presentation gun for the same reason her father did?"

"Whose father?" asked a new voice.

"Ah, Nathan! Betty! I'm so glad you're here."

Mayhew quickly introduced Nathan Benton and Betty Coates Ramos, chairman and treasurer, respectively, of the Morrow House board of trustees. "The Bentons and the Coateses were two of Shaysville's earliest families," he told the lawmen. He hastily described for the new arrivals how he had entered the library to turn on the lights in case there were any visitors today. "I thought I would lay the updated Morrow genealogy on the table—people always want to know the dates of our ghost—and that's when I saw the empty case."

Mrs. Ramos was a tall attractive blonde who appeared to be in her late fifties or early sixties. Her ski pants and leather boots were black and she wore pearls and cashmere beneath a quilted white parka. She had pushed the hood back and her short hair was a windblown tangle of loose but well-styled curls. Diamonds flashed on her fingers as she pulled off her gloves and extended her hand, first to Radcliff, whom she seemed to know already, and then to Dwight.

"Major Bryant? Are you Jonna's—?" She hesitated, searching for the tactful term.

"Her ex?" Dwight said bluntly. "Yes, ma'am."

"And has she really taken the guns?" asked Mr. Benton, who looked to be in his mid-sixties.

There was something so familiar about the man that Dwight almost felt as if he should salute.

He was roughly five-nine, but carried himself with the authority of someone taller. Trim of body, with piercing blue eyes, iron gray hair, and a neat gray mustache, he wore brown slacks and a brown leather jacket over a white shirt and tie. The brown clothes only added to his military air, and that was when Dwight pegged his familiar look. Nathan Benton could have stepped out of one of those old war movies that he and Deborah liked to watch, central casting's idea of a stiff-upper-lip British colonel whose gruff, no-nonsense demeanor would inspire his men to feats of heroism.

"We only just arrived ourselves," said Chief Radcliff. "It's too soon to know who did what. Sounds as if they could have been taken anytime during the last month."

"Nonsense," Benton said crisply. (Dwight wondered if he heard a faint English accent.) "The cleaning man would have noticed. *I* would have noticed."

"Mr. Benton donated the derringer and the World War I Colt," Mayhew explained for those who had not made a connection between this trustee and the labels beneath two of the indentations. One read, "(L-46.3) Derringer Black-Powder Pistol, ca. 1872. Originally owned by Letitia Morrow Carter, daughter of Peter Morrow." The other was simply described as "(L-46.2) Government Model Colt automatic pistol, ca. 1912." Both labels carried the line, "Gift of Nathan Benton."

"And I distinctly remember seeing all three guns in the case as recently as last week," Benton told the two lawmen.

"Wait a minute," said Dwight as he straightened from reading the label. "Black powder? Did the presentation gun use black powder cartridges, too?"

"Well . . ." Mayhew deferred to Benton, who said, "No, it's post–Civil War. Used .36-caliber cartridges, I believe, although that gun was never meant to be fired."

"And yet it was," Radcliff said grimly. "At least twice that we know of."

"Twice?" asked the puzzled Mrs. Ramos.

"Jonna's great-grandfather killed himself with that gun," Mayhew said in a half-whisper, as if repeating scandalous gossip. "So did Eustace Shay."

"Jonna's father?"

Mayhew nodded.

"But that's awful!" Betty Ramos looked distressed. "How can Jonna stand its being here?"

"In the first place, she was only a baby when it happened," said Mayhew as he repositioned his glasses. "In the second place, does she even know?"

His question was directed at Dwight, who said, "I never heard about the first death, only that her father had shot himself accidentally. She never described the gun, though."

Benton raised a skeptical eyebrow. "Surely she must know. Someone in the Historical Society told me the gun's history when I decided to give the derringer. It doesn't seem to be a huge secret."

"Well, I certainly didn't know," said Mrs. Ramos. "Of course, I've only been on the board since Thanksgiving."

"Mrs. Ramos and her husband donated our new heating and cooling system," Mayhew said in a parenthetical murmur. "And she's been a supportive Friend of the Morrow House for years."

"But it wasn't until the children grew up and moved away that I've had time to become more involved. I can see that I still have a lot to learn."

"The guns were unloaded, right?" asked Dwight, trying to get them back on track. "And there are no bullets for them?"

"Not to my knowledge," Mayhew said.

"That's what you were talking about when Betty and I came in, wasn't it?" said Benton. "You're afraid she's going to follow the family tradition."

"That's ridiculous," said Mrs. Ramos. "I've been helping her take inventory this past month and there is noth-ing—absolutely *nothing*!—like that on her mind."

Radcliff's pager buzzed and he excused himself to walk out into the hall.

"When was the last time you talked to Jonna?" Dwight asked Mrs. Ramos.

"Day before yesterday."

"Thursday?"

"Today's Saturday?" The treasurer for the board of trustees counted back on her fingers. "Yes, Thursday morning."

"What time?"

"Around nine-thirty. We had both planned to come in and work on the inventory while it was quiet." She cast a brief apologetic glance at Mayhew, who stiffened slightly at the implication that he was a distraction of any sort. "But I had to go out of town for an emergency and I came by to say I'd be in on Friday—yesterday—to help get ready for Sunday . . . tomorrow."

"Oh my God!" Mayhew moaned. "Tomorrow! The SHGS!"

"What happens tomorrow?" asked Dwight.

"The Shaysville Historical and Genealogical Society is supposed to meet. It's our gala reception for the instal-lation of officers. Jonna was going to become the new president. We even have a guest speaker coming from the Smithsonian."

"We'll have to call him and cancel it," Benton said firmly. "We cannot go on now."

Mayhew looked shocked at the suggestion. "We can't do that without consulting with the other officers. We have to—"

He broke off as Paul Radcliff returned. He moved with purpose and spoke decisively. "I'm afraid we're going to have to put this room off-limits for the time being, Mr. Mayhew. Do you have a key for it?"

"I'm not sure, Chief."

"There's one in the key cupboard," said Mrs. Ramos. "Shall I fetch it?"

"Here," said Mayhew, fumbling with his keyring. "You'll need the cupboard key."

"That's okay," said the woman, already moving through the doorway. "I'll use the one in the vase."

Mayhew looked at her in consternation and Dwight threw an amused glance at his friend. She had only joined the board at Thanksgiving? So much for the director thinking no one knew about that spare key.

But Radcliff did not return his grin. He gave one of the uniformed officers orders to lock the room and bring him both keys and told Futrell to pack up his bag and follow his car.

"What's up?" asked Dwight as they stepped out into a wind that seemed to be blowing straight out of the Arctic.

"Jonna's car's been found," he answered tersely, moving rapidly toward his patrol car.

"Is she okay? What about Cal?"

"Sorry, pal. No sign of him. Just her."

He got into the car and Dwight followed.

"Well, what does she say? What's she done with him?"

"I'm sorry, Dwight," Radcliff said again. "She's dead."

CHAPTER
11

Let us consider the fatal effects of excessive cold.

—Theophrastus

SATURDAY NOON, 22 JANUARY

Jonna Bryant's blue Honda was parked in a crowded junkyard at the edge of town. It had been found by two teenage brothers who were searching the lot for a door to match the one they'd smashed to hell and gone when they slid their Mustang into a waist-high concrete gatepost during Wednesday night's snowfall. When they finally located a Mustang with a viable door, it was jammed in between a 1972 Pinto and a late-model Accord. Both the Pinto and the Mustang were clearly banged and scarred, but the Accord looked pristine under its sheet of ice.

"We saw the shape of something weird in the front seat, but we couldn't tell what it was," said one of the brothers, "so we used a screwdriver to pry loose part of the ice on the driver's side and oh, man! We 'bout near died ourselves."

Beneath the red of their wind-chapped cheeks, both boys were pale and shaky, but nervously excited, too, as they told it over and over again to anyone who would listen.

The owner of the junkyard was wary and belligerent, afraid he was going to be blamed for this. He claimed total ignorance as to how or when the Accord had been added to his inventory. And he certainly knew nothing about the dead woman slumped stiffly over the steering wheel, her left hand dangling free, a silver-plated antique gun on the floor as if it had slipped from her lifeless hand after she put the barrel to her head and pulled the trigger.

Dwight took one look and it was like a sucker punch to the heart.

"She's wearing a red jacket," he said.

Paul Radcliff nodded grimly and thumbed his radio. "Jack? Start a Code Amber on Cal Bryant. Here's his dad. He'll give you the details and a description of the woman who took him." Then, much as he hated to have to turn this over to the Virginia state police, he added, "And when you've finished with that, call Captain Petrie and tell him I'm officially requesting their assistance to process a crime scene."

Dwight looked up in protest, but Radcliff shook his head. "You know I've got to, pal. They have the resources. We don't."

Bone-chilling winds swept down from the snow-covered hills, straight through the open lot, and those lawmen too macho to wear gloves or hats jammed their hands into their pockets and hunched deeper into their heavy jackets.

While they stamped their feet on the frozen, dirty snow in an effort to stay warm until the crime scene van arrived, Futrell took pictures of the car from all angles, documenting what Dwight already knew. This car had not moved and its doors had not been opened since last night's freezing rain cemented them in place. It was un-likely that Jonna was the woman in a blue parka who took Cal yesterday. Nor could she have been the one who was in the house last night, not with ice this thick all around the door.

His own brain felt cased in ice. How would Cal handle her death? Was the woman he went off with Jonna's killer? If not, what was their connection? There had to be one. Otherwise, it would be one hell of a coincidence that his son was taken the same day his ex-wife was mur-dered. But why take the boy if they were going to kill the mother? Had Cal inadvertently seen something the killer was afraid he would tell?

He bent down again to peer through the hole that the teenagers had made. Half of the window's ice had broken away in one sheet so that the interior could be clearly seen even on this dull gray morning.

His first thoughts were of the woman who lay there on the other side of the glass, stiff and frozen and beyond the warming touch of any human hand; the woman who had been his wife, who had given birth to their son, who had walked away from their marriage. And yeah, maybe that was because she knew he did not love her or maybe it was because she had never really loved him. The reason did not matter, had not mattered for years. The mutual lack of passion had made their divorce feel like the polite disso-lution of a business arrangement that no longer paid dividends. She had cared too much about appearances for Dwight's liking, but she was not a bad or stupid woman. He had felt guilty for not trying harder to save their marriage for the sake of their son; yet, at the same time, he had been so grateful that she wanted out that he had not fought her over the terms of the settlement. And despite their growing struggle over Cal these last few years, he was filled with deep sorrow that she had ended like this.

Then his training took over. As he read the blood-spattered note that lay in her lap, his fears and regrets were displaced by a cold rage.

"See the note?" Radcliff asked in his ear.

"Yeah."

The spiky letters wavered, but they were in Jonna's handwriting: *He won't divorce her and I don't want to go on living.*

"The bastard made her write her own phony suicide note," Dwight said as he straightened up. "What did he say to her? Threaten to kill Cal? Where the hell *is* he, Paul?"

"We'll find him," Radcliff said. "I promise you we'll find him."

Yesterday's canvassers had returned the pictures of Cal, so Dwight handed one of them back and Paul signaled for an officer to take it to the station and get it out on the Internet.

"I'll ride along with him," Dwight said. "Pick up my truck."

"You don't want to wait for the van?"

"What for? To watch your BCI techs try to find trace evidence that'll take days to analyze?" He jerked his head toward the car. "You're reading this phony setup same way I am, right? A shot to the left temple when she was right-handed? No blowback blood spatter on either hand and none on the interior window glass?"

Radcliff was right there with him. "The shooter probably held the gun on her through the window while she wrote the note, then shot her, put the gun in her hand so it'll have her prints, rolled up the window, and was on his way."

"Or her way," said Dwight.

"Or her way," Radcliff agreed. "I have to wait for the state guys, but there's no reason you can't go talk with Jonna's neighbor again, see if you can get a better description of the woman."

———

Leonard Carlton was dismayed to hear that Jonna was dead and indignant to think that Dwight felt he'd misled them by saying it was she who took Cal the day before.

"I told you. She had on those big wraparound sunglasses and her hood was up, so it never occurred to me that it was anybody else. Same build, same looks. You sure it wasn't her?" He gestured to the side door clearly visible through his large window. "She came out of that door right behind the boy and he went off with her like I've seen them do a hundred times."

"I don't suppose you happened to glance over last night about the time someone let themselves into the house?"

"I don't mind other people's business," said Carlton in frosty denial. Then curiosity cut the high ground out from under him. "A burglar? I thought you stayed over there last night."

"I did. Somebody slipped in while I was asleep."

"And you call yourself a police officer?"

"Hell of a note, isn't it?" Dwight said wearily.

Carlton shook his white head and, to Dwight's surprise, pulled a Palm Pilot out of the pocket of his impeccably tailored trousers. "Perhaps it's time I did start taking notice." With stylus held firmly in his wrinkled hand, he looked at Dwight expectantly. "Give me your cell number. If I see your boy or that woman or anybody else going in, I'll call you."

After thanking the man, Dwight walked back to the front of Jonna's house, unlocked the door, and walked through to see if last night's intruder had returned. The light was blinking on the answering machine by the kitchen door, and he pushed the play button to listen to the new messages.

First came Mrs. Shay's voice: "Jonna, sweetie, where are you? Why haven't you called? You're not still mad at me, are you? I need a few things from the grocery store and it's too icy for me to go out. Besides, I think I'm catching a cold. Call me right back. You hear?"

That message was followed by an unfamiliar woman's voice. She sounded slightly annoyed: "Hey, Jonna, it's Lou. Did you forget that Cal and Jason had a playdate this morning? Call me."

In the utility room, Bandit was whining to be let out. Dwight knelt and petted the little dog, who seemed hungry for attention, then he turned the dog into the yard for a brief run. While he waited for Bandit to return, Dwight began to have second thoughts. Until an ME gave them the time of death, it was theoretically possible that the woman in the blue parka had indeed been Jonna; that she had taken Cal somewhere yesterday afternoon, changed into her red jacket, then driven to meet her killer.

But where would she have taken him?

There was only one place that seemed logical. He called Paul Radcliff. "I'm going around to Jonna's mother again. See if she's got Cal. You got a problem with me telling her about Jonna?"

"I don't," came his friend's guarded reply, "but the state guys might. They've officially bumped me off the case and they want to talk to you."

"*Me?* Hell, Paul, I've been chasing my own tail since I got to town yesterday. I don't know what was going on in her life or who— Oh," he said, finally thinking like a cop instead of a distracted and apprehensive father. "Yeah. Of course. Ex-husband. Fighting over the kid. No alibi for last night. Right."

"I gotta go now, but listen." Paul's voice dropped another level. "Do what you want about telling Mrs. Shay, but I promised 'em that you'd meet us at the station at one o'clock."

"I'll be there," Dwight said.

———

A thin mixture of rain and snow began to fall as he drove over to his former mother-in-law's house. It suddenly seemed so reasonable that Jonna would have brought Cal to her mother's that Dwight half expected his son to answer the doorbell when he rang.

Instead, it was Mrs. Shay. "Oh, Dwight! I'm so glad to see you! Did you find Jonna? She's not answering her phone."

"Cal's not here?" asked Dwight.

"No, I told you. I haven't heard from them since Thursday morning and I'm beginning to get quite worried. Have you eaten lunch? I made a pot of soup in case they do come by. On these cold days, don't you think a nice hot bowl of soup is the perfect meal? Warms you right up, doesn't it? My stomach hasn't been right all week, and soup is the only thing that would agree with me today. Come on back to the kitchen. I'm embarrassed to admit that I sometimes don't go to the trouble of carrying everything into the dining room when it's just me."

Dwight knew that for Mrs. Shay, "embarrassed" was not a mere figure of speech. She was a woman who clung to the standards by which she had been raised. Only the live-in housekeeper and yardman ate in the kitchen of her childhood, never her parents; and even though her own housekeeper and yardman had dwindled to a weekly cleaning woman, old habits died hard. She brought out a second linen placemat, a fine china bowl and silver soup spoon, then went to a cupboard for more crackers, which she placed on their own bread plate. For Mrs. Shay, setting the box on the table would have been "*déclassé*," a term Jonna had murmured more than once when offended by some of his country ways, until he was driven to find a French dictionary. "You saying I'm common?" he had asked.

While Mrs. Shay bustled around reheating the soup, chattering about her health, the weather, and where on earth Jonna could have gotten herself to, Dwight examined the kitchen for some sign of Cal. A rubber baseball sat amid oranges and apples in the fruit bowl on a side counter and there was a colorful picture on the refrigerator of an ornately decorated tree and wobbly cursive letters that spelled out "Merry Christmas to Nana—Love Cal." But there was no jacket or gloves; and, most tellingly, there was no place set for him at this table.

Mrs. Shay filled his bowl and seated herself in the chair opposite his, clearly prepared to continue making polite conversation. Knowing that he would get no more information out of her the moment he told her Jonna was dead, he said, "When you talked to Jonna Thursday morning, what exactly did she say?"

"Exactly?" Mrs. Shay frowned. "Well, let me think. We talked about the snow. The boy who usually shovels my walk has the flu. He was supposed to send his brother, but he never came and I almost slipped going down my steps that night. The brother finally came this morning and now here it is snowing again. I'll be so glad when Cal is old enough to do it for me. He's such a nice child. And so mannerly. Don't you think Jonna's doing a good job with him?"

"Yes, ma'am," he said. Never mind that she had tried to turn Cal against him for remarrying. "Did she say what her plans were for the day?"

"She was going over to the Morrow House to work on the inventory. There hasn't been one in twenty years and so much has been donated to the house since then. It was my grandparents' home, you know. I don't remember my grandfather, but I was well in my teens when my grandmother died so I spent many a night there before we closed the house and the Historical and Genealogical Society took it over. Did you know she's their new president? She's really looking forward to tomorrow. You haven't touched your soup, Dwight. Don't you like it?"

He looked down at the steaming bowl. He had not felt

hungry before, but now the aroma of creamed vegetables and smoked ham made him suddenly ravenous.

Gratified by his evident enjoyment, Mrs. Shay rattled on about how she used to take the girls over when she was helping the SHGS document the original furnishings that had been there during her own girlhood, especially those that had belonged to the pre–Civil War Morrows. "They loved to run around and hear their little voices echo in those big empty rooms." She crumbled a half cracker over her soup and dipped her spoon in.

"Grandmother sold quite a few of the later things, but she had a firm sense of history and she wouldn't part with any of Peter Morrow's possessions, not even the ivory toothpick he brought with him from Philadelphia back in eighteen-twenty-three," she said proudly. "I plan to leave my great-grandmother's rocker to the house and Jonna is going to return the portrait. We may not have as much money as some of the new donors, but *our* pieces are originals, not period replacements."

Dwight tried to draw her out about Jonna's friends and whether there was anyone she would have left Cal with.

"No, dear. If she's gone away for a couple of days, she's surely taken Cal with her. Otherwise, he would be here with me. Not that she does go away without him very often. And not that she would go away this weekend with her big day coming up tomorrow. I keep telling her she should get out more, meet new people. I understand that you've remarried?"

Dwight nodded.

Mrs. Shay pursed her lips. "I was younger than Jonna when my husband died and left me with two difficult little girls to raise. It was too much to ask of another man, although there were two or three who professed themselves willing." She gave a coy smile. "Jonna only has the one and Cal's so easy. But she doesn't want to hear me talk about it."

"So she isn't seeing anyone?"

"I didn't say that and it's hardly proper for you to ask, is it?"

"Cal's my son, too, Mrs. Shay," he reminded her. "And I need to find him."

"I shall certainly have Jonna call you as soon as they return." She pushed back from the table and stood up. "Now, are you sure I can't offer you dessert or something to drink?"

Dwight knew that this was his cue to excuse himself and leave and there was nothing he would have liked better. He looked down at his watch.

12:20. Less than forty-five minutes before he was due to turn up at Paul's office. It was now or never. He took a deep breath. There was never an easy way to say what she had to be told.

"Are you all right?" she asked when he continued to sit there.

"I'm so sorry," he said, "but I'm afraid I have bad news."

As he spoke, her eyes grew wide, then filled with tears. She sank back down in her chair and shook her head in disbelief and denial.

"No," she whimpered. "Not Jonna. Oh, please, not Jonna."

"Is there someone I can call for you?" he asked. "Your other daughter?"

Knowing that Jonna considered her sister, Pamela, a

total flake, he wasn't sure how much comfort she could be to Mrs. Shay or how quickly she could get here from—where was it? Tennessee?—but she, too, would have to be told and surely she would come.

"Not Pam," said Mrs. Shay, trying to choke back the sobs that nearly strangled her. "My cousin Eleanor. She's right around the corner."

She managed to give him the number. The cousin was shocked and said she would come immediately. True to her word, she was there within minutes, a sturdy woman with salt-and-pepper hair who folded Mrs. Shay in her arms and rocked her back and forth. Mrs. Shay lifted her ravaged face to Dwight.

"Cal," she said. "Oh dear God, where *is* he?"

"I'll let you know as soon as we find him," Dwight promised.

He wrote down his numbers again. Mrs. Shay's cousin matched his promise to call if there was any news and then she raised him one. "My husband owns the local radio station. We'll have everyone in the valley keeping an eye out for him."

CHAPTER
12

However these informants were guilty of a further important piece of ignorance.

—Theophrastus

SATURDAY MORNING, 22 JANUARY

While Jack Jamison headed back to Cotton Grove to question some of the people known to have had run-ins with J.D. Rouse, Mayleen Richards asked Raeford McLamb to go with her to interview Nita Rouse again. "They might talk to you quicker than to me alone," she said.

McLamb arched an eyebrow. "Because I'm black?"

"I doubt if that'll help," she said with a grin. "I was thinking more because you're a man and her brother struck me as pretty macho when we talked to him Thursday night."

"So you're gonna let me do all the talking?"

"Heck, I'll even let you drive," she told him.

A small neat sign on the shoulder of the road modestly announced that this was Diaz y Garcia, Landscape Design and Lawn Service. When she was there before, it had been quite dark and Richards had been so aware of Major Bryant that she had not paid much attention to the Garcia family setup. Now, in the morning light, she was rather impressed by the compound they had created. Two double-wide mobile homes were separated by a driveway wide enough for larger trucks. Both homes backed up to a pleasant variety of hollies and tall evergreens, interspersed with accents of golden cypresses, that completely screened them from the road. The shrubbery continued all around the lot so that the head-high chain-link security fence was almost indiscernible. Across the courtyard were equipment sheds for some trucks, a couple of low trailers, a midsize tractor, and several riding lawn mowers. More esoteric bits of equipment stood along the back walls. Four or five little dark-haired children were clambering over the machines, pretending to drive. They ducked down out of sight as soon as they saw the unfamiliar car.

An older, single-wide trailer abutted the sheds, probably a bunkhouse for seasonal workers; and judging by the curtains in an upper window, Richards guessed there was an apartment over one of the sheds. Tucked into the remaining corner of the open lot was a henhouse. The run was split in half so that as soon as the chickens finished off the winter oats on one side, the new oats in the other half would be big enough to feed them. Eight or ten Rhode Island Reds pecked away at the greens beneath their feet and their combs were a bright healthy red in the thin wintry sunlight.

Through the closed chain-link gate at the rear of the yard Richards could see their tree nursery. In all, she estimated that the compound and nursery occupied slightly less than six acres.

"Nice," said McLamb as he parked in front of the double-wide on the left. "Boy, I'd love to have me a dozen of their eggs. I bet the yolks aren't that pitiful pale yellow you get in the grocery store. Your folks still keep chickens?"

Richards shook her head. "Nobody wanted to shovel out a henhouse anymore."

He laughed. "No pain, no gain."

She laughed, too. She loved her job and had no desire to ever again mess with gummy green tobacco or to deal with the backaches and heartbreaks a subsistence farm could generate. Nevertheless, the sight of those glossy brown hens made her suddenly homesick for the life of her childhood, chicken droppings and all.

Before they had the car doors fully open, two men emerged from the house. Both were dressed in heavy red plaid wool jackets and both wore black leather cowboy hats. Richards recognized the shorter man from two nights earlier.

"Señor Garcia," she said, extending her hand. In halting Spanish, she reminded him of her name and that she had been there before with Major Bryant.

He nodded acknowledgment and she introduced Detective McLamb, then moved back a half-step as if in deference.

In turn, Garcia nodded to the taller man beside him. *"Miguel Diaz, mi cuñado."*

With absolutely no idea what *cuñado* signified, Richards and McLamb smiled politely.

Diaz grinned at them. "I'm his brother-in-law," he explained in lightly accented English. "His wife is my sister. Have you come to tell us who killed his other *cuñado*?"

"Wish we could," said McLamb. "We were hoping to talk to Mrs. Rouse again and we have a few questions for Mr. Garcia here, too. I'd sure appreciate it if you could translate for us."

"Of course." He turned and spoke rapidly to Garcia, who hesitated, then gestured to the concrete table and wooden benches that sat under the bare branches of a nearby oak. While Diaz led the way, Garcia went back inside, presumably to fetch his sister. At least that was what Richards thought she understood as she followed the other two men over to the picnic area. In summer, this would be a pleasantly shady place to sit and talk. Today, the sun shone through the bare limbs and kept them from being uncomfortably cold.

As they sat down, McLamb laid a yellow legal pad on the table and wrote the time and place at the top before asking, "How well did you know J. D. Rouse?"

"Only so well as he would let us, which means not well. You have seen where they lived?"

His question was aimed at Richards and she shook her head.

"They live in a field. No flowers. No bushes. One ugly tree. When he married the sister of *mi cuñado*, we wanted to landscape the yard for their wedding gift. He would not allow it."

"Why?" asked McLamb.

Diaz shrugged. "For that you must ask another."

The morning was warming up rapidly and Mayleen

Richards slipped back the hood of her coat. Her shoulder-length cinnamon-colored hair blazed in the sunlight and Miguel Diaz's dark brown eyes widened in appreciation.

"Muy hermosa," he murmured.

Her hair? *Beautiful?* Richards flushed a bright red, which made him smile beneath the brim of his hat.

Fortunately McLamb missed the byplay because his eyes were on the door of the double-wide as Gerardo Garcia escorted his sister out to them.

Juanita Rouse was dressed in black from the scarf on her head to the boots on her feet. Her eyes were sad and there was a deep purple bruise on her left cheek; and yes, she told them, clearly ashamed of the bruise, J.D. had gotten violent with her once or twice, but only once or twice. All right, yes, maybe three or four times. He was not a bad man, though. Nor a bad husband. Not really. Only when he drank too much beer or when things had gone badly at work. She turned to Diaz and spoke rapidly in Spanish with hand gestures to illustrate vocabulary words Richards had barely read, much less heard pronounced.

"She says that these things happen between a man and wife before the man settles down into marriage, when he still fights himself because he is not young and free." Diaz's tone was completely neutral. "She wants you to know that he was a good father to their daughters."

At that, Garcia growled and spat on the ground in disgust, which would indicate that he knew more English than they realized.

Mrs. Rouse's dark eyes flashed. "Never once does he hit them, Gerardo. Not even when he have much beer. He brings candy, he plays with them, he makes them laugh."

Garcia's words were scornful and Diaz translated them, too. "A good father does not hit the mother of his children."

"What about his own fight with Rouse?" asked McLamb.

Back came the reply through Diaz: "A man does what he must for the honor of his family."

"Would that include killing the man he feels has dishonored the family?"

"It could. But not like that. He says it was a coward who shot him, not a man of honor."

"All the same, we have to know where he was Thursday evening."

"He was with me," Diaz answered directly. "We have the contract for Orchard Range. You know where that is?"

McLamb nodded.

"We are planting around the entrance sign and the berms. You can speak to our men. They will tell you the same."

"I'm sure they will," said McLamb. "Anybody else who could vouch for him? Besides those in your employment?"

"Will the Anglo who employs us do for this? He came by around five to talk to us about using more holly instead of cypress."

McLamb asked for the developer's name and telephone number and jotted it down on the yellow legal pad, then turned back to Nita Rouse. "Do you yourself know of anyone who would want your husband dead?"

"No," she said, but as McLamb continued to look at her steadily, her eyes fell. As if it were too painful to try to say it in English, she spoke through Diaz.

"There is a woman," he told them. "Her name is Darla. This is why they fight so much now. She is married, too. Her husband has been in the war. Now he is home again. Maybe if he knew?"

His name?

Nita Rouse denied knowing it.

McLamb had been watching Diaz as he translated, but Mayleen Richards had watched the woman and had seen the small twitch of satisfaction at the edge of her lips. As they drove out of the compound back onto the highway, she said, "If that soldier does know about Rouse and his wife, guess who got word to him?"

"You think?"

"Five'll get you ten."

"No bet." The car's interior had warmed up while standing in the sun and he reached over to turn the heater down a couple of degrees.

As McLamb drove, Richards called Jamison and told him to ask about a Darla-last-name-unknown.

"Long as we're out this way, let's stop by the Harper woman's house and see if she's remembered anything else."

———

In Cotton Grove, Jack Jamison felt as if he were batting 0 for 3. The first suspect seemed genuinely surprised that anyone would think he'd shot a man simply because of a barroom brawl that happened over a month ago. "Hell, it was Christmas. The holidays. Everybody was drinking too much. Yeah, me and J.D. mixed it up a little out in the parking lot, but we was both so drunk, falling on our faces did more damage than our fists. I chipped a tooth when I hit the concrete. Cost me four hundred dollars by the time the dentist got through with me."

He was more interested in talking about that tooth than any grudge he might have been carrying for Rouse, but he did furnish the full name of the woman—Darla Overholt.

So where was he Thursday evening?

"Driving back from High Point with my boss. We got in around seven. Here, I'll give you his number."

The second suspect was helping a friend change the carburetor in his truck. He freely admitted he wasn't sorry to hear Rouse was dead, and no, he didn't have a real good alibi. "Darla Overholt? Yeah, she lives down near Makely. Comes up this way to do her playing. Too close to Fort Bragg the other way."

His friend came out from under the hood with a big grin on his face. "You say Rouse was shot? From *how* far away? Ol' Ken here couldn't hit an elephant less'n it was standing close enough to squirt him in the face. Ask anybody."

Jamison found their third suspect at a fund-raising fish fry outside the fellowship hall of a local church.

Boiling grease bubbled in one of the portable vats as the man dropped in battered catfish fillets one by one, then scooped crisp hushpuppies from an adjacent vat into a large colander. The air was redolent with the smell of fish and hot cornbread.

"I was at a planning session for today," he told Jamison as he dumped the hushpuppies into a metal tray that one of the kitchen helpers took over to the serving line. An awed look spread over his face. "I never fried fish for a church before and I didn't really want to do it this time, but my wife talked me into it. She said it would prove a blessing to me. Well, damned if it didn't, right?"

———

As they neared Rideout Road, Richards recognized the name on a street sign as being the same as the address for Orchard Range and quickly told McLamb to turn onto it. The development consisted of large boxy houses nearing completion. From a cursory drive through, it looked as if all that was lacking was the installation of appliances and the usual minimal landscaping. The berms that gave a semblance of privacy from passing traffic and the newly planted entranceway were both getting a thick mulch of pine straw from the Diaz y Garcia Landscaping crew. Indeed, Miguel Diaz himself had arrived and was standing by his truck when the two detectives got back to the entrance. He was talking to an older white man whose own truck bore the logo of the consortium that owned this development.

When introduced, the man confirmed that he had indeed spoken with Garcia on Thursday, although he did not think it was as late as Diaz had led them to believe.

"It was probably only around five because the sun was still up when I left," he said. "I remember 'cause it was right in my eyes but too low for the visor to do any good."

Richards felt Diaz's eyes on her, challenging her. Confused, she avoided his gaze and pointed to the woods that lay on the far end of the development. "What's on the other side of those trees?"

"Over yonder?" asked the man. "That would be Rideout Road."

———

Mrs. Harper had just given her corgi a bath when the two detectives rang her bell. She met them at the door with the wet dog wrapped in a towel and invited them to come in while she finished drying it off.

They sat in the living room and she held the dog on her lap to dry between its toes.

"Are you any nearer to learning who did that awful thing?" she asked, moving on to the little dog's ears.

"We have a few leads," Richards told her, "but we were hoping you might have remembered something more that might help us. For instance, did any vehicles pass you going the other way just before he was shot?"

Mrs. Harper shook her head. "Not that I noticed. I'm sorry. I'm afraid I get quite single-minded when I'm out there. I'm only looking for the next bottle or can or scrap of paper."

"It's really nice of you to do the whole road all by yourself," said McLamb.

She shrugged away his praise. "It's barely a mile and it's the least I can do to honor my father."

"Is that him?" asked Richards, glancing at the portrait over the couch.

The older woman nodded and her face softened as she, too, looked at the man in uniform. "The Colonel was such a good person. Kind and considerate of everyone. He was the one who actually started trying to keep the road clean. I never had his patience. 'Why bother?' I'd ask him. 'You know some slob's going to trash it again.' He said it gave him something to do while I was at work. Said it was giving a little something back to the world."

"You must miss him a lot," said Richards.

"It'll be three years on Monday since he died," she said simply. "As soon as I took early retirement, I knew this is what he would want me to do."

"Getting back to Thursday night," said McLamb, "did you happen to notice the time of the shot?"

Again the woman shook her head. "I wasn't wearing a watch."

The dog yawned and curled up on the towel and fell asleep in her lap. "Poor Dixie! Baths just wear her out."

"But the sun was still up, right?" Richards persisted.

"Just barely. I could see pretty good, but it was almost completely dark when I got home, and I started back as soon as I knew you people were on the way."

———

On the return drive to Dobbs, Raeford McLamb said, "What time is sunset these days anyhow?"

Mayleen Richards logged onto the Internet and in less than a minute was able to say, "Sunset for Thursday in this area was five-twenty-nine. And twilight till five-fifty-six."

"Wouldn't take a person but maybe ten or fifteen minutes at the most to walk through the woods from Orchard Range to Rideout Road."

"True," Richards agreed. "But it's not like Rouse was keeping to a split-second timetable. If it was Garcia, how would he know for sure that Rouse would be driving past in that short window of time?"

They were still batting scenarios back and forth when they got back to the office. Jamison came in right behind them, waving a fragrant brown bag with grease stains.

"I brought lunch," he said. "Catfish."

They were munching on hushpuppies and sharing their findings when one of the uniforms stuck his head in the door. "They just posted a new Amber Alert from Virginia. Eight-year-old white male. Calvin Shay Bryant. Isn't that Major Bryant's boy?"

CHAPTER
13

I have to go, whether the north wind sweeps the earth or winter shortens the snowy day.

—Horace

I got home a little before one and was trying to decide which I least wanted to do: fold laundry or get started on an ED for a divorce I was supposed to hear next week. Equitable distributions are the most time-consuming part of modern divorces. Everything has to be evaluated, from the family silver to the family Tupperware. Each party makes its own evaluation and then it's up to the judge to reconcile the two. If the values are close, I can just split the difference, but sometimes they'll vary by hundreds of dollars. That's when I go browsing on eBay to get an idea of what's fair and equitable.

I decided that the laundry could wait and was heading for my laptop when the house phone rang.

"Mrs. Bryant? Judge Knott?" asked the vaguely familiar voice of someone who wasn't sure if I was still using my maiden name.

"Speaking," I said.

"This is Deputy Richards, ma'am. We were wondering if you could tell us what's happening? I mean, we didn't think we should call Major Bryant directly, but we're all worried for him and his son."

"Worried?" I parried, wondering how she had heard about Jonna jerking Dwight's chain.

"Yes, ma'am. That Code Amber just came across our computer screen, but all it says is that he was taken yesterday afternoon by an unknown white woman in a blue parka and sunglasses and not by his mother as they first thought."

"What?"

"Oh, gosh," she groaned, instantly realizing that I didn't have a clue what she was talking about. "I've done it again, haven't I? I'm so, so sorry!"

I knew she was referring to a piece of confidential information that she had blurted out at a dinner the sheriff's department had given Dwight and me right before Christmas. Dwight had roasted her over the coals for that, but what was this?

Before I could respond, my cell phone rang and I grabbed it. Dwight's number was there on the screen. I promised Richards that I'd call her right back and pressed the talk button.

"What's going on up there?" I asked, not quite sure whether I was angry at being left in ignorance while all hell seemed to be breaking loose in Virginia. "I thought you said it was Jonna that took Cal."

"How do you know about that?" he asked.

"You do an Amber Alert and you don't expect me to hear about it? I'm your wife, Dwight. Why am I hearing about this from somebody else?"

"It just went out and this is the first real chance I've had to call you."

"Where's Jonna?" I said, ready to go rip her eyes out. "Who does she think has Cal?"

There was a long silence.

"Dwight?"

"Jonna's dead," he said, and I listened in stunned silence as he told me all that had happened since we talked earlier that morning.

I was aghast and wanted to go over every detail, but that wasn't going to happen. "Sorry, Deb'rah. I've got to be in Paul's office in about three minutes or the state guys will probably have a warrant out for my arrest."

"What?"

"Bad joke. But they do want to talk to me."

The pain in his voice decided me. "I'm coming up," I said. "I'll be there before dark."

He started to protest, but I wasn't about to listen.

"For better or worse," I reminded him. "Besides, you probably need fresh underwear and socks."

"Well . . ."

"Anything special you want me to bring?"

"No, but call my mother, would you? She needs to be told before she hears about it like you did."

"I'll tell her," I said. "You go to your meeting and I'll see you in a few hours."

I called Mayleen Richards back and told her the bare minimum, then I called Miss Emily.

As soon as she heard my voice, she said, "Oh,

Deborah, I was just fixing to call you and Dwight." She bubbled with happy anticipation. "Rob called. He and Kate are on their way to the hospital. The baby could be here anytime now!"

I hated to lick the red off her candy, but I couldn't not tell her. She listened with small murmurs of dismay.

"Poor Jonna," she said when I'd finished. Cal's disappearance terrified her, too, but she wasn't going to think the worst before she had to.

"Dwight will find him," she said, even though a slight quaver in her voice betrayed her surface calm.

Minnie was shocked when I phoned but instantly volunteered to tell Daddy and the others. "You sure you don't want someone to ride up with you?"

"I'm sure," I said. "I'll be okay."

"Promise you won't speed," she said. "I just saw the Weather Channel. It's snowing up there and I want to be able to truthfully tell Mr. Kezzie you promised not to speed."

"I promise," I lied.

Finally, I called Roger Longmire, my chief judge, and explained why I needed to take a week of personal leave.

After that, I packed enough clean clothes to get us through the week, and at the last minute tucked a dark suit for Dwight and a black dress for me into a garment bag even though it was too soon to know when, or even if, there was to be a formal funeral.

I was on the road within an hour after Dwight's call.

CHAPTER
14

The wounds and blows inflicted by men . . . render them less able to bear the afflictions of heat and cold.

—*Theophrastus*

SATURDAY AFTERNOON, 22 JANUARY

For all the times he had sat in the burn box while defense attorneys nitpicked his testimony—"How can you possibly say, Major Bryant, that this wrench, sold by the thousands at hardware stores throughout the country, is the exact same wrench purportedly owned by my client before his girlfriend's tragic death?"—and despite the many suspects he had cross-questioned himself, Dwight was not looking forward to this session. Paul might call it a formality, but these men were here to find Jonna's killer, and as the ex-spouse, he was a ready-made natural suspect. He told himself to just suck it up. Pointless to get their hackles up by a show of impatience or hostility. The sooner this was over, the quicker he could get back to the search for Cal.

Yet, for all that, it began pleasantly enough. When he arrived at the police station a minute or two before one o'clock, the others were settled in Paul Radcliff's office and they made no move to take it down the hall to the interrogation room, for which he supposed he should be grateful. At the moment, the two state police officers were acting as if this were nothing more than a pro forma meeting of professionals.

Dwight smiled when Paul introduced him to Special Agents Nick Lewes and Ed Clark of Virginia's Bureau of Criminal Investigation. "I guess y'all've heard all the jokes."

"Jokes?" Lewes asked blankly. He looked at his partner, who shrugged.

"Never mind," said Dwight. If they were putting him on, then let it ride. He shucked his jacket and hung it on the back of the remaining empty chair.

Lewes was probably his age, mid-forties, and Clark looked to be a couple of years younger. Both were muscular six-footers, although Lewes was somewhat heavier. Both wore leather shoulder holsters over casual civvies. Their heavy navy blue utility jackets with insignia and shoulder patches were draped over their chairs. Lewes had a receding hairline and pouches under his eyes like a sleepy bloodhound, while Clark's pointed face and bright button eyes reminded Dwight of a poodle he had once known.

"Sorry about your boy," Lewes said. "Hell of a situation you got here."

"We understand he went with his abductor willingly?" asked Clark.

"Sounds like it," said Dwight. "That's why we thought she was Jonna."

As they finished with the small talk, Clark set a tiny tape recorder on the desk corner nearest him. "You don't have a problem with us taping this, do you, Major?"

"Fine," said Dwight.

Clark recorded the time and place and the names of those present, then asked, "When was the last time you spoke to Mrs. Bryant?"

"The twenty-ninth of December, when I brought our son back from North Carolina."

"Not since then? Not even on the phone?"

"No."

The two looked at him expectantly, as if he were a nice fresh bone to gnaw on, but seeing no reason to elaborate, Dwight gazed back, maintaining a relaxed posture.

"How would you characterize your relationship with the victim? Good, bad, antagonistic?"

He hesitated. "I didn't think of it as a relationship. She was the mother of my son, so we kept it polite. He was the only thing we had in common."

"Why'd y'all split up?"

"That was almost eight years ago and it's not relevant to this situation," he said, willing himself to maintain his composure. If he were sitting in their seats, he would certainly think his questions were hitting home if the suspect suddenly crossed his arms protectively over his chest.

"A little cheating on the side, maybe?"

"No cheating on either side and I didn't remarry till this past Christmas," Dwight said, sidestepping the spirit of Clark's question, because yes, when you got right down to it, wasn't wanting Deborah the whole time he was married the same as cheating on Jonna? (*"Whosoever looketh on a woman to lust after her hath committed adultery with her already in his heart."*)

Not that these men would suspect that he'd had to wait seven years after the divorce to do anything about it. (*"And Jacob served seven years for Rachel . . . for the love he had for her."*)

"She got custody," said Clark. "Did you resent that?"

Dwight shook his head. "Cal was a baby. It made sense for her to have him."

"I'm talking about recently, now that he's older."

"He's only eight. He still needs his mother."

Saying the words drove the truth of it home like the blow of a sledgehammer.

How's Cal going to deal with this? Or does he already know that Jonna's dead? Dear God, was he there? Was he used as a bargaining chip in a game Jonna had already lost? Forced to watch while someone put a gun to his mother's head? And what about Deborah? She loves Cal, but she's not Jonna. She can't be for him what Jonna—

"Major Bryant?"

"Sorry," he said. "Look, could we do this later? My son—"

"Every law agency in a five-state area has your son on their computer screens," Clark said mildly, "and I believe Chief Radcliff has officers out questioning neighbors and friends?"

Paul Radcliff nodded.

"So unless you know where he's likely to be, it'll help him more if you finish bringing us up to speed. Now, we understand you got into town yesterday morning and your wife—sorry, your *ex*-wife—was already missing?"

Dwight nodded. "Cal said he hadn't seen her since she dropped him off at school Thursday morning."

With the tape recorder running, he repeated everything Cal had told him, from their breakfast of bacon and pecan waffles and the drive to school, to his coming home to an empty house and how she hadn't answered her cell phone.

"And you spent yesterday looking for her?"

"I tried." He told of his visits to Jonna's mother and to the Morrow House and how he had come up colder than the slushy rain pounding on the skylight above them. "Her mother said she planned to go in to work that morning, and that jibes with what one of the trustees—"

He glanced at Radcliff, who helpfully supplied the name. "Betty Ramos."

"Yeah. Mrs. Ramos said she saw Jonna briefly when she stopped by the Morrow House Thursday morning."

"Anybody else see her there?"

"When I spoke to the director the first time, he said he hadn't seen her since the weekend before," Dwight said. "I didn't exactly lean on him, though."

"And when we were there the second time," said Radcliff, "we were more concerned with the guns."

They described Mayhew's discovery of the missing antique guns, as well as the bloody history of the presentation pistol that had killed Jonna.

Lewes lifted his sorrowful bloodhound eyes to Radcliff. "Who knew about that?"

"We're not sure. Mayhew thought Mrs. Bryant might not know, but Nathan Benton—he's chair of the trustees—says someone in the Historical Society told him. On the other hand, Mrs. Ramos says she never heard it before today."

Lewes started to ask another question but Clark had moved on to a different subject. "How did you feel about your ex-wife's affair?"

"What affair?" asked Dwight.

"The one she wrote about in that suicide note."

"There was no affair and she didn't kill herself."

"You don't think it's her handwriting?"

"Oh, it's her handwriting, but this whole phony suicide was staged by whoever shot her."

"Phony?" said Clark.

"You guys are joking, right?"

"Why would we joke?" asked Lewes.

"You saw the setup. No blood spatter where you'd expect it? Besides, if there's one thing I know about Jonna, it's that she'd never kill herself over any man and she certainly wouldn't do it without making sure Cal was taken care of."

"Maybe she did make sure. Maybe that's who took your son," said Clark. "She knew you'd remarried, right? Could be she resented it. Or did you resent the idea of your boy having a new stepfather?"

His shiny black eyes reminded Dwight even more of that poodle he had once known.

Known and, as he now remembered, hadn't particularly liked.

He felt his jaws tighten.

"Tell you what," he said. "This isn't getting us anywhere. Why don't y'all go talk to people who know what her life was like up here? If she really was having an affair with a married man, somebody will know. Shaysville's not that big."

"He wants us to explore other routes," Lewes told his partner.

"Map out a different expedition," Clark agreed with a slight smirk on his poodle face.

"Jesus H!" said Dwight, slapping his hand down so hard on the desk that Clark had to grab for the tape recorder to keep it from bouncing off. "My son's missing, his mother's dead, and you're playing games with me?"

"Sorry," said Clark, "but hey, you did ask, and yeah, we've heard all the jokes."

"Fine," said Dwight. "Glad I could give you some more laughs." He stood up angrily and reached for his jacket.

Lewes put out a placating hand. "Just a minute, Major. Chief Radcliff tells us you're staying at Mrs. Bryant's house. We're going to want to take a look."

"When?" he asked, still frosted.

"Now works for me."

"It's been contaminated since Jonna disappeared," Dwight warned him grudgingly. "I slept there last night and someone came back for Cal's sweater."

"Huh?"

This was clearly something Radcliff had not told them, so Dwight gave a quick recap.

"Anything missing besides the sweater?"

"Maybe something from the medicine cabinet. And that reminds me." He pulled out the bottle of antihistamine tablets that had been prescribed for Jonna late last summer and turned to Radcliff. "This Dr. Brookfield. Where can I find him?"

"How about you let us handle that?" said Clark and held out his hand for the bottle. "And how 'bout you remember that you're a couple of hundred miles out of your jurisdiction?"

"Oh, I don't think we need to get too official," said Nick Lewes, playing the ameliorating good guy as he, too, stood and put on his jacket. "We're all on the same team here. I'll go on out to the house with him and maybe you could see what's happening with the wagon. Oh, and Chief. Didn't you say your people lifted the abductor's fingerprints at the house yesterday? Maybe Ed could take what you have back for our lab to process."

"Sure," Radcliff said sourly.

———

Rain mixed with snow continued to fall as they left the station. Special Agent Lewes borrowed one of Radcliff's squad cars and followed Dwight's truck over to Jonna's house. They stood on the porch out of the icy wet and Dwight pointed to the stone that had hid the now missing key. "When Cal and I came back yesterday, whoever was in the house could have watched from behind the blinds as Cal got it and then put it back."

He unlocked the door and held it open for the other officer. "We didn't search the house when we came in, so she could have been hiding anywhere downstairs here."

He went on through the house to the utility room and let Bandit out of his crate. The little dog barked sharply when he first saw Lewes, but then wagged his tail and approached for a friendly pat.

As Dwight opened the outer door to turn Bandit into the snow-covered yard, he glanced across the two driveways and saw Jonna's neighbor, Leonard Carlton, at the window.

"Any news?" the old man called.

"Nothing," Dwight called back. "You?"

"Sorry."

"That the guy saw your son leave?" asked Lewes.

Dwight nodded. Before he could close the door, Bandit scooted back through his legs. Between the wet and the chill, he had finished his business in record time.

"And the dog didn't bark last night?"

"Not that I heard. He sleeps at the foot of Cal's bed and that room's at the top of the stairs. If he came down when he heard the key, I'm pretty sure I'd've heard him bark."

"Yeah, he's got a shrill voice," Lewes agreed. "And it's not like you weren't on edge about your son. I'm guessing you'd've rared up if they'd made any noise."

"I slept through the door closing," Dwight said bitterly.

They walked up the carpeted stairs and Lewes swung the door back and forth on its hinges with the tip of a gloved finger. It moved easily with no giveaway squeaks.

"You touch that knob this morning?"

"Not on this side, I didn't."

"Good. I'll have it checked out."

"I was careful about opening the medicine cabinet, too," said Dwight.

"They took a chance coming up here. Must've been something they really wanted. Only how would they know? Your son on any special medication?"

"Not that I'm aware of. And I think Jonna would've said."

"What about her?"

Dwight shook his head. "Maybe her mother would know."

"Why don't you ask her? And we'll check out her doctor."

Dwight heard the subtext of what Lewes was saying, and whether or not this was more good-cop tactics to soften him up, he was nevertheless grateful.

"Thanks."

The other man shrugged. "Hell, I figure you're gonna keep digging no matter what we say. I know I would. But you gotta share anything you find, okay?"

"Of course."

Lewes looked at the football posters on Cal's wall. He touched the small trophy on the bookcase and half-smiled at the old brown plush teddy bear squashed into the bottom shelf of Cal's bookcase. "My kid's ten," he said.

CHAPTER
15

Good heed must be taken to the local conditions
of the region in which one is placed.

—*Theophrastus*

With only a generic description of the woman who had taken Cal—Caucasian, five-six, slender build, wearing a blue quilted parka with black fur trim, and without even a car color much less a make to go on—the Amber Alert had produced no fruitful sightings. There had been one call from a supermarket in Shaysville itself, but when an officer checked it out, he knew both the boy and his mother. Four more calls came from a large shopping mall off the interstate that served the whole valley, and the responding officers sighted a surprising number of blue fur-trimmed parkas. The women wearing them ranged from skinny teenagers to hefty matrons and the parkas covered the full spectrum of blue, from pale aqua to dark navy. Two even had small boys in tow, and they were at first indignant at being stopped and asked to prove that the boys were their sons; but their indignation quickly melted into compassion for the missing child when the officers explained.

"Oh, that poor woman," said the first mother, putting a protective arm around her son's shoulder.

The second, who moments earlier had scolded her son for losing his gloves and then spilling catsup on his jacket, decided abruptly that maybe she would get him that action figure he wanted after all.

———

After leaving Nick Lewes to go through Jonna's papers while he waited for the evidence truck, Dwight was grimly amused to find no parking spaces near Mrs. Shay's house. It was still small-town South here. Only three hours ago, he had told his former mother-in-law that Jonna was dead, yet word seemed to have spread through her circle so quickly that he suspected a highly efficient telephone tree. As he slid his truck into an empty space on the next block, more friends and neighbors hurried up her walk, umbrellas slanted against the slushy rain, bearing food and words of comfort. Like the U.S. Postal Service used to be, he thought—neither snow nor rain, nor heat of day nor gloom of night, would deter them. Even though Jonna's body was by now headed away from Shaysville for a complete autopsy, a local funeral home had already arranged for a spray of white carnations for the front door, and a register stood in the foyer for callers.

Inside the house, a cone of silence followed behind him as people realized who he was; and when he asked to speak to Mrs. Shay, it was her cousin Eleanor who came down to escort him up to the bedroom where Mrs. Shay lay weeping on a blue velvet chaise longue, attended by three or four of her most intimate friends. On the hearth nearby, gas logs burned in a cast-iron grate. No doubt it was meant to be cheerful, but it made the room feel oppressively warm to someone who had just come in out of the cold and wet, and the different floral scents worn by some of the women contributed to the hothouse effect. Yet Mrs. Shay had a fleecy shawl wrapped around her shoulders as if she was chilled to the bone.

"Oh, Dwight!" she moaned. "What's happening? Have they found Cal?"

"No, ma'am, not yet. The police here have put out an Amber Alert and they're questioning the neighbors again." Mrs. Shay's bedroom was one of those ultra-feminine rooms full of spindly furniture and breakable knickknacks that always made him feel like the Durham Bull in a tea shop and he tried not to bump anything as he crossed the thick white rug. "I was wondering if I could speak to you privately for a few minutes?"

Chirping and twittering, the elderly, well-mannered women immediately began to leave, but Mrs. Shay put her feet on the floor and sat up to reach for her cousin's hand. "Whatever you have to say may be said in front of Eleanor."

Eleanor Prentice tried to disengage her clasping fingers, but Mrs. Shay was insistent. "Please, Eleanor, I can't do this alone. You know my heart can't take much more of this."

"It's okay with me," Dwight told her. Today was the second time he had met this cousin, and he was impressed by her calm demeanor and soothing air.

"Of course, I'll stay if you want me," she said and brought Dwight the sturdiest chair in the room. He sat down gingerly and she joined her cousin on the chaise.

Quietly, Dwight told them how someone had entered Jonna's house during the night. Mrs. Shay murmured and exclaimed, and Dwight was struck anew by how little he had actually known of this woman before today. She had flown out to Germany for their wedding, the only member of Jonna's family to come, but there had been no time then to get to know each other. When he and Jonna returned stateside, Jonna had always come back to Shaysville alone and Mrs. Shay had visited them in Arlington only once, an overnight stay necessitated by a relative's funeral. Indeed, this weekend was the first time they had met since the divorce, and except for Cal, there was no real shared mutuality. At times, in exasperation, Jonna had called her a spoiled hypochondriac, but that had not stopped her from hurrying home whenever Mrs. Shay called. He thought of Jonna's financial records and the monthly bank draft from Mrs. Shay's bank. Quid pro quo?

Trying to get information from her was like trying to hold smoke in his hands, yet when he said that the intruder had taken Cal's sweater, she looked at him with sudden hope in her eyes. "But that's good, isn't it? I mean, it shows that Cal's being tended to, doesn't it? Warm clothes? You don't steal a sweater if you're going to hurt— Going to— Oh, surely he's still alive?" Her voice broke and she couldn't continue.

"Something was also taken from the medicine cabinet. Was Cal on any medication?"

"Not now. He had a real bad cough last week and the

doctor prescribed a cough syrup, but it made him so sleepy that Jonna got scared and stopped it after a couple of days."

"What about Jonna?"

"Only for her allergies."

"Nothing more?"

"Certainly not!" Mrs. Shay said. "What are you implying, Dwight?"

He heard something defensive in her tone and his curiosity was pricked.

"I'm not implying anything. I'm just trying to understand what's going on. Cal's dog didn't bark, so it was probably someone familiar with the house, who knew where Jonna kept medication, because those were the only two things taken. Can you think of anyone it could have been?"

"None of Jonna's friends would do such a thing," protested Mrs. Shay. "Sneak around in the dead of night? Rummage through her medicine cabinet?" A sudden thought struck her. "Oh, Dwight! Could it have been Jonna?"

"We won't know for several hours, but we're pretty sure she died sometime before then."

Yet even as he said it, Dwight found himself wondering if there were any chance in hell that it *had* been Jonna after all. That was the simplest explanation. Who else could be able to walk in and out of the house without alarming Bandit or crashing into furniture? Who else would have gone straight to the medicine cabinet? Had he been mistaken about the thickness of the ice around the Honda's doors and windows?

"We're also trying to locate some of her friends.

Maybe you could tell us who she was close to? For instance, there was a message on her machine from someone named Lou with a son named Jason?"

"Lou Cannady," said Mrs. Shay. "And Jill Edwards. They've been friends since kindergarten."

He didn't press for addresses. Surely one of them was bound to be in Jonna's address book, and as Deborah had reminded him, one friend would probably lead to others.

As he stood to go, he asked again, "Are you sure you don't know of any medications Jonna was on?"

"Absolutely not."

"One more thing. There was a message on Jonna's answering machine from you, too, Mrs. Shay. You asked if Jonna was still mad at you about something. What was that about?"

"I—I don't remember," she said, but her blue-violet eyes, so like Jonna's, fell before his steady gaze and she started to cry again.

Awkwardly, Dwight promised to keep her informed. As he turned to leave the room, Mrs. Prentice opened the door and the faithful intimates who had waited there in the hall streamed back in.

"I'll just see him out, Laura," said Mrs. Prentice, but when they reached the landing, she touched his sleeve. "Major Bryant—Dwight?" She looked up into his face and whatever she saw there decided her. "You do know that there have been periods when Jonna took tranquilizers, don't you?"

"Tranquilizers? When?"

"Since adolescence, I think."

"What?"

"You really didn't know?"

With a worried frown, she opened a door down the hall and ushered him into an empty guestroom. It was chilly and appeared not to have been used in some time. Although there were fragile ornaments here as well, they were fewer and a window seat offered a sturdy place for him to sit. There was a heating vent on one wall but Mrs. Prentice did not open it. Instead she drew her wool cardigan more tightly around her and pulled a chair close to him so that she could speak in confidential tones.

"Laura doesn't like to talk about it, not even with me. She thinks it's something shameful. Jonna's depression was never as severe as Pam's, though, and—"

"Wait a minute," said Dwight. "Her sister has depression, too?"

"With psychotic episodes. You really didn't know?"

"We never met. I mean, Jonna used to talk about her crazy sister, but I thought that was just an expression."

The older woman clicked her tongue in gentle exasperation. "Jonna was as bad as Laura. Pam is fine as long as she takes her meds. Frankly, I never thought Jonna really did have depression, but you can't blame Laura for worrying. First Stacey and then—" She paused. "If you didn't know about this, perhaps you don't know about Stacey?"

"Eustace Shay? Jonna's dad?"

Mrs. Prentice nodded.

"Jonna told me it was an accident, but from what I've heard today, it was suicide, wasn't it?"

"Again, this is nothing that Laura ever wants to talk about. Officially it was an accident. The story was that the gun was old and unstable and that it went off while he was packing up his office. In truth, that gun was a family heirloom and it was Laura's pride and joy. She kept it in their library at home until that last day when he took it to the office."

She sighed. "Stacey was a sweet man, but with no head for business. He should have sold the company the day after he inherited it, but he was too prideful. He couldn't admit that he didn't have his father's business sense and it wore on him. Looking back now, I would guess that this is where the girls inherited their tendency to depression."

"And not from the Morrows?"

"You heard about that, too?"

"Same gun, they tell me."

"Did they tell you that he had gambled with Shay money?"

"Stock market losses, right?"

Mrs. Prentice shook her head. "He lost most of his own fortune in the crash of 1929, but he didn't shoot himself till two years later when it turned out that he'd been embezzling money for his gambling debts. He would have gone to prison. That was the disgrace he could not face. The Shays covered it up and put the best face on it they could because they didn't want to besmirch the Morrow name. I'm not sure that Laura knows about her grandfather even to this day."

"You're not a Morrow?" asked Dwight.

"Oh, good Lord, no! Laura's mother and mine were Ansons, not a speck of kin to the Morrows except by marriage."

"Mrs. Prentice—"

"Call me Eleanor," she said. "After all, we're connected, you and I, through Cal. I'm sorry we never met before. I can't get over how much Cal looks like you."

Before he could reply, the door opened and one of the elderly friends poked her white head into the room.

"So this is where you disappeared," she scolded. "Laura needs you. You know how she asked Mr. Thomas to bring pictures of caskets? Well, he's come and she wants you to help her choose."

"Oh dear," said Eleanor Prentice, rising at once. "I thought she agreed to wait till Pam was here. Will you show Major Bryant out for me?"

CHAPTER
16

*Again, if during a storm from the north there is
a white gleam from that quarter, while in the
south a solid mass of cloud has formed, it gener-
ally signifies a change to fair weather.*

—*Theophrastus*

SATURDAY AFTERNOON, 22 JANUARY

The woman who escorted Dwight down the wide staircase of Mrs. Shay's house was a hand-wringer who
wanted to pause on almost every step to bemoan Jonna's
death and the unlikelihood of finding "that poor little
boy" unharmed "because, oh dear, everyone knows why
little children are taken and it's just *wicked*!" Grimly, he
saw that more women waited in the foyer so that they
could add their own commiserations.

Except that they didn't. Once again he had made a
stereotyped assumption about ineffective, hand-wringing
women; and once again, practical women like his mother
or Deborah's Aunt Zell were there to haul him up short.

The blue-haired ladies who met him at the bottom of the steps handed him two large flat boxes. "We know you can't stay and eat something now," one of them said briskly, "but we want you to take this back to Paul Radcliff's office and share it with the officers who are trying to find Cal. It's way too much food for Laura's small family and there's no sense in having it go to waste, you hear?"

"Yes, ma'am. And thank you. I know they'll appreciate it."

He certainly did, he thought as he carried the boxes back to his truck. He could smell hot biscuits and fried chicken. Despite his anxiety about Cal, his stomach rumbled. The small bowl of soup Mrs. Shay had given him at noon was long gone.

His phone rang just as he put his key in the ignition, and when he answered it, Bo Poole's voice said, "Dwight? What the hell's going on up there, boy?"

As concisely as possible, he told his boss about Cal's disappearance and the discovery of his ex-wife's body.

The sheriff listened quietly, asked a couple of questions, then said, "What about those state police agents? They giving you a hard time? Say the word and I'll speak to an old buddy of mine in Richmond."

"That's okay for now," Dwight told him. "If things get dicey, I'll let you know. How's the Rouse case coming? Any breaks yet?"

Poole repeated the report that Mayleen Richards had given him a little earlier. "She's shaping up to be a right good detective, isn't she? She still hasn't found much of a loose string to pull on, but they'll keep on it. She and McLamb left a little while ago to go interview Rouse's married girlfriend down near Makely. I'll let 'em know what you've told me. They're all concerned about you and Cal. Gotta run. My pager's beeping, but you keep in touch, hear?"

———

Back at the police station, the fried chicken and biscuits soon disappeared as the cold and hungry canvassers came in from the streets. The second box contained two or three pounds of cold cuts and several packages of rolls, and they were going fast, too.

Munching on a ham and cheese sandwich, Paul had to report that there was no word on Cal. "Clark told me that they've asked the ME to expedite Jonna's autopsy in light of Cal's disappearance. And for what it's worth, the prints we lifted off the doorknob yesterday don't match Jonna's, but they do match the ones on the medicine cabinet. We've run them through the system. No hits."

No hits. He didn't know whether to be glad or dispirited by that. "A match would've given us a name and a description," he said, stating the obvious.

"On the other hand," said Paul, striving for something optimistic to give his friend, "no match means it wasn't a hardened criminal that took Cal. I keep trying to understand why he went with her in the first place. You and Jonna both must have warned him about going off with strangers. And he wouldn't fall for the old trick about helping to look for a lost pet, would he?"

"No, but he might fall for the line that Jonna was hurt and calling for him. Not ordinarily, but yesterday? When we'd been looking for her and he was already worried and upset? And the woman couldn't have been a stranger.

Not if she was in the house. She has to be someone he was familiar with and trusted. Mrs. Shay named a couple of her friends—Lou Cannady and Jill Edwards."

Radcliff was familiar with both names.

"Lou Cannady's husband owns the local Honda dealership and Jill Edwards is president of the PTA." He handed over the address book that Dwight had given him earlier. "They're both in here. I had a couple of clerks call every nonbusiness name just in case somebody had any suggestions about Cal. They came up dry."

He paused as an attractive woman appeared in his doorway. She wore a short red car coat, black slacks, and boots. Her dark blond hair was damp from the rain and the wind had turned her cheeks as red as her coat. Dwight dropped his sandwich and stood up so quickly that he almost knocked his chair over as he reached for her.

"I was about to call you when I spotted your truck parked out front, so I—"

The rest of her words were muffled against Dwight's chest.

Paul grinned. "I guess this means the Marines have landed?"

CHAPTER
17

But if a tree stands sideways to the north with a draught round it, the north wind by degrees twists and contorts it, so that its core becomes twisted instead of running straight.

—*Theophrastus*

SATURDAY AFTERNOON, 22 JANUARY

The news about Major Bryant's missing son and murdered ex-wife had the makings of a seven-day sensation within the department, but as Deputy Mayleen Richards reminded them, "The best way to help him right now is to clear up the shooting down here so he can concentrate on what's going on up there."

She contacted Sheriff Poole to advise him of the situation in Virginia. Then, while Raeford McLamb and Jack Jamison batted around possible scenarios and polished off the rest of the catfish and hushpuppies, Richards called the only Overholt in the Makely area listings. Michael Overholt.

The phone rang so many times that she expected to hear it switch to an answering machine, but after ten rings, she broke the connection.

"Maybe we should ride down to Makely and see what we can dig up."

Jamison still had people and places to check out along the Rideout Road area, so McLamb volunteered to go along with her.

When they were fifteen minutes from Makely, a male voice finally answered the phone. "Sergeant Mike Overholt here."

"May I speak to Mrs. Overholt, please?" Richards asked without identifying herself.

"Sorry," he said. "She can't come to the phone right now."

"Is she there?"

"You a friend of hers?"

"No. I'm with the sheriff's department up in Dobbs," she said smoothly. "We wanted to get a statement from her about a traffic accident she might have witnessed. When would be a convenient time for me to see her?"

There was a long silence. "I'm getting ready to check in at the base now. How 'bout you give me your number and I'll tell her to call you?"

Richards rattled off her mobile number, but told McLamb to keep driving. "If he's going out and she's there, it'll give us a chance to talk to her without him knowing."

Makely was in the next county south, on the way to Fayetteville and Fort Bragg, but its calling area included a narrow swath of Colleton County, and according to the county map that lay open in her lap, the Overholt residence fell inside that swath. After several turns from the main highway, they wound up in a sparsely settled neighborhood that was a mixture of small stick-built houses interspersed with older mobile homes, the kind that resembled boxcars with windows rather than the newer ones that mimicked regular houses.

The Overholts' flat-roofed trailer was set back from the road in a stand of pine trees. It was painted khaki green and someone with more enthusiasm than artistry had painted a screaming eagle on the wall beside the door. A black Subaru sedan sat in the graveled driveway. As they drove past, a white soldier in desert cammies came out of the trailer and got into the sedan.

They continued slowly along the level flat road until they spotted an empty house with a "For Sale" sign near the mailbox. Playing the part of a prospective buyer, McLamb hopped out of their unmarked car and appeared to scrutinize the roof as the Subaru passed them. Before he was fully in the car again, he saw the Subaru turn around and head back past them to the trailer.

"Did he forget something or do you think he made us?" asked Richards, suddenly conscious that their car carried the permanent plate of an official department rather than the usual blue-and-white "First in Flight" design of civilian plates. Looking in her side-view mirror, she saw the soldier emerge from his sedan, unlock the door of the trailer, and disappear inside.

"Get your notebook and pretend you're taking notes on the house," said Richards as she reached for her own notebook and got out of the car.

Like the trailer, this shabby little house was also sheltered by tall longleaf pines so prevalent in southeastern

North Carolina. Here in January, the grass was a dull auburn brown, almost hidden beneath a thick layer of pine straw. More brown needles had dropped on the steps and shallow porch. A cool wind ruffled her red hair but the air wasn't quite cold enough to require hat or gloves. Together the two deputies walked up on the porch and peered through the dirty windows while Raeford McLamb made a show of pointing out various architectural features.

As Richards nodded feigned agreement, the phone clipped to her jacket rang. "Richards here," she answered automatically.

"Yeah," said a tight male voice. "I had a feeling you were the same bitch as called before. Take your jungle bunny and get your lying ass the hell off my road."

Richards turned and faced the trailer. Staring back at her through the large front window was the cammie-clad soldier with a phone to his ear.

"Sir, we're here on official business. All we want is to interview your wife about an accident that—"

"Cut the crap, bitch!" he snarled. "I know why you're here. You want to ask her about that bastard she was whoring around with while I was out there putting my life on the line. Well, he got what he deserved and so has she."

"Shit!" said McLamb, who had heard every word.

They both knew the statistics. The abuse and murder rate for children in military communities was double that of civilian communities elsewhere in the state. For wives, it was even higher. The macho mentality. The deadly training. Add mangled pride and you had a volatile combination that could blow without warning any time, any place.

"Sergeant Overholt," she began again in her most diplomatic voice. "If we could just talk?"

"I'm through talking!"

The sound of breaking glass was all the split-second warning they got. As they both dived for the ground behind the car, Richards registered the report of the rifle at the same instant that her right side erupted in fiery pain.

From the nearest houses and trailers, doors opened and people yelled.

"Police officers!" McLamb yelled back. "Stay inside!"

Another burst of shots raked the side of their car, and pebble-sized bits of shatterproof glass rained down on them.

From her position flat on the cold ground, Mayleen Richards saw a neighbor farther down the street step out into his yard. He wore Army fatigues and a brown sweatshirt and he yelled, "Mike? What the hell's going on, buddy?"

The man took one more step, then the rifle barked and he crumpled to the ground. A woman screamed and ran to him but she never got there. Overholt's next bullet spun her around and she dropped in midstride.

By then, Richards and McLamb were both on their phones calling for backup.

A second later, he realized that she had been hit, too. "Officer down! Officer down!" he screamed into his phone.

Suddenly gunfire blasted from the house next door to them and diagonally across from the Overholt trailer. Several automatic rounds sprayed the trailer.

"I'll hold him down," yelled the soldier who lived there. "Y'all run around to the back of my house. The door's open."

There was no way Mayleen was going to try to run, and McLamb was not going to leave her. "Stop the goddamned shooting!" he cried.

An eerie silence fell over the neighborhood. Long minutes passed and they heard one of the shooting victims groan. Impossible to say which it was. Dogs barked and children were crying. A woman's hysterical voice called to her friends and they heard her beg someone to let her go help them. It seemed like half a lifetime before the blessed sound of sirens reached them from a distance, coming ever closer until the air was full of raucous wails. No sooner did the first patrol cars swoop down the street than a chopper appeared overhead and hovered like a protective guardian angel.

The ground troops piled out of their cars and took cover, but nothing moved behind the shattered windows of the Overholt trailer. A SWAT team arrived on the heels of two rescue trucks and one of the team members immediately came over to get briefed by Richards and McLamb. While rescue workers hurried to the other shooting victims, one EMT stanched the blood in Richards's side.

"Lucky," he grunted as he finished bandaging it. "You need stitches, but looks like the bullet passed right through the fleshy part without nicking anything major."

He went back to the truck for a shot of painkiller and wanted to transport her to a hospital in Fayetteville, but she refused.

"What about the other two that got shot?" she asked.

"Through the heart," said the tech. "The woman's still breathing, but I doubt she'll make it. Most soldiers are good with a rifle, but they say this guy's a Ranger with a really high proficiency rating."

Someone on a bullhorn called for Overholt to come out with his hands over his head.

There was no answer and no sign of movement inside.

Sheriff Poole arrived about the time they lobbed a tear gas canister into the trailer. A moment later, the SWAT team stormed it.

"All secure! Two down!" someone called from inside.

Richards had been sitting on the ground while the painkiller took effect, and now, with a hand from McLamb, she stood upright and walked over to join the other law officers who were milling around the front of the ravaged trailer.

A raised ten-by-ten concrete square served as a front patio and was level with the door. A single shallow step led up to it, and when the two deputies approached, they saw that strings of tiny multicolored Christmas lights still dangled from the top edge of the trailer. The front door stood wide, as did a rear door to help disperse the tear gas fumes.

While they waited, Richards stepped to one side of the patio and looked in through what had been the picture window. A single long shard of glass remained, and as she watched, it slid loose from the caulk and crashed to the concrete, making several men jump. Inside, a woman lay face up on the couch. Darla Overholt. Late thirties, thought Richards, automatically cataloging. Bright red lipstick, blue eye shadow on the closed lids. But the blood that caked and stiffened her blue sweater was dry, and Richards heard one of the EMTs say to another, "What do you think? Twelve hours?"

"At least," said his colleague.

Overholt's body lay crumpled between the couch and the window.

Too soon to say whether it was the neighbor across the street who had taken him out or if he died by the M16 rifle they were going to have to pry out of his cold dead hands after they finished taking pictures to document the scene.

The neighbor's rifle had already been confiscated and would be subjected to a thorough examination by ballistics experts.

Overhead, two TV helicopters, one from Raleigh, the other from Fayetteville, circled overhead like two buzzards looking for fresh roadkill. On the ground, Richards recognized a familiar face among the SBI agents in the crowd—Terry Wilson, a longtime friend of Major Bryant's. As soon as he spotted her, he came right over. But it wasn't the two bodies inside that concerned him at the moment.

"Hey, Richards," he called. "What the hell's this Amber Alert on Cal Bryant?"

CHAPTER
18

It is always possible to find a [local] observer, and the signs learnt from such persons are the most trustworthy.

—*Theophrastus*

"You must be Paul," I said, when I finally untangled myself from Dwight's welcoming arms.

Chief Radcliff had a grin as big as Virginia on his broad face as he shook my hand. "And I'm guessing you're Deborah?"

"Any word about Cal?" I asked.

His smile disappeared and a quick glance at Dwight's face gave me the answer.

"What about Jonna's killer?"

"Not yet," the police chief said grimly.

"Driving up, I kept thinking that Cal wouldn't have gone with just anyone, would he, Dwight? Is it possible that Jonna felt threatened? She didn't know you were coming up, so did she maybe send someone he trusted—someone *she* trusted—to take him and keep him safe?"

"Would—could—might—we just don't *know*!" he said, worry and frustration in every breath he took. "That's what's driving me nuts. I want to think whoever has him believes they're doing what Jonna would want, but who the hell would it be? And why wait so long to take him? Jonna disappeared Thursday morning. Cal wasn't taken till yesterday afternoon around two-thirty."

As he spoke, he glanced up at the clock over Paul Radcliff's door. It was a couple of minutes before five, which gave him something less serious to worry about. "I thought you were driving, not flying."

"Flying's a waste of time," I said, happy to distract him, even if it meant getting growled at. "If I'd tried to fly, I'd probably be touching down at the Roanoke airport about now and it'd be another two hours to rent a car and drive back down here. Don't fuss, Dwight. The roads were in good shape."

In truth, the interstates had been just fine. Icy secondary roads had probably produced enough fender benders to keep the commonwealth's troopers too busy to worry about free-flowing traffic, so I hadn't had to lose time wheedling my way out of any tickets. It wasn't until I took the Shaysville exit that things got a little hairy, and even then I only fishtailed once. Okay, twice if you count sliding in beside Dwight's truck, but that was because I was almost past before I recognized it and I'd braked too sharply.

"I don't suppose you stopped for food," he said, offering me the rest of his sandwich.

"Or anything else," I admitted. "So point me to a restroom first."

When I came back, refreshed, I wasn't hungry but I welcomed the mug of hot coffee Paul had poured for me.

"I called Sandy," he said, "and she told me that if I didn't bring both of y'all home with me, I didn't need to come either."

They brought me up to speed on everything they'd learned since I'd spoken to Dwight earlier, including the unexpected news that Jonna occasionally took anti-depressants, which may have been what last night's intruder was after.

Shortly before six, as I turned to ask Dwight what our plans were, Paul's phone rang. He listened intently, but with his hand over the receiver, mouthed, "Nick Lewes."

I looked at Dwight and he murmured, "Special agent, Virginia state police."

"What about the boy?" Paul asked.

A moment later, he replaced the phone on the hook and gave us a regretful look. "No word on Cal, but they've had a call about the ME's preliminary findings. Jonna's body was pretty much frozen solid, so the usual indicators don't help. What did help was that you could tell them when and what she had for breakfast Thursday, because that was her last meal. They're thinking she was shot no more than four to six hours later and that death would have been instantaneous."

"While I was at work down home," Dwight said.

I squeezed his hand. We could tell each other forever that he wasn't really a suspect, but it was good to have it proved.

"Also, what lividity there is would indicate that she hasn't been moved."

"Probably talked her into meeting somewhere close to

the junkyard and forced her to drive there, then walked out," Dwight speculated.

"Lewes said they were questioning the owner again."

"Good." Dwight stood and pulled me to my feet. "We'll get settled in and be over around seven, okay?"

"You're staying at the house?" Paul asked with a sidelong glance at me.

"You don't mind, do you, Deb'rah?" Clearly he hadn't given this much thought and I had assumed we'd go to a motel. "If Cal did get away, that's where he'd run."

"Of course I don't mind," I lied.

I seemed to be doing a lot of that today.

"Great. Just let me check in with Bo and we'll be on our way."

Checking in with Bo proved to be more complicated than he'd expected. No sooner did Dwight identify himself than he fell silent, absorbed by whatever Sheriff Bowman Poole had to tell him.

"Jesus H, Bo!" he exclaimed at last. "Is she okay? . . . Good. Did they find the forty-five? . . . Tell her to call as soon as they know more . . . Yeah, thanks, Bo."

"What?" I asked as soon as he hung up.

"They got Rouse's killer," he said. "He's the guy that was shot in his pickup Thursday night that I told you about," he reminded Paul, who nodded. "Some soldier out of Fort Bragg, just back from Iraq. He found out that his wife and Rouse were getting it on while he was gone. My people went down to Makely to question her— Richards and McLamb," he told me in an aside. "Soon as the guy spotted them, he went ballistic. Literally. Started shooting at them. Killed two neighbors who tried to break it up. They called in reinforcements. A SWAT team. SBI.

The works. By the time the smoke cleared, the soldier was dead, Richards was winged, and they found the wife's body on the living room couch. Dead at least twelve hours."

"Damn!" said Paul.

"What about Richards?" I asked.

"Bo says the bullet just nicked her in the side. She's a gutsy woman. Wasn't going to go get it stitched till Bo ordered her to."

"Well, at least that's one thing off your plate," Paul said.

———

The slushy mix of rain and snow had finally quit falling, but the wet streets were starting to freeze when I followed Dwight's truck through Shaysville, which looked to be somewhere between Cotton Grove and Dobbs in size. In the residential section, streetlights on alternate corners shone through the leafless trees. Jonna's house was a story-and-a-half bungalow, probably built in the late fifties or early sixties. The evergreen foundation plantings were precisely clipped into green balls and triangles. Two dogwoods and a maple stood in the small front yard. The porch was narrow, yet deep enough to shelter three or four people.

We parked on the street out front because a Virginia crime scene van (they call theirs an evidence truck) was parked in the side driveway in front of an unmarked cruiser with permanent Virginia plates, and it looked as if the four agents were about to leave when we arrived.

"Don't crack wise on their names," Dwight muttered as two of the men approached us; and yes, Lewes and

Clark was an amusing combo, but I was too brain-dead from the drive to think of an original comment when he introduced me, and I was sure they'd probably heard all the dumb ones.

We made polite noises at each other, then Lewes looked at us with small sharp eyes. "You heard about the probable time of death?"

Dwight nodded. "But what about my son? Any sightings? Any calls?"

"Sorry, Bryant. Nothing substantial yet."

"Turn up any leads in the house?"

"Not really," they said vaguely. "What about you?"

He told them about Jonna's bouts of depression and that her cousin suggested that she might have been taking antidepressants. "But that's probably what her doctor told you, right?"

"Wrong," Clark said. "He hasn't prescribed anything like that in over five years." He moved away toward his car.

"See you tomorrow?" asked Dwight.

"Probably," said Lewes, following his partner. "Good night, Judge."

"How does he know I'm a judge?" I asked as we carried our suitcases into the house. Dwight had introduced me merely as "my wife."

"Probably the same way you figured out how to get to Shaysville," he said wearily.

"He Googled you?"

"Quicker than going through channels."

———

We set our bags in the entryway and I looked around while Dwight switched on lights and turned up the heat.

Jonna's taste seemed to have run to genteel Old South: drop-leaf side tables, brass candlesticks, an old hand-pieced patchwork quilt used as a wall hanging, lots of polished mahogany. Most were reproductions of antique pieces, though no doubt some of them would turn out to be authentic. Old but still beautiful oriental area rugs lay atop wall-to-wall carpeting.

A framed sampler hung opposite the quilt. The linen was tattered and badly foxed and the embroidery was so faded that I had trouble reading that it had been made in 1856 by "Eliz. Morrow. Age 10 yrs. 7 mos."

"That's new since my time," said Dwight, reading over my shoulder. "I bet she's the ghost."

"Ghost?"

"At the Morrow House, where Jonna worked. It's supposed to have the ghost of one of the Morrow daughters, who died of a broken heart during the Civil War." He put his arms around me and, in an effort to ease our fear and tension over Cal, said, "Would you die of a broken heart if I got shot?"

I didn't want to joke about something like that. Instead, I turned in his arms and let my lips meet his. His jacket was unzipped and I slid my arms inside to feel the warmth of his body as we kissed again. Only thirty-six hours since he left yesterday morning, yet it felt as if we'd been apart for weeks.

He kissed me again and said, "I'm glad you came."

Before we could get into the specifics of just how glad we were to see each other, I heard a sharp bark from deeper in the house.

"Bandit," Dwight said. "I'd better let him out."

I tagged along past the dining room (Sheraton table,

centerpiece of artificial fruit, lyre-back chairs, glass-fronted china cabinet, two oil portraits), through the kitchen (corner breakfast table, dated oak cabinets, standard appliances), out to the utility room (usual coat hooks, washer, dryer, closed cabinets). The dog was cute—a small terrier with brown eye patches that did look a bit like a bandit's mask. Dwight told me that he was only a year old and lived in this large wire crate whenever Jonna and Cal were both away. He barked at me a couple of times, then wiggled his little docked tail to show he really didn't mean it.

Dwight let him out into the fenced backyard and kept the door open for me. "Come meet one of the neighbors."

We walked across the frozen ground and I saw a white-haired man sitting at the window of the house next door with a dim reading lamp over his shoulder. Dwight gestured for him to open the window. "Mr. Carlton, this is my wife. She came up to help us look for Cal."

"A pleasure, ma'am," he said with old-fashioned courtesy. "Although a sad occasion."

"Mr. Carlton's keeping an eye on the house in case Cal comes back or anything odd happens."

"That's very kind," I said. "Thank you."

"No bother. This is where I usually sit to read anyhow."

It was too cold for an extended chat through an open window so we followed Bandit back inside, where Dwight discovered that his hands were black from the fingerprint powder left on the doorknob. He picked up the duffel bag I'd packed for him and announced that he was going to take a shower and change into fresh clothes.

There was a powder room off the entry hall and a full bath that serviced both bedrooms above.

I followed him upstairs to Cal's room with its single twin bed, and that's when Dwight finally realized that yes, Houston, we did have a problem.

"I guess you're not going to want us to sleep in Jonna's room, are you?"

I shook my head.

"That's okay. You can have Cal's bed and I'll sleep on the couch."

"I don't suppose it opens up?"

He gave me a blank look.

"You take your shower. I'll check."

While Bandit sat outside the bathroom door, I went down to lift one of the sofa cushions and discovered that we were in luck. There were sheets and extra blankets in the linen closet upstairs. Only one extra pillow, though, so I grabbed Cal's as well.

I tried not to let myself dwell on his room—the boyish treasures, the books, the posters, the school papers on his desk, the once loved, outgrown teddy bear on a bottom shelf. My heart turned over, though, when I caught sight of a champagne cork on his nightstand and realized he had kept a souvenir from our wedding last month.

Unlike many children of divorce, Cal had no illusions that his parents would ever get back together. They had separated before he was a year old, so he had no memory of Dwight as part of a threesome. With his base in Virginia secure with Jonna, he had been okay with our marriage and seemed ready to fit me into his North Carolina family. But now that Jonna was gone? *Just let us get him back safely and I'll do whatever has to be done*, I promised.

Pushing down my fears, I busied myself with the task at hand. The coffee table and a couple of chairs had to be shifted before I could open up the couch. Oddly enough, it already had sheets and a blanket in place, and I saw a short dark hair where the white sheet had been folded back over the top of the blanket. I knew Jonna had worn her hair long. Had her guest been a man or a woman? I pulled the sheet back and saw another short dark hair. And pulling back the sheet also revealed that whoever slept here last had used a musky perfume with floral overtones. Something sweet. Not magnolia or roses. Honeysuckle? Gardenias? It was too faint to be certain.

So, Jonna, I thought. *You don't change the sheets after an overnight guest?* And here I'd been under the impression that she was a neat freak.

I stripped the mattress, stuck the used sheets in the washer, and by the time Dwight came downstairs, had made it up with fresh sheets and blankets, ready for us to crawl into when we got back from Paul's.

From what I had seen so far, Jonna's taste in decor was unadventurous and a little too girly, but the overall effect was attractive enough, and certainly in keeping with someone whose ancestors had founded the town.

Nevertheless, the whole house made me uncomfortable as hell. Its owner was dead and I had no right to be here, looking at her things, making judgment calls on her taste and intelligence or level of cleanliness. Dwight is a good detective, but men simply do not look at houses the same way women do. I want our marriage to work and I didn't want to start comparing what his marriage to her must have been like. And although I believe him when he says he didn't love her at the end, he must have loved her at the beginning, so what sort of woman had she actually been?

No way would I ever ask Dwight. Not when there were others I could question.

"Have you spoken to any of Jonna's friends yet?" I asked as we drove over to Paul Radcliff's house.

"I haven't, but Paul's office did a quick-and-dirty call around. Maybe you could talk to some of her closest friends tomorrow? See if they know more than they've told?"

"Sure," I said.

Sometimes it's too easy.

———

Like Paul, Sandy Radcliff's brown hair was going white early and she wore rimless bifocals instead of the usual contact lenses. Dressed in dark blue sweats over a green turtleneck, she was generously built and equally generous in her welcome. Even before we took off our coats that evening, I knew that I was going to like her, especially since she was obviously fond of Dwight. I soon learned that they'd all known one another in Washington.

Their youngest son, Jimmy, was a grade level ahead of Cal although they were only a few months apart in age. Their daughter, Michelle, was fifteen and son Nick was thirteen.

When we got there, Nick and Jimmy were watching a DVD and Michelle was messaging back and forth to her friends on the computer, which sat in the family room with its screen visible to whoever passed by, a policy subscribed to by all my kin with kids in the house. ("Putting an online computer in a child's room is like giving him a big bowl of candy bars and expecting him to eat only one a day," says April, my sister-in-law who teaches sixth

grade. "No matter how much they promise, they can't resist going where they shouldn't, bless their sneaky little
hearts.")

All three responded politely as I was introduced, but
before returning to her computer, Michelle said, "We're
really sorry about Cal, Mr. Dwight. All my friends are
keeping an eye out for him."

"Mine, too," Jimmy chimed in.

"At the mall today," said Nick, "my friend and me?
There was a kid with this woman in a blue parka. We
were sure it was going to be Cal, but it wasn't."

"Thanks, guys," said Dwight. "I hope you'll keep it
up."

We went on through to the big eat-in kitchen, where
we sat down at the round oak table. "I fed the children
early so we could hear ourselves talk," Sandy said.

She took a lasagna out of the oven and let it sit a few
minutes to firm up, while Paul poured red wine and she
passed bread and olive oil to go with our salads. Although
the talk kept circling back to Cal and Jonna, we also compared backgrounds, exchanged anecdotes from earlier
years, and engaged in the usual small talk that lets close
friends open their circle to a stranger.

Sandy was a good cook but neither of us had much ap-
petite and we turned down dessert. So did Michelle, but
both boys pulled up chairs as Paul put on the coffee and
Sandy brought out the chocolate cream pie she'd baked
that afternoon.

"Either of y'all tour the Morrow House with a scout
troop last month?" Dwight asked.

"That was me," said Jimmy.

"Our class did it last year when we were studying the

Civil War," said Nick, who wavered between being too cool to evince interest while still kid enough to want to be included.

"Did you see the guns?"

Both boys nodded. "Swords, too," said Nick.

"Is there really a ghost?" I asked.

"Nah," said Nick.

"Is too!" Jimmy said. "Cal showed me." His face reddened in instant guilt.

"Showed you what?" Nick challenged as he dug into his pie.

"Nothing," said Jimmy, scrunching down in his chair.

"Is this about you and Cal sneaking off from the rest of the Cubs?" Sandy asked, eyeing him sternly over the top of her glasses.

Paul frowned at his youngest, who looked as if he would gladly slide under the table.

"Cal must know the house really well," I said, "since his mom worked there."

Encouraged, Jimmy nodded. "And his grandma used to stay there when she was little, and his mom played there, too, Cal said. She lets him go anywhere he wants to as long as he doesn't mess with anything, so when Mrs. Hightower wasn't looking, we went all the way up to the third floor and he showed me her bedroom."

"Whose bedroom?" asked Nick scornfully.

"The ghost's. Elizabeth Morrow's. That was her name and she was sixteen when she died. Cal said she would've been his great-great-great-great-aunt or something like that, only she went and died because her boyfriend got shot and killed. And he told me to smell and I did and it really was gardenias, Mom. Cal said that was her favorite flower and every time she walks, people can smell them, even in the middle of winter, and that was a little before Christmas."

Nick rolled his eyes. "Oh, right."

The others laughed, but when the boys had returned to their movie, I said, "Did Jonna use gardenia perfume?"

Dwight looked blank and Sandy shrugged.

"You think she pretended to be Cal's ghost?" asked Paul.

"Or brought the ghost home with her." I told them about opening up the couch and finding used sheets that smelled faintly of either honeysuckle or gardenia. "Gardenia must be a fairly common scent, though. Maybe a docent at the Morrow House? Assuming it has docents?"

"Only in the summertime, I think," Sandy said doubtfully, looking at Paul for confirmation.

"Something else to check out tomorrow," Dwight told me.

"Not you, hon?" asked Sandy.

"I've been told officially that this case belongs to the state guys," Paul told her. "But Cal's his son, so they can't really shut Dwight down."

We moved on to other topics, but later, when I helped Sandy clean up the kitchen, I asked about Jonna. Not directly of course. I didn't have to. Sandy knew what I was angling for and she spoke candidly as she moved back and forth from the table to the refrigerator, putting away the food.

"Dwight and Paul were assigned to the D.C. area about the same time," she said, "and we all wound up living on the same side of Arlington. We had them over to the house for cookouts and stuff, and we'd go there occasionally or to the O Club, but Michelle and Nick were little, so it was hard to get out much, and frankly, she made me uncomfortable. She was beautiful, but beautiful in a way that made me feel frumpy, and she was very class conscious, if you know what I mean? Very proper. One of those people who clobber you over the head with their own good manners? I always felt as if she was watching to catch me using the wrong fork or something, so I didn't try very hard to make her my best friend even though Paul and Dwight clicked. Besides, from the first time we all got together, I could see that their marriage was withering on the vine. Especially after Dwight left the Army and joined the D.C. police."

She began rearranging things in the dishwasher so as to fit in a final bowl, and I added a stray fork and serving spoon to the utensil basket.

"What about when she got pregnant with Cal?" I asked.

"Could've knocked me over with a feather," Sandy said. "Frankly, I was surprised they were even sleeping together. I was still carrying Jimmy, and Dwight asked me to visit her. He was worried because she was having terrible morning sickness and she didn't seem to have any friends. The day I dropped in, she was feeling so miserable that she was almost human. Her breasts were sore, her skin was blotchy, she felt bloated, she was throwing up every morning, yet she was so happy about being pregnant that for the first time I could understand why Dwight married her. It was a good visit and I felt as if we'd really connected. We went shopping for baby things a time or two and the four of us even got together for dinner about a week before Jimmy was born. Afterwards? I don't know. Maybe it was my fault for not trying harder, but with two kids and a new baby, I just didn't have much time or energy to give to the friendship, and by the time I could put my head up and look around, she was gone. I never saw her again till Paul took this job and we moved to Shaysville. Even though Jimmy and Cal are Cubs together and they play on the same Pop Warner team, she ran in a different circle from mine—the town's old money and old blood, women she was in playschool with."

"No male friends?"

"Boyfriends? I wouldn't know about that. Haven't heard any gossip."

She closed the dishwasher door and pushed the on button. "I'll tell you one thing for sure, though: if there was anything going on in Jonna's life that led to this, you can bet that Jill Edwards or Lou Cannady knew about it."

CHAPTER
19

*Dreams are difficult, confusing, and not every-
thing in them is brought to pass.*

—*Homer*

Although we were tired and emotionally drained, sleep
did not come easily. Part of it was sharing the couch with
Bandit, who seemed bewildered by Cal's absence; but an
even bigger part was our fear and dread. The night re-
vived old memories of my eighteenth summer when I
would wake from troubled dreams with a heart that was
heavy even though my mind had temporarily forgotten
why. There would be a two- or three-second disconnect
between effect and cause and then the cause would come
rushing back.

Back then, it was *Mother's dying*; tonight, it was *Cal's
missing*.

Being together helped. We were too distraught to make
love, but just holding on to each other was a comfort, and
eventually we did drift off. We slept so lightly, though,

that each time one of us stirred, the other would wake. Around two a.m., Dwight finally fell into a deeper sleep. At that point, I eased off the couch, thinking that he might continue to sleep for a couple of hours if I wasn't there tossing and turning beside him. Bandit followed me out to the kitchen, where I switched on a light over the stove and poured myself a glass of orange juice. Weird to know that Jonna had bought this juice only a few days ago. Had bought the eggs and butter and everything else in this refrigerator.

"Mooning over groceries isn't going to find her killer or get Cal back," said the pragmatist who lives in my head.

"You need to find something useful to do," agreed the preacher who shares the same quarters.

I looked around the kitchen. Except for a bowl and spoon in the sink, it was completely tidy. I opened drawers: utensils neatly compartmentalized. Cupboards, ditto. She probably ran the dishwasher only once a day because Thursday's dirty breakfast dishes were still there, but no pots and pans.

Over the phone was a calendar with squares for each day. Today was supposed to have been a playdate with someone named Jason. There had been a PTA meeting earlier in the month. A notation about choir robes last Sunday. A dental appointment next Tuesday. "Lunch w/L&J" was penciled in for the coming Wednesday.

What really stood out on the calendar, though, was a line drawn through this weekend from Thursday to Monday, a line Jonna had labeled "MH." Saturday and Sunday, yes. Those were the winter opening days for the Morrow House, according to Dwight. And the director had told him they usually worked a third day, either Friday or Monday. So why would Jonna have five days marked off like this?

Out in the utility room, all the laundry products were stored according to their function, with dog care items on their own shelf. No jackets or scarves on the coat pegs, but a pair of little-boy boots stood on a mud tray beside the door, and the sight of them tore at my heart. The temperature was below freezing. Was Cal out there somewhere this bitter winter night, shivering with cold and fear? Surely no woman that he trusted would be so cruel?

I finished drinking my juice and put the glass in the dishwasher. Then, with Bandit at my heels, I crept back through the living room and up the stairs, grateful for the carpeted steps. Between the reflective snow that covered the ground outside and the streetlight down the block, I had no trouble finding my way without switching on extra lights. Dwight and Paul had made a lot out of the fact that someone had entered the house and gone up to the bathroom without stumbling over furniture, but once my eyes adjusted, it was no problem.

I went on down the hall to Jonna's room and felt along the inner wall till I located a switch. A lamp came on beside the double bed, a perfectly made double bed. Despite the evidence of the couch, my first impression wasn't wrong. She *had* been a neat freak. No rumpled coverlet, no gown or pajama top hanging from the bedpost, no slippers kicked off in the corner. And yeah, yeah, I know the theory that tidying up as you go is the secret of an orderly home, but damn! This wasn't just orderly, it was downright military. I looked around and wondered if maybe this is one area where Dwight actually does compare me to her.

"You work full-time," the preacher comforted me, making excuses.

"Get real," said the pragmatist. *"Living in a bandbox couldn't be important to Dwight or he wouldn't have married you. He knew he wasn't getting Martha Stewart."*

Martha could have decorated this room, though. There were more frills here than downstairs—ruffles on the floral bedskirt and pillow shams, ruffles on the curtains— and the furniture was of the same style: four-poster mahogany bed and matching chest and dresser. No computer on the corner desk or, now that I thought about it, anywhere in the house. Luddite or too frugal to buy one?

The desk had clearly been examined by the state police and I wondered what they had taken. One of the desk drawers was for hanging files. The one labeled "Bank" was empty and I didn't see a checkbook either. It might have been in her purse, though. Had her purse been in the car with her?

Something else to check on.

A diary would have been helpful, but who keeps one these days? If Jonna had, it was no longer here, and from the things her house was telling me, I doubted she was the type. A quick thumb-through of the hanging files in her desk drawer showed little of the sentimental. Cal's folder contained his medical records, his school reports, group pictures from kindergarten and first grade, and one funny Mother's Day card. Unless those two state agents had taken them, she did not seem to have saved personal letters from friends or family either.

On the other hand, there were several photo albums on the long shelf above the desk. No boxes stuffed with unlabeled snapshots for Jonna. Each picture was carefully dated and the people identified. No denying it: she had been a beautiful bride, and the picture of her and Dwight on their wedding day took my breath away. I had forgotten how skinny he'd been back then. And that regulation haircut! Her dark hair had been much longer then, and in their picture, one strand had fallen over the front of her white satin gown almost to her waist. She was looking down at her flowers and presumably at her new wedding band, too. He was looking at her.

With love in his eyes.

"It was their wedding day. Of course he loved her," said the preacher.

"She left him," whispered the pragmatist. *"He didn't leave her. The divorce was her idea."*

Despising myself for the ugly jealous thoughts that coursed through my head, I quickly returned that album to the shelf and took down a later one. Ah! Pictures of Cal shortly after his birth, a tiny infant held by a man's big hands. Dwight's hands. But blessedly, no head shots of Dwight in this album. It covered the first five years of Cal's life even though there were other occasions. Birthdays. Christmases.

I thought of my brothers' wives. Most of them could produce a foot-high stack of pictures to document their firstborn's first year. No way would a whole year fit in one album, much less five. Which is not to say Jonna didn't dote on Cal as much as they doted on my nieces and nephews. He has the sunny good nature of a child who is loved and his room was cheerfully messy, which would indicate that she had not too rigidly imposed her own standards on him. Tidiness might have been instinctive to her and not necessarily a conscious choice.

As I flipped through the pictures, two faces kept re-appearing: Lou Cannady and Jill Edwards. At a lake, at a luncheon, at a baby shower. There was a studio picture of Jonna with an older woman—Cal's other grandmother? And another of those two with a third woman who had the same family features. Probably Jonna's sister.

Also on the shelf were four high school yearbooks that had been looked at so often that they were almost falling apart. I took down the last one and flipped to the back. Guess who had been homecoming queen twenty-five years ago?

And part of her court? Lou Cannady and Jill Edwards. Only back then, they were Lou Freeman and Jill Booker.

The Three Musketeers.

To my amusement, her junior year annual fell open to a picture of the girls and damned if it wasn't labeled "The Three Musketeers of Shaysville High."

A sheet of paper slipped from the yearbook. It was an alphabetized list of over a hundred names and seemed to be the kids who had graduated in Jonna's class. She had methodically drawn lines through four of the names and written "dead" beside them. For the rest, she had entered married names and current addresses, highlighting those whose addresses included "S'ville." It would appear that a twenty-fifth reunion was in the offing and that she was chair of the class gift committee.

Soon someone else would be chairing that committee. A line would be drawn through Jonna's name, and sometime during the reunion evening there would be a moment of silence for the classmates no longer there. Then the laughter and chatter and remember-whens would resume with nothing more than a brief shadow over the gathering.

I sighed and turned back to the file drawer in Jonna's desk.

A Morrow House file contained a sheaf of faded Xerox copies that had started to cornflake around the edges. The top sheet identified it as the bicentennial inventory of the Morrow House, and it appeared to list every teacup, law book, or artifact in the historic house. Different hands had added items since 1976 and I recognized Jonna's writing in a few places. Within the past six months, a Nathan Benton had given a CSA brass belt buckle, circa 1863; a Catherine D. Schmerner had donated a lady's hand mirror; and a Betty Coates Ramos had given a letter written in April of 1893 to one J. Coates from P. Morrow. There was a question mark beside the hand mirror, then, in a different-colored ink, but still Jonna's writing, she had added, "Ebony, inlaid with silver, ca. 1840." All four items had been entered under the proper room, along with a dated accession number. I seemed to remember some mention that Jonna was taking inventory. Maybe that was why she had scheduled extra days at the Morrow House?

Another folder held the paperwork to her divorce from Dwight. No way was I going to look at those, although clearly the police had, judging from the way the papers were jammed in so crookedly.

It was none of my business. It was old news, over and done with before Dwight came back to Colleton County. It was—oh, well. What the hell?

She had saved the ED pages, and as I had suspected, they showed that she had royally screwed Dwight. The valuations on her share of their marital possessions were much lower than the ones on his. She got all the furniture and the car; he got his clothes, a lawn mower, some books and tapes, the smaller of their two televisions, and the truck he'd owned back then. That was basically it. Nevertheless, he somehow wound up having to pay her a few thousand extra to attain what the presiding judge had deemed "equitable."

Well, I'd known all along that he hadn't fought the settlement. His reasoning was that anything she got would make life better for Cal, and who can fault a father for that?

Digging deeper in the file, I realized that Dwight was still paying child support based on his D.C. salary, which seven years later was still a little higher than what he currently earns with the Colleton County Sheriff's Department. Now, *that* I hadn't known, and it made me angry to think how he had occasionally taken on extra work so as to afford something Jonna said Cal needed.

But Jonna had known about the salary difference because here was a printout of the base salaries for Colleton County employees. Public records. And damn! Here was the salary range for district court judges with an approximation of my salary circled and added to Dwight's. More question marks in the margin. Dollars to doughnuts, she was planning to go back to court and ask that Cal's child support be raised on the strength of Dwight's increased household earnings. I wasn't clear on Virginia law, but good luck with that, I thought. Wait'll Portland hears.

And then, abruptly, it hit me anew that Jonna was dead. This was never going to come to court.

Clipped to the salary sheet was an account of our wedding that had appeared in the *Ledger*, Dobbs's biweekly paper. A couple of papers later, I found a printout of the write-up the *Raleigh News & Observer* had carried.

It occurred to me that Jonna either had someone looking stuff up for her on the Internet or that she used a computer at work and was no babe-in-the-woods Luddite. This would also explain how Agents Lewes and Clark knew I was a judge.

There was a hanging file labeled "Medical Records." An empty hanging file. They must have taken those to discuss with her doctor.

By now it was almost three-thirty, so I switched off the light and, rather than disturb Dwight, crawled into Cal's bed. Bandit curled up at my feet and promptly went to sleep. I lay there with my eyes wide open trying to understand why such a thoroughly normal—even rather dull—small-town mother should have been killed.

Then I fell asleep, too.

Sometime later, I felt Bandit jump off the bed. I had a vague awareness that Dwight was moving around in the doorway—probably checking to see where I was—but I was too far under to do more than mumble sleepily, "I'm fine. Go back to bed."

I heard him brush against the papers on Cal's desk, and then I was gone again, dragged down and down, back into a dream in which Dwight and Cal and I were walking through a summer garden full of flowering bushes. . . . *We aren't running but we do have a destination in mind and we are anxious to get there, yet Cal keeps stopping to smell the gardenias. "Stay up with us, buddy," Dwight says, but Cal stops again to break off one of the creamy white blossoms. "Smell, Daddy," he says. He gives me a big handful. "Smell, Miss Deborah." And all around us, the air is heavy with the sweet, sweet fragrance of summer . . .*

CHAPTER
20

Make money, money by fair means if you can, if not, by any means money.

—Horace

When next I woke, the sun had not yet risen. Looking up through the bare limbs outside Cal's window, I knew it soon would, though, because I could see faint stars in a cloudless sky. I glanced at my watch—6:05—then pushed back the covers, visited the bathroom, and splashed cold water on my face. And yes, there were faint circles under my eyes. Not enough to scare the horses, though.

Downstairs, Dwight was still stretched out on the couch, but he opened his eyes and smiled when I came into the room.

"I was just about to come looking for you," he said.

"Like you didn't know where I was," I said, sliding in beside him to feel his scratchy face against mine as we kissed. "Were you able to get back to sleep okay?"

He frowned. "What do you mean?"

"After you checked up on me sometime this morning."

He shook his head. "I haven't been upstairs since we got back last night."

"Sure you did. I heard you . . . didn't I?"

We looked at each other in dawning comprehension and I suddenly remembered my dream.

"Gardenias! She was here again!"

It took only a moment at the front door to confirm that someone else had indeed been here.

"Unlocked," said Dwight, "and I know I locked it when we came in."

"What was she after?" I wondered aloud as we headed upstairs.

I wasn't familiar enough with the house to spot what, if anything, was missing. Jonna's room looked the same as I'd left it and so did the bathroom. The sliding mirror doors of the medicine cabinet were completely closed.

"I distinctly heard the papers on Cal's desk move," I told him, "and I smelled her perfume, so she must have come into the room. But why? What was worth the risk?"

Dwight looked around the room and shrugged. He started to turn away, then stopped in his tracks, his attention riveted on the bottom shelf of the bookcase. "Carson!"

"Carson?"

"Cal's old teddy bear. I noticed it yesterday morning, and now it's gone. You didn't move it, did you?"

I shook my head. "It was there last night before we went to Paul's."

"Cal used to sleep with it when he was little. He's too old for it now, but Jonna told me that he still wants it when he's sick or unhappy about things."

"It has to be the same woman who took Cal!" I said, feeling an unwarranted rush of optimism. "She knows it will comfort him. Wherever he is, he has to be okay or why would she come for it?"

"Because he's sick?" asked Dwight. "Because he's hurt?"

He went back down for his phone to call Paul, and it startled us both by ringing in his hand before he could dial.

"Bryant here," he said. "Oh, hey, Mama . . . No, still no word . . ."

As he listened, a smile softened his grim face. "That's great! How's Kate? . . . And how's Rob holding up?"

By which I knew that his brother's baby boy had been born.

In the midst of death, we are in life.

With his hand over the mouthpiece, he said, "Seven pounds, two ounces," then gave me the phone so that Miss Emily could tell me all the details while he used my phone to call Paul and leave a message for Agents Lewes and Clark about our nocturnal visitor.

Despite our overriding concern for Cal, it was impossible not to feel happy for the safe arrival of Robert Wallace Bryant Junior, and I gladly listened as Miss Emily described the long night, how the labor pains completely stopped at one point as if the baby had lost interest in getting himself born, but then, as the doctor was about to send Kate home, around three this morning, he'd changed his mind and popped out at four.

"I waited as long as I could to call you," she apologized.

"It's okay," I assured her. "We were awake. Do they know what they're going to call him?"

"At the moment, it's a toss-up between Bobby and R.W."

I sent our love to them and promised we'd call that night even if there was nothing new to report. As long as I had a phone in my hand, I decided to call the farm. Daddy hates talking on the phone, so I knew I could give him the facts and get off and that he'd spread the word to the rest of the family.

"I'll tell 'em," he said. "And Deb'rah?"

"Sir?"

"You and Dwight, y'all don't need to take no chances, you hear?"

"We'll be careful," I promised.

At the time, I really meant it.

———

There didn't seem to be any coffee in Jonna's kitchen and Dwight confirmed that she was a tea drinker, so we finished dressing and found a pancake house that was open for breakfast.

The waitress offered coffee before she even handed us a menu, then brought it immediately and left the carafe. My kind of waitress.

Over sausage and scrambled eggs, we planned the day. I was torn. I wanted to tackle Jonna's two best friends right away, but we also needed to check out her work-space at the Morrow House.

"Should we split up?"

"Not right away," said Dwight, slathering grape jelly on his biscuit. "It's Sunday, remember?"

"So?"

"So where do proper ladies spend their Sunday mornings?"

"Oh," I said. "Right. And me without a single pair of dress gloves in my suitcase."

He grinned. "I said *proper* ladies."

It was almost like our normal banter, but I heard the worry beneath.

"Sunday's also one of the days the Morrow House is open during the winter," he said, pulling out his phone. "Let me see if I can get the director to open it up early."

From Dwight's side of the conversation, I gathered that Mr. Mayhew wasn't thrilled to have been awakened before eight on a Sunday morning. Nevertheless, he agreed to meet us there at nine.

I gave Dwight my biscuit and half my grits and we lingered over a third cup of coffee while the restaurant became busier with the pre-church breakfast crowd. As three women passed our booth on their way to a table at the back, one of them paused.

"Major Bryant?"

She was an attractive woman, late forties or maybe early fifties, with soft brown hair that was beginning to go lightly gray.

Dwight automatically came to his feet even though she kept saying, "No, no, please don't get up," as if that would stop a son raised by Emily Bryant.

Her face was concerned and she held out her hand to him. "I don't want to interrupt your meal, but I heard about Mrs. Bryant and I'm so worried about Cal. Is there any word?"

"Nothing yet," he said.

Her hazel eyes went to me and Dwight said, "This is my wife, Miss Jackson. Deborah, Miss Jackson is Cal's teacher."

The woman's smile widened in genuine warmth. "You're Cal's Miss Deborah? A judge, right? I'm so pleased to meet you. Cal's had such nice things to say about you."

"Really?" I was absurdly pleased to hear her say that because I so want him to like me and you never really know what's going on in an eight-year-old's head. Her two friends were already seated in a booth on the far side of the restaurant and had begun taking off their heavy winter coats but I scooted over on the seat. "Won't you join us for a cup of coffee or something?"

"Oh, no. I'm—" She gestured toward the others, then hesitated. "On the other hand, I did plan to get in touch with you, Major Bryant. It's probably nothing, but still—"

"Please," I said, and Dwight signaled to the waitress for another cup.

"Okay. Just let me tell them what to order for me."

Unbuttoning her gray wool car coat as she went, she left it with her friends and soon rejoined us. Yet once she was there, with a cup of steaming coffee before her, she seemed unsure how to begin. "I hope you won't think I'm gossiping. But if the children trust you, they'll sometimes tell you things that I'm sure their parents would be embarrassed about if they knew."

Again the hesitation.

"Was Cal worried about something?" I asked.

"He's such a conscientious little guy," she said. "Caring and kind." She looked at Dwight. "They say that his mother was killed on Thursday. Before school was out. That Cal was left alone in the house all night. Is that true?"

Dwight nodded grimly. "That's why he called me.

Why I came up yesterday. Not that I knew she was gone. He just said that he had promised you I would come, nothing about his mother."

"No," she said, stirring her coffee thoughtfully. "He wouldn't. He's very loyal to her, even when—"

"Even when what, Miss Jackson?" I prompted

"Please. Call me Jean." Her smile was bittersweet. "It's not as if we're going to have much of a parent-teacher relationship, are we? You'll be taking him back to North Carolina, won't you?"

Dwight nodded.

"But we'll need his school records," I said, determined to keep thinking positively, to assume that in the end our only worries would be mundane things like reading and math levels and whether we had all his transcripts.

She took a deep breath. "When I heard that Mrs. Bryant had been killed, I couldn't help wondering if it had anything to do with the fact that she had been worried about money."

"Money?"

"This past Tuesday, Cal stayed after school to ask me if there was anything a boy like him could do to earn a lot of money. I suggested that maybe his mother might let him do extra chores around the house and he said no, that he needed the money for her. He told me that he heard her talking on the phone with his grandmother one night and she was crying because she really, really needed five thousand dollars and his grandmother wasn't going to give it to her. He was afraid something bad was going to happen if she didn't get the money."

"Something bad?" Dwight asked sharply.

Jean Jackson nodded. "He said that her face was going

to get hurt if she couldn't get five thousand dollars by the end of the month."

I was shocked. Someone threatened to wreck her beautiful face if she didn't pay up?

"Did he say who was going to do that to her?"

"He didn't know, but he was genuinely upset. I told him I thought he ought to talk it over with his mother, make sure he hadn't misunderstood or something. I mean, Mrs. Bryant and her friends, they're all very well-to-do, aren't they? I couldn't understand how she could be crying over five thousand dollars. It would make a difference to me—I live on a teacher's salary—but she's a Shay, for heaven's sake. And sure enough, Cal was okay on Wednesday. He said his mother told him she had all the money she needed and everything was fine. Only now she's dead . . ." Her voice trailed off in doubt. "I couldn't help wondering if maybe the two are connected?"

CHAPTER
21

Of all the icy blasts that blow on love, a request for money is the most chilling and havoc-wreaking.

—Gustave Flaubert

Cal's teacher left us to join her friends and Dwight asked me if I had seen Jonna's bank records when I was looking through her papers last night.

"No. Those state agents must have taken them."

"Well, *I* saw them and I don't know where Miss Jackson's coming from, because Jonna certainly wasn't rich. In fact, she was living right up to the edge of her resources. There was less than seven hundred in her checking account and about five hundred in savings. She was basically working at the Morrow House to pay for medical insurance."

"You mean she lived on what you sent for child support?"

"Not entirely. I think there's a small family trust fund

that her mother controls, because she was getting a five-hundred-dollar draft from Mrs. Shay's bank every month. No credit card debt, though. In fact, no debt at all except for her mortgage. Remember that speech W.C. Fields makes in *David Copperfield*?"

"Mr. Micawber?"

"Yeah. How the difference between happiness and misery is whether you spent sixpence under your income or sixpence over?"

I nodded. As a boy, Dwight hung out at the farm so much that I grew up thinking of him as just another brother, so when we wound up in Dobbs, both of us single, we used to make popcorn and watch old videos together whenever we were both at loose ends.

"First time you and I watched that movie, I flashed on Jonna. She always knew exactly how much she had to spend and she'd spend to the limit, but she never went a dollar over. She wanted Cal's support raised, but that was for him, not for herself. When you think about it, it's pretty amazing how well she managed on practically nothing."

I was instantly and painfully aware that Dwight and I are still working out our own finances and that he's not particularly impressed with the way I handle money, but I bit my tongue before I said something bitchy, like, if money was so damn tight, why didn't she get a real job?

"This is not the time to tell him that Cal's support payments were based on his old D.C. salary," whispered the preacher.

"Especially not when he's in the middle of measuring Jonna's head for a halo," said the pragmatist with spiteful jealousy.

"If Cal heard what he thought he heard and if Jonna really did need a quick five thousand, I don't know where she would get it. Especially if Mrs. Shay wouldn't give it to her. She left a message on Jonna's machine yesterday morning. Wanted to know if Jonna was still mad at her."

"Because of the money?"

"Maybe. When I asked her about it, though, she claimed she didn't remember saying it."

"So what about her two best friends? Sandy Radcliff says they both have wealthy husbands. If I suddenly needed money, Portland would get it for me in a heartbeat, so wouldn't they?"

He shrugged. "But five thousand or she'd get her face smashed in? What the hell is that all about and what does it have to do with Cal?"

The heaviness had settled back in his voice, and I was out of suggestions. All I could do was reach across the table and clasp his hand and try to keep the optimism flowing.

"We'll get him back," I said briskly. "And at least he has Carson to hang on to for right now, so let's go do the Morrow House, get that out of the way, and then talk to her friends."

―――

The Morrow House anchored what Shaysville was pleased to call History on the Square, the square itself consisting of a small town commons complete with massive old oaks and a bandstand of filigreed ironwork painted white. The house and grounds originally took up the whole block across from the commons. After passenger service was discontinued here, the town's nineteenth-century railroad station had been moved onto the south end of the grounds and turned into a combination senior center and craft workshop. The two structures were separated by a commodious parking lot.

Directly across the street, on the other side of the square, was the old Shaysville High where Jonna must have gone to school. Set back from the street, it boasted a wide flagstone terrace with benches and a rather ugly central fountain that I later learned had been a gift of the last class to graduate from there. The front looked out of balance to my untrained eye, what with its fairly ornate main entrance on one side and a plain blank windowless wall on the other. Built around 1920 from native stone that matched the Morrow House, it still looked like a school on the outside.

Dwight gamely tried to play tour guide. "The old classrooms are subsidized apartments for the elderly," he said as we circled the square. "And its auditorium is a community theater now."

This early on a chilly Sunday morning, the sidewalks bordering the square were empty of pedestrians, and only a few cars were about. Despite the bright sun, last night's ice had only grudgingly begun to melt from the parking lot and walkways, and I was glad for my boots, not to mention Dwight's strong arm, when I almost lost my footing.

The Morrow House surprised me. For some reason, I'd been expecting one of those antebellum Taras so prevalent in tidewater Virginia and the lower South. Instead, as I soon came to hear from the Morrow House's unquenchably informative director, the first Shaysville Morrow had erected a stone version of his grandfather's brick house back in Philadelphia: "a foursquare, three-story Federalist that was gracefully elegant within its chaste constraints," according to Mr. Mayhew, a thin, stooped-shouldered man with rimless glasses that kept sliding down on his nose.

Dwight went straight to Jonna's desk, but Mayhew was clearly eager to show the house to new eyes and I thought it wouldn't hurt to get to know the man Jonna had worked with. I also thought it might be helpful to get an overview of the place where she had spent so much time. Unfortunately, Mayhew was one of those single-minded enthusiasts who miss the woods because they're too busy documenting every leaf on every tree.

He wanted to discuss the finer points of each object his eyes lit upon and he proudly caressed a cut-glass syrup pitcher on the dining room sideboard that he himself had donated to the house. To my eyes, it looked like something you could buy in any flea market or antiques mall, but for Mayhew it was his personal link to this house because it had originally belonged to a female ancestor of his, "the sister of Peter Morrow's daughter-in-law." It seemed to be a lifelong regret that he was only collaterally related to the Morrows and that none of his own people were in the direct line.

As we passed from room to room, I soon realized that he had an ulterior motive for trying to infect me with his own enthusiasm. With Jonna dead, he knew that if Cal was found—not *if*, I mentally protested, but *when*!—we would be taking him back to North Carolina and he wanted to make sure I fully understood what Cal would be leaving behind, "because you do see that this is young Cal's heritage, too?"

"Heritage" was one of the man's favorite words, and he used it when alluding to the two portraits that Jonna had hanging in her living room. Nothing so crass as "probate" or "trust" passed his thin lips that morning, but I was given the distinct impression that he rather thought Jonna's will would include a bequest to the house.

A sizable bequest. Not just the portraits but money, too.

Evidently, Mr. Mayhew labored under the same misconception as Cal's teacher. I wasn't sure if Jonna had actually made a will. I certainly hadn't seen a copy in her papers, and it suddenly occurred to me that unless there was a legal document saying otherwise, then her house and everything else she possessed would automatically go to Cal, which meant that Dwight—and by extension, I as his wife—would decide what to keep and what to let go, including those portraits and any other Morrow heirlooms. I was repelled by the man's single-mindedness, because he had surely worked it out that if anything did happen to Cal, then as the boy's next of kin, Dwight would be in line to inherit whatever estate Jonna had left. This was such a disturbing thought that when we got to the library, I almost didn't connect Peter Morrow's missing presentation gun with the gun Jonna's killer had used.

"I was rearranging things when you rang the bell. Chief Radcliff kept this room locked until closing time last night so I wasn't able to get in here to move this," Mayhew said, touching the display case on the center table in the library.

"Must have been an awfully big handgun," I said, looking at the shape left on the velvet by the gun that had shot Jonna.

"It was an early Colt revolver," said Mayhew. "One of the first postwar models. Post–*Civil* War," he elucidated. "And yes, it's big. Weighs over two pounds. The original presentation case seems to have been lost, but the gun itself is a beauty. Silver plate over brass and quite elaborately engraved. Have you seen it yet?"

I shook my head. "A forty-four?"

"Actually, I believe Nathan Benton—he's the chair of our board of trustees and very knowledgeable about guns—he says it's a thirty-six caliber."

"Tell me again why this Peter Morrow was presented with the gun?"

"For all that he did for Shaysville after the war. He was a judge, too, you know."

"Really?"

"Oh, yes. A true politician in the best sense of the word. Even though he didn't own any slaves and thought it was an abomination on the South, he was a Reb through and through. Nevertheless, he had Yankee relatives and he was very careful not to burn all his bridges to the North. He had been a representative in Congress and this part of the state had a lot in common with what became West Virginia, so he had good friends in high places in Washington. That's how he got appointed to a seat on the western court here. That position enabled him to use his Philadelphia connections to lighten Shaysville's burdens of Reconstruction. As Shelby Foote was fond of saying, there was no Marshall Plan for the South, but Judge Morrow used the law to keep the worst of the carpetbaggers out, then he used his influence to get the railroads up and running again. He helped Thomas Shay secure contracts to ship furniture-grade oak and maple all over the Northeast. That's where the Shays first made their fortune. In the lumberyards here. A little later, they went into the furniture business themselves and made even more. That created so many jobs that Shaysville was quite a prosperous place for the time and its citizens were grateful to the man who had made it possible."

He lifted the case and slid it under the table, where it was hidden by the green felt cloth that hung down almost to the floor.

"Such a shame that all three guns were taken. Our guest speaker was looking forward to examining them. I don't suppose there's a chance that Chief Radcliff will let us have the presentation piece back today?"

"I wouldn't count on it," I said, chilled by such insensitivity. I found it hard to believe he would actually want to display so quickly a gun that had killed his colleague, I don't care how historical the damn thing is. Was he that cold-bloodedly obsessed with this house?

"It's just that today was supposed to be so special."

"Oh?"

"The Shaysville Historical and Genealogical Society usually meets here on the fourth Sunday of each month at five o'clock. But the January meeting is always at four with an opening reception for the public at three. As chairman of the board, Mr. Benton thought perhaps we ought to cancel in consideration of Jonna, but as Mrs. Ramos pointed out, we've already announced it in the paper and on the radio that someone is coming over from the Smithsonian to talk about family treasures, so we're expecting quite a large crowd. Thirty-five people, maybe even fifty if it stays sunny."

"How many members in your local group?" I asked.

"Technically, we have forty-five on the rolls, but many are too elderly to participate any longer and some live out of the state. Our core group of actives is around twenty. Jonna was so looking forward to today. She was to take office as president of SHGS and I'm sure she would have wanted us to go ahead as planned. We will have a tribute to her, then the presentations."

"Presentations?"

"That's what makes today so special. Mrs. Ramos is donating a set of drapes and a counterpane for Elizabeth Morrow's bedroom that she had made up in High Point, and Mr. Benton is giving us a perfectly exquisite perfume bottle of cameo glass such as Elizabeth might have used. He found it in a yard sale down in Winston-Salem, if you can believe it. The man has *the* most amazing eye! He's picked up at least a dozen bibelots for us these last few years since he moved to Shaysville. But Mrs. Santos is closing in on him. Not that it's a contest, but every item helps. Except for two of the bedrooms, the upstairs is rather bare. We've acquired enough major pieces from the mid- to late eighteen-hundreds to furnish them sparsely, but very few of the grace notes that finish a house." He gestured to the period mirror over the mantelpiece and to the ornate matched vases that sat on the mantel. "So much was sold before the house came to us."

He looked around as Dwight stuck his head in and said, "Sorry to interrupt, but where is Judge Morrow's office?"

"Through that door. Is there something I can help you with?"

At that moment, the doorbell rang. Mayhew automatically looked at his watch and muttered, "It's much too early for them," as he went to answer the door.

"Found something?" I asked, noting the papers in Dwight's hand.

"Yeah," he said grimly. "I was skimming through these old inventory sheets and—" He broke off as Agents Lewes and Clark followed Mayhew into the library.

Here in daylight, I was struck anew by what a similar type so many lawmen can be. Like Dwight, these two agents were muscular six-footers, and, like him, they were casually dressed in jeans and leather jackets. Dwight had more hair than both of them put together, though. Clark's hair was thinning rapidly across the crown and Lewes's had retreated well behind the crest of his forehead.

"Major Bryant," said Clark. He nodded to me. "Judge. I had a feeling we'd find you here."

"Any news of my son?" Dwight asked.

"Sorry, Major. You know how it is. A flurry of false alarms that turn out to be nothing, but we'll still check out every one of them. What about you?"

Dwight handed Lewes the inventory and pointed to an item down near the bottom of the page. "According to this, a box containing five thirty-six-caliber cartridges is stored in the safe in Judge Morrow's office."

"Bullets?" Mayhew looked shocked.

"Show us the safe," said Lewes.

The director obediently opened a door in the far wall. There were very few books in the library, but Peter Morrow's office was a grander version of my own and the shelves here were packed with law books of every description.

While we watched, he moved aside a set of Blackstone's *Commentaries* to reveal a small wall safe with a combination lock.

"Now let me think." Mayhew went over to the huge mahogany desk that dominated the room. He hesitated and looked at each of us with a nervous laugh. "I suppose all of you can be trusted not to speak of this?" It was less a question for us than a reassurance to himself. He pulled out a side drawer, turned it over, gave an annoyed click of his tongue, and tried the adjacent drawer. There on the bottom was the combination. "In Judge Morrow's own writing," he told us.

Agent Clark took a penlight from his jacket pocket and carefully examined the exterior of the safe before touching it. I heard him mutter, "Hell. Knob and handle both too grooved to hold prints."

His partner held the drawer up so that he could read off the numbers while he twirled the dial. Clark tugged on the handle and the door of the safe opened smoothly. The diameter was only about eight inches yet surprisingly deep. He aimed his penlight inside. "Empty."

"Empty? That's impossible!" Mayhew exclaimed, almost elbowing the two bigger men aside so that he could look in.

"Don't touch," Clark said sharply as Mayhew put out his hand to the safe.

"Peter Morrow's signet ring," Mayhew moaned. "Elizabeth's gold locket. Catherine's mourning parure."

"What's a parure?" asked Clark.

"A matched set of jewelry. In this case, a necklace, bracelet, and earrings of onyx and braided hair."

Clark frowned. "Hair?"

"It was her daughter Elizabeth's hair. I know it sounds morbid, but people used to take comfort from wearing the hair of a loved one."

"Is the set valuable?"

"To the Morrow House, it's priceless. On the open market? It's a matched set of known provenance and the glass cases of the bracelet and necklace are set in twenty-four-carat gold with intact hinges, so perhaps two thousand dollars. The hairwork is incredibly fine."

"And those other pieces? The signet ring? And gold locket?"

"No more than five or six hundred. We kept them in the safe simply because we have no secure way to exhibit jewelry yet."

"Is this the ring?" asked Clark. He held out a small domed box that had once been red velvet but was rubbed down almost to the cardboard backing. Inside was a heavy gold ring inset with an onyx signet.

"Yes! Where on earth did you find it?"

"In Jonna Bryant's pocketbook," said Lewes.

"In her purse? I don't understand. And what about the locket? The mourning jewelry?"

"Sorry. This was it."

CHAPTER
22

*Every plant, animal, or inanimate thing that
has an odor has one peculiar to itself.*

—Theophrastus

It was only 9:45 when we left the Morrow House that morning, pointedly invited by Lewes and Clark to take ourselves elsewhere while they gave Jonna's desk and computer a thorough examination. They had also called for their evidence truck to process the wall safe on the off chance that Jonna or someone else had left prints.

Mr. Mayhew had feebly denied that Jonna would have stolen from the safe, yet insisted that only the two of them knew that the combination was written on the underside of that drawer.

"He said the same thing about the keys to the locked key cabinet, too," Dwight told me, turning his own key in the truck's ignition, "and he's only been there eight or ten years, so somebody had to show him. One of the board members or someone in that Historical Society, maybe."

"Did she take them to sell?" I wondered aloud. "Raise the five thousand that way?"

"Never happened." He sounded angry at me for even suggesting such a thing. "I don't care how desperate Jonna was for money. It would never cross her mind to steal. Period."

I knew better than to argue, but that didn't stop my rebellious thoughts. Only last week, he had arrested one of his mother's most trusted employees. Miss Emily was the principal at Zachary Taylor High School and it turned out that the manager of the school's cafeteria had embezzled almost thirty thousand over the last two years. Both of us have put too many pillars of the community behind bars to say for sure who would or wouldn't break the law, but if Dwight was on his white horse and riding in defense of his lady wife's reputation, anything I said could and probably would be used against me, so I kept my mouth shut.

"The shooter must have put that ring in her purse to make us think it was a falling-out of thieves in case the suicide note didn't work," he said as we drove out of the communal parking lot.

"What about the other pieces? And the guns?"

"Probably kept them to sell somewhere out of the area. The signet ring and guns would be too easy to identify, but it sounds as if those weird hair things are pretty common and gold lockets must be a dime a dozen. Could be she caught the thief in action and threatened to tell. Maybe that's why she was killed."

And maybe she offered to meet her killer in an out-of-the-way place so she could sell him the things she herself had stolen, I thought, but did not say. Nor did I say, *Or what if they were the first installment on that five thousand she needed so urgently?*

What I did say was, "We forgot to tell them about Jonna needing money."

"Yeah, well, it's not like we won't be seeing them again," he said grimly.

"So where are we going now?"

Dwight glanced at his watch. "It's still too early for church to be over. You mind coming with me to talk to her mother so I can ask her about the money again? She'll always be Cal's grandmother, so you probably ought to meet her."

"Sure," I said gamely, even though I had a feeling that this was going to be really awkward.

———

Mrs. Shay lived in the older and wealthier part of town, only a block or two from the Morrow House, and close enough that Cal had probably been allowed to walk back and forth if he wanted. Hundred-year-old oaks and maples towered above the rooftops in this neighborhood and there was a lot of elbow room between the houses. According to Dwight, Jonna said that they had moved to this smaller house after her father's death. Smaller? It looked plenty big to me, almost as big as the old farmhouse I had grown up in, and our house had held fourteen of us. Mrs. Shay and her two daughters must have rattled around here, and now it was just Mrs. Shay.

Dwight said the house had been full of people yesterday afternoon. Only one woman was there this morning.

She looked to be mid-sixties, with short salt-and-pepper hair that waved softly over her head, and she wore tailored black pants and a black silk turtleneck accented by an unusual silver pin on the upturned collar. I myself seldom use perfume except for dress-up occasions, so I immediately noticed the light, spicy scent she wore. Her strong face was somber when she first opened the door in response to our ring, but then she smiled and said, "Oh, Dwight! Come in. Any news?"

"Not yet," he said. "I've brought my wife to meet y'all. Deb'rah, this is Mrs. Shay's cousin, Eleanor Prentice."

We said the usual things and she led us out to the kitchen. "I was just making tea and toast for Laura. She insisted on staying alone last night, but I knew she wouldn't eat a thing this morning if I didn't come around and fix it for her."

She put the plates and cups on a large silver serving tray and hesitated when Dwight offered to carry it up for her.

"Well . . . only to the top of the stairs, though," she said. "I'm sure she'll want to put on a pretty dressing gown and fix her face before seeing you. If you like, Deborah, do make you and Dwight a cup of tea, too. The cups are in that cupboard and you'll find tea and sugar in those caddies beside the stove. There's milk and lemon in the refrigerator. If you don't see what you need, just root around."

Left alone, I did exactly that. I opened drawers and doors and looked inside. It was clear where Jonna got her tidiness. Even the gadget drawer was neat. Silverware, both sterling and stainless, occupied their own sections in separate drawers. In the pantry, one shelf held soup, another canned tuna and salmon, another pickles and relish, etc. etc. No mixing of soups with pickles. Yet she was also a doting grandmother if the Christmas picture that Cal had drawn for her meant anything. Here it was almost a month past Christmas and the picture still hung on her refrigerator door. The one he made for Dwight and me still hangs on our refrigerator, too, I thought sadly.

I added more water to the kettle and turned on the flame, then set out porcelain cups and saucers for Dwight and me when it became clear that there were no mugs in this kitchen. No tea bags either and Eleanor Prentice had taken the teapot with her, but a flameproof measuring cup made a serviceable substitute. By the time Dwight came back down, the loose tea leaves had steeped enough to strain into the cups.

He sighed as he retrieved a rubber baseball from the bowl of fruit on the counter and sat down at the table, where he absently tossed the ball from hand to hand. I sensed that he was wondering if he would ever again play catch with Cal. Nothing I might say could change that. The best I could do was try to distract him.

"Eleanor seems nice," I said. "How's she related to Mrs. Shay?"

He frowned. "I think she said their mothers were sisters. So that makes them what? First cousins?"

We talked about degrees of kinship and how Eleanor would be Cal's first cousin, twice removed—idle meaningless talk to fill up the silence that seemed to be growing between us.

He finished his tea and stood up to stretch and flex his arms, then stared out the window into the backyard that was beginning to show patches of brown grass beneath the melting snow. "I just feel so damn helpless," he said with his back to me. "We're running around in circles while Cal's out there somewhere and there's nothing I can do."

"We'll find him," I murmured.

"You keep saying that!" His voice was harsh with frustration. "Dammit, Deb'rah, what if we don't?" He turned and the anger drained from his face, leaving it bleak and despairing. "What if we don't?" he said again.

Before I could answer, the cousin returned to say that Mrs. Shay was ready to see us.

"For some reason, she seems to be doing much better today," Eleanor said as she led the way upstairs. "She's still heartsick about Jonna, of course, but she's decided that Cal's going to be all right in the end. I think it's a combination of prayer and the power of positive thinking."

————

Mrs. Shay's corner bedroom was quite spacious and nicely proportioned with high ceilings and classic molding, yet despite tall windows on two sides, it felt almost airless. Too much polished wood furniture, too many ruffles, too many knickknacks. I charitably decided that it probably seemed like a cozy retreat to her.

Two delicate wing chairs upholstered in the same blue velvet as a nearby chaise sat in front of the fireplace, where small gas logs burned in the grate. The silver tray with the remains of Mrs. Shay's toast and tea sat on a low table between the two chairs.

Mrs. Shay herself sat on the chaise under one of the windows, and after I was introduced she gestured for us to take the wing chairs while Eleanor Prentice sat down beside her.

There was very little family likeness between the

cousins, but having compared that family picture in Jonna's bedroom with recent pictures of Jonna herself, I knew that Mrs. Shay had been equally beautiful in her youth. Even now, with wrinkled face and age-blotched hands, she was still pretty and still as slender as a young woman. Her eyes were widely spaced and so blue that they were nearly violet, and they made her seem innocent and somehow vulnerable. I could well understand why her husband had catered to her and had tried to shield her from the sordid details of his financial failures. Nevertheless, there must have been a lot of money left from the wreckage if she could afford to live like this for so many years. No wonder the Mayhews and Jacksons of the town thought Jonna had money to spare.

Dwight confessed that we were yet no closer to finding Cal, but she gave a serene smile and lightly patted his arm.

"Put your trust in the Lord, Dwight. That's what I've done. There's nothing He can do now for Jonna, but last night I began to feel absolutely certain that Cal will come back to us safely."

I had expected to find a mother and grandmother shattered by grief, but this woman seemed oddly removed from it. Yes, tears came to her eyes whenever talk turned to Jonna, but no tears for Cal, even though I'd been told that he was her only grandchild.

As I sat there quietly listening, a strange feeling of déjà vu began to take over my senses, and when she mentioned last night, I pinpointed the reason.

"Your perfume is very nice," I said, leaning forward to make sure I wasn't mistaken. "Is it gardenia?"

"Why, yes, it is," she said, struggling to play the

polite hostess. "All the women in my family are quite fond of it."

"Not me," Eleanor said crisply as if alluding to old family rifts. "And not Mama."

"Nor Jonna," Mrs. Shay conceded sadly. "It began with Elizabeth Morrow," she told me. "You know about her ghost?"

I nodded. "I heard that her gardenia perfume can be smelled whenever she walks."

"I've often wondered who the maker was that it could last for over a hundred years," Eleanor said.

Mrs. Shay gave a mournful smile. "Eleanor doesn't believe in ghosts, so Elizabeth doesn't believe in her. She's never let Eleanor smell her perfume."

I thought at first she was joking, but her regretful tone was clearly meant as condolence for her cousin's exclusion from an inner circle. It reminded me of the pitying look my Aunt Zell gave a newcomer to Dobbs who was so clueless as to openly desire to join the town's oldest book club, a club limited to the female descendants of the original 1898 founders.

Talk turned to funeral arrangements now that Jonna's body had been released for burial. The day and time were yet to be set, but probably Tuesday or Wednesday. "Surely Cal will be back with us then," Mrs. Shay said hopefully.

"When does her sister arrive?" Dwight asked. "She *is* coming, isn't she?"

"Of course she will come," Mrs. Shay said sharply. "Pam was devoted to Jonna. To Cal, too. It was such a shock. To her, to me."

"To all of us," said Dwight. "And I hate to have to

bring this up again, Mrs. Shay, but that message you left on her answering machine, when you asked if she was still mad at you. Was it because she had asked you for money and you told her no?"

Tears filled those dark blue eyes. "Oh, Dwight, how can you be so cruel?"

Her glance bounced off me and then away, and I realized that she was embarrassed that he'd asked something so personal in front of me.

I immediately stood. "Y'all need to talk privately. I'll wait downstairs."

Eleanor started to rise herself, but Mrs. Shay begged her to stay.

"It's okay," I said. "I know the way. Why don't I just take this tray back to the kitchen and fix myself another cup of tea? It was good meeting you, Mrs. Shay. I'm just sorry it had to be under these conditions."

I knew I was babbling, so I shut up and grabbed the tray. Dwight opened the door for me and I made my escape.

———

It was almost a half hour before Dwight and Eleanor came back downstairs.

As they entered the kitchen, I heard her say, "I don't know the address, but let me find a piece of paper. I can give you directions and draw you a rough map."

She opened the drawer beneath the wall-hung kitchen phone, took out a notepad, and quickly sketched a simple map, explaining turns and landmarks as she drew.

Dwight asked a couple of questions, then tucked the map in his pocket and turned to me. "Ready to go?"

"Not till Mrs. Shay tells us what the hell she's done with Cal." I was so angry that I couldn't stop my voice from shaking.

"What?"

I stormed across the kitchen and threw open the door to the utility room. There, hanging on one of the pegs amid a collection of scarves and knitted headwear, was a dark blue parka. Its hood was trimmed in black fur and the smell of gardenias permeated the cloth.

CHAPTER
23

Grief teaches the steadiest minds to waver.

—Sophocles

Eleanor Prentice was bewildered as Dwight jerked the parka from its peg, sending hats and jackets flying.

"I don't understand," she said. "Why would you say that Laura took Cal?"

"Didn't you hear the description of the abductor?"

"Only that you thought at first it was Jonna and then someone else."

"This is the coat the woman was wearing," Dwight said, almost shaking it in her face.

"But it's not Laura's. Her parka's black, not navy."

"There's no black parka," I said, gesturing toward the pegs beside the outer door of the utility room.

"But I know Laura. She was genuinely upset when Cal disappeared."

"Then explain the gardenia perfume," I said. "Oh, Dwight, she *must* have been the one who took Carson.

That's definitely something a grandmother would think to do."

Eleanor threw up her hands. "What on earth are you talking about?"

"I slept in Cal's room last night and somebody sneaked in and took his teddy bear. I thought I was dreaming, but whoever it was wore gardenia perfume. The same perfume as Mrs. Shay. And you said yourself that she was here alone last night. No wonder she's not worried about Cal. She knows where he is."

"Oh, dear Lord," she said, sinking down on the nearest chair. "Pam?"

Now it was our turn to look bewildered.

"Pam? Jonna's sister?" I asked.

"She uses gardenia perfume," said Eleanor, "but I thought she was still in Tennessee."

"Is she here? Is this her coat?"

"I don't know."

Dwight was already turning the pockets inside out and found nothing except some loose change and a used tissue. He fumbled through his own pockets for the number Agent Lewes had given him last night, grabbed the kitchen phone, and dialed it. As soon as Lewes answered, he immediately described what we had found and where. "Yes, my ex-wife's sister . . . Pam . . . wait a sec. What's Pam's last name?" he asked Eleanor.

"Morgan. Mrs. Gregory Morgan, but Laura says she may go back to Shay if it does come to a divorce."

Dwight relayed the information, then turned again to the older woman. "What kind of car's she driving?"

"The last time she was here, it was white. A white sedan."

"The make?"

She shook her head helplessly.

"Would Mrs. Shay know?"

Lewes must have said something about Tennessee's DMV because Dwight said, "Yeah, of course, I'm not thinking straight . . . It's Knoxville, right, Eleanor?"

She nodded, then gathered her wits and said, "Laura's address book is in that drawer. It probably has Pam's home phone number."

Dwight pulled the drawer out so hard that it slipped off its rails and crashed to the floor. I began picking up the pencils and pens, rubber bands, and scratch pads that tumbled around his feet and put them back in the drawer while he plucked a leather-bound address book from the pile and soon was reading off all the numbers and street addresses listed for Pamela and Gregory Morgan. There were even two cell phone numbers, one labeled "P" and the other "G."

"I'll try the 'P' one right now," said Dwight. "What? . . . Yeah, we'll be here. Damn straight we'll be here."

He broke the connection and dialed the number for Pam Morgan's cell phone. A moment later, he said, "Crap!" and hung up the phone. "That number's out of service."

He grabbed up the parka that had fallen to the floor and headed back upstairs with the two of us close behind. And no, he didn't bother to knock at Mrs. Shay's bedroom door. She was standing in her slip in front of her open closet, and as we entered she gave a ladylike gasp and reached for her robe.

"Really, Dwight!"

But Dwight was in no mood for niceties. He thrust the parka toward her and said, "It's Pam's, isn't it? You lied when you said she was still in Tennessee. Where is she? What's she done with Cal?"

Every word was like a slap across her face and she was so shocked that she clutched the robe to her chest as if it could protect her. Moaning, she held out a hand to Eleanor, but her cousin said, "No more false pride, Laura. You have to tell us."

"Is she here in the house?" Dwight asked. "Dammit, where's my son?"

"I didn't lie," she whimpered. "I told you she would be at Jonna's funeral. You never asked if she was already here."

Eleanor was dismayed. "Oh, Laura. Why didn't you tell us?"

"She's here? In the house?" He started for the door, but Mrs. Shay called him back.

"They're not in this house, Dwight. I don't know where they are, honest. She wouldn't tell me."

While Dwight paced like a caged tiger that smells blood, Mrs. Shay told us how Pam had blown into town two weeks ago. "She left her husband. She wanted to stay here, but she wasn't taking her pills, so I couldn't have that. Not with my friends in and out and she acting so—so—"

"Crazy?" asked Dwight.

"She's not crazy!" Mrs. Shay cried. "She's not, she's *not*! She's bright and funny and just as sane as you and I when she's taking her pills."

"And when she doesn't take her pills?" I asked quietly. "Is she violent?"

"She would never hurt Cal," Mrs. Shay said, instantly grasping the concern beneath my question. "She adores him."

"But she hears voices," said Eleanor, "and sometimes those voices tell her to do"—we watched her search for an alternate term for "crazy" that wouldn't set her cousin off again—"to do . . . irrational things."

"The only person she's ever hurt is herself," Mrs. Shay said.

I thought back to the used sheets on Jonna's couch. "Did she stay with Jonna?"

Mrs. Shay nodded. "When she first got to town, she did. Jonna let her stay a whole week, but then, with the voices and all . . . You know what Pam's like, Eleanor, and this was a busy time for Jonna. Taking inventory out at the Morrow House, working on her class reunion, committee members coming to the house. And Jill and Lou are such gossips. It would have been all over town. We called Gregory, but he wouldn't come get her this time. He said he was through trying to keep her on her medication."

"So where did she go when Jonna kicked her out?" Dwight asked impatiently.

Mrs. Shay was once again affronted by his choice of words. "You make it sound as if we're coldhearted and uncaring, but Pam knows she would be more than welcome if she stayed on her pills and—"

Dwight stopped pacing. He's six-three and solid, and as he towered over his former mother-in-law, there was such thunder in his face that she quit talking in midstream. "You know something, Mrs. Shay? I don't give a flying frick about your problems with your daughters.

This is my son. Now you tell me what the hell's she done with him or I'm going to take this town apart house by house and you can damn well believe that every one of your snooty friends will be told exactly why."

"But I don't know!" she wailed. "Honest. Jonna got one of our Anson cousins to invite her up to their cabin up in the hills and she did go, but she was afraid of getting snowed in up there and left before it started falling Wednesday night. William—that's our cousin—called the next morning to see if she was okay, but when I talked to Jonna on Thursday morning, she hadn't seen Pam either. We thought maybe she'd gone on back to Tennessee."

Thought? I wondered. Or hoped? Out of sight, out of mind. Whited out like the snow.

Even though she had taken Cal, I nevertheless felt a sudden compassion for Jonna's poor unstable sister. Delusional people like her cycle in and out of my court every week, one of the Reagan legacies you seldom hear mentioned. I'm told that we used to have a halfway decent system of community mental health centers, but Reagan ended all the federal funding for them as soon as he took office, which is why so many demented, homeless people roam our streets these days. And they want to carve his face on Mount Rushmore? Jeez!

"So where did this parka come from?" Dwight asked.

Mrs. Shay took a deep breath. "Pam must have taken mine by mistake. She was here around two this morning. I couldn't sleep so I came down for cocoa and a few minutes later she came walking through the kitchen door just as if she were a teenager again coming home from school."

"She still has a key?" Eleanor asked.

"Well, of course she does. Both my daughters . . ." She choked up as the realization hit her anew that now she only had one daughter.

"Why didn't you call me?"

"At two in the morning? I'm sure Kenneth would have liked that."

"Mrs. Shay," said Dwight, and from his tone, I knew he was about to lose it again.

"She knew about Jonna, Dwight, and she was heart-sick. Said she knew it was going to turn out bad."

"Knew what was going to turn out bad?"

"She wasn't making sense. She said that Jonna would be a ghost now, too. She would be a guide to freedom. That the trains were running and Jonna would be on one, riding to glory and freedom. Her voices had told her so."

"Did you ask her about Cal?"

"I tried, Dwight. I really tried. She said he was asleep in the arms of Jesus."

Ice formed around my heart. "Oh God!"

"No, no," she assured me. "He's not dead and not hurt, because she wanted me to give her some crackers and soda for him. She took a banana, too, and she said there was one more thing she wanted for him, but she would have to be a ghost to get it. It was all such a muddle. I couldn't tell what was real and what was her voices. They had told her that she had to watch out for the blood-hounds. Can you believe that? *Bloodhounds!* Nobody in this town has a bloodhound and the trains quit running years ago. I tried to tell her that, but she said she had to keep him hidden till it was safe to bring him out. She promised me that she would bring him back. I told her he must be scared and cold, but she said no, that she and Jesus were keeping him warm." She looked at Eleanor helplessly. "And you know she was never religious. It's those voices in her head."

"She would have to be a ghost?" Dwight asked.

"That's what she said, but it was just nonsense. It was so distressing. I'm sure this is not good for my heart."

"Did you come over to Jonna's house last night and take that teddy bear from Cal's room?"

"Of course not!"

"So it was Pam. Bandit knew her. And she knew the house because she stayed there last week."

The doorbell rang and I hurried down to answer it. I expected it to be Agents Lewes and Clark. Instead it was two attractive women, who looked to be a couple of years older than me. They were expensively dressed in an understated way—wool topcoats, cashmere scarves, high-heeled boots. One carried a large dish garden of mixed green plants in a beautiful ceramic bowl. I recognized a prayer plant, a peace lily, and some variegated ivy. It was accented with a huge white silk bow.

"Is Mrs. Shay receiving callers?" one of them asked. "We're old friends of Jonna's. I'm Lou Cannady."

"And I'm Jill Edwards," said the other.

It would appear that church was over.

CHAPTER
24

It is better to be envied than pitied.

—Herodotus

"Come in," I told the two women. I took the plant and, after making sure the bottom was completely dry, set it on the hall table beside the funeral home's guest register. "Mrs. Shay hasn't come down yet, but I'm sure she would want to know you're here."

"Are you one of the Anson cousins?" asked Lou Cannady as she signed the register. She automatically peeled off the numbered tab beside her name and stuck it on the dish garden so that next week sometime, Mrs. Shay would know exactly who should be sent a graceful little handwritten note of thanks for it.

"No, I'm Deborah Knott, Cal's stepmother."

"Really?" said Jill Edwards. "Is there any news? Everybody's so worried."

"Nothing official," I said.

Her small china blue eyes swept over me, and I knew

she was cataloging my clothes, my hair, and my looks, which was okay since I was doing the same with both of them. The Three Musketeers had not been three of a kind. Jonna had been a brunette and easily the prettiest of the three. Jill was a natural blonde with a square face, while Lou Cannady had a long thin face and dark red hair. Both women had the ease and confidence of those born to privilege. And yes, it might be the small-town version, but it was no less real than what I'd seen drifting in and out of chic stores in midtown Manhattan after Mother died and I tried to run away from school, from family, and, most of all, from a world she no longer inhabited.

In a demonstration of long familiarity, these two hung their coats in the hall closet before I could offer to take them and moved into the living room, almost as if they were the hostesses.

"How's she doing today?" Lou asked.

"Between Jonna's death and Cal's disappearance, that poor woman looked as if she was about to collapse yesterday," said Jill, taking a seat on the couch.

Her straight blond hair was asymmetrically cut and had a tendency to fall over one eye so that she had to keep pushing it back. Would've driven me crazy, but it did help disguise the squareness of her face. It wasn't just her hair that occupied her restless hands, though. She was someone who constantly straightened her collar, rearranged the folds of her skirt, touched her earrings, and fiddled with her rings (obligatory large diamond solitaire and a really nice emerald about half the size of Ireland).

Usually redheads are stereotyped as volatile and flighty, but Lou Cannady was much more composed than her friend. She sat gracefully in one of the period side chairs and she didn't fidget, but her hazel eyes were watchful as we discussed Mrs. Shay's losses.

They were both still in shock that Jonna had been shot in what appeared to be a deliberate, cold-blooded murder, and they were dismayed to hear that I had no inside information on why anyone would want her dead.

"I believe Cal's dad is a sheriff's deputy?" she asked, moving on to the other aspects of this situation. "Is he involved with the investigation?"

I nodded. "We're both doing everything we can."

"Oh, that's right," said Jill, brushing blond hair from her eyes. "You're a judge, aren't you?"

Again I nodded. Well, it was natural that Jonna would have spoken of us to her closest friends. Portland Brewer and I certainly would have.

"I saw the yearbooks in Jonna's house," I said. "The Three Musketeers. You three have been tight forever, haven't you?"

"Since Miss Sophie's Playschool," Lou said sadly. "Grade school, high school, college. It was such a shock when she went off to visit a friend in Germany and wound up marrying an Army officer instead of someone here in town. Of course, he *was* very good-looking."

"Still is," I said, smiling.

"And really, Lou, who was left here?" asked Jill, adjusting the gold loop in her earlobe. "You and I got the best of her leavings and she was too picky for anyone else."

I like to think I have a poker face but that catty remark must have registered because Lou smiled and said, "You'll have to excuse Jill. She never got over the fact that Forrest proposed to Jonna first and Jonna turned him down."

"Oh, and like Dale wasn't in love with her first, too."

"Every boy in our crowd was in love with Jonna first," Lou agreed calmly as she tucked a strand of red hair behind her ear, "but not all of them got down on bended knee with a ring."

Jill Edwards had a blonde's fair skin and she flushed in annoyance. "I'm sure Judge Knott isn't interested in all this ancient history."

Lou gave a wicked grin. "I bet she is. I certainly would be."

I laughed outright and Jill gave a grudging smile.

"You're right," I said. "I can't help feeling that the more I know about Jonna's life here in Shaysville, the better I'll understand Cal."

Sudden tears pooled in Jill's blue eyes. "Poor kid."

"How can we help?" asked Lou. "What do you want to know?"

I told them to call me Deborah, and at first I just listened to what they had to say about their murdered friend, the shock of it, their sense of loss. It wasn't that no one had ever been murdered in Shaysville, rather that no one they knew had. They were warm in their praise of Jonna and had funny stories about the mischief they had gotten into as kids. I gathered that she had been their leader since the Miss Sophie days. She was the prettiest, her people had founded the town and had produced its most illustrious sons, so her blood was the bluest. She had the best sense of style and she was acknowledged to be the smartest of the three. Maybe not academically, although her grades had been decent enough in school, but she was savvy about people and situations, which was probably the real reason why she had married so far outside their crowd, Lou said candidly, as if realizing for the first time how claustrophobic "our crowd" could be. They had not been surprised, though, that the marriage had failed "because after all," Jill said, "this is where her roots were and what would a lawman like Dwight Bryant do here?"

Not that there was anything wrong with being a lawman, they quickly assured me, but the opportunities here were so limited that they didn't really blame him for hastening the end of the marriage by not wanting to come to Shaysville with Jonna.

I didn't bother to explain that coming to Shaysville had never been an option so far as I knew. Evidently Jonna had given them a slightly different version of the divorce from the one Dwight had told me.

"Who are you going to believe?" asked the preacher. *"The man you've known all your life or the secondhand reports of her partisan friends?"*

The pragmatist remained silent, withholding judgment.

"What about her sister?" I asked. "Was she part of your crowd?"

"Oh, sure," said Jill as she removed a stray thread from her skirt. "She was a year ahead of us in school, but in some ways it was as if Jonna were older. Pam seemed to look up to her instead of the other way around. But she was popular in her own way, very cute and funny. She and Jonna used to be really close."

"Used to be?"

"You don't know?"

They exchanged glances, then Lou said, "Maybe she didn't talk about it with Dwight."

"Probably not. She didn't like to talk about it even with us," Jill said earnestly. "See, Pam always liked to party, but when she went off to UVA, she got into alcohol pretty heavy. Turned into a real lush. Flunked out of school. Maybe even did drugs for a while. Totally freaked Jonna out. She didn't want to have anything to do with her. She wouldn't even apply to UVA, which is how we wound up going to Hollins."

"Which may have been another reason she left Shaysville, now that you think about it," said Lou.

Evidently neither woman had ever connected the two. "But it's true that even though Pam hadn't lived here since high school, Jonna didn't come home to stay till Pam was safely married to someone out in Tennessee. We haven't seen Pam in . . . when *was* the last time?" Jill asked her friend.

"Three or four years ago?" Lou hazarded. "Poor Jonna was so embarrassed. She thought Pam had totally dried out, but all she had done was switch to vodka so you couldn't smell it on her breath. Remember how crazy she acted that day?"

Jill nodded. "It was sad. They had to call her husband to come get her."

Crazy, I thought. Dress it up with all the politically correct terms: "unstable," "schizophrenic," "psychotic." The world would still call it crazy and people like Jonna would still prefer that people think she had an alcoholic sister rather than one who heard voices in her head.

"Who were Pam's friends?" I asked. "Who would she turn to here?"

They both looked blank. "I don't think she has any friends left here. She and Missy Collins were pretty close during high school, but Missy married someone in the State Department and they live in Italy, the last I heard."

"Why are you asking about Pam?" asked Jill. "Hasn't she come yet?"

"She's been in town almost two weeks," I told them.

They were not as surprised as I'd expected.

"Ah," said Lou. "That's why Jonna canceled the meeting. I wondered what the real reason was. She must have been dealing with Pam. Is she drinking again?"

"Meeting?" I asked, sidestepping the question of Pam's problems.

"Our twenty-fifth high school reunion's coming up this spring," said Jill.

I remembered the list of names and addresses in Jonna's files and that she had chaired the class gift committee.

"It's not official yet, but we're pretty sure that Pam's the one who took Cal," I said.

Jill's face lit up in relieved delight. "Oh, thank heavens! I've been so worried about him. Afraid that it was Jonna's killer or some pervert that had taken him. But if it's Pam . . . I mean even if she is back on the bottle, she would never hurt him."

Lou agreed. "But why would Pam take Cal? Unless—?"

"Unless what?"

"I know it sounds irrational, but could she be thinking of trying to get custody? Keep Dwight from taking him back to North Carolina? She can't have children of her own and she was always sending him books and toys."

"Have both motels been checked?"

"Chief Radcliff put out the word as soon as they realized Cal really was gone," I said.

"By now she could already be back in Tennessee with him," said Jill.

Lou shook her head. "She wouldn't leave before the funeral."

The custody theory was something they could easily believe and I didn't see the point of disabusing them.

"Was Jonna seeing anyone?" I asked.

"Boyfriends? I don't think she's gone out with anyone in a couple of years," said Jill.

"No," said Lou. "Remember that guy last fall? What was his name? Selby?"

"That's right. I'd forgotten Jim Selby. But he was so not our crowd that she dropped him after two dates."

The doorbell rang again, and this time the room did fill up with law. Dwight and Eleanor Prentice came downstairs, but Mrs. Shay refused to leave her room, so Jill and Lou went up to see her while Dwight and I told the two state agents about finding Pam's parka, how Pam had visited her mother alone last night, and how she must have been the one to sneak back in the house for Cal's teddy bear.

"Like a ghost," I said, repeating what she had told Mrs. Shay.

"The car's a Honda Accord, same model as the victim's, only white. Tennessee plate." Agent Clark rattled off the number and Dwight jotted it down on one of the cards in his wallet. (I had given him a proper leather-bound notepad and pencil as a stocking stuffer at Christmas, but does he remember to carry it? File under "Rhetorical Questions.")

Dwight told them about Pam's mental condition, I elaborated on how her friends had been told she was alcoholic, not psychotic, but that they agreed with Mrs. Shay that Pam was truly fond of Cal. "They think she took him because she hopes to get custody of him."

Dwight was outraged by that until I reminded him that this was a woman listening to inner voices about bloodhounds and ghosts and trains that no longer ran.

All five of us were at a loss to think of where Pam could be. No friends, Jonna dead. "Are you sure she's not here in the house?" asked Lewes.

"I checked every room upstairs," said Dwight.

"And I checked the basement before I found the parka," I confessed. "Eleanor?"

She shook her head. "I can't imagine. Unless the Anson cousins are hiding her? I'm her only other relative here and you're welcome to search my house if you like."

"You're just around the corner, right?" asked Clark. "No offense, ma'am, but if you're sure you don't mind, maybe I could just take a quick look?"

Eleanor was understandably offended. "Of course," she said frostily. "Let me get my coat."

As the two of them left, I remembered that the only reason I was downstairs alone long enough to search the place was so that Dwight could question Mrs. Shay about the money.

"Did you tell Agent Lewes about Cal's teacher?"

"Not yet."

"Something new?" Lewes asked.

Dwight explained how we had run into Cal's teacher at breakfast this morning. "On Tuesday, Cal told her that someone was going to smash his mother's face in if she didn't come up with five thousand and that she was crying because his grandmother wouldn't give it to her."

"Someone threatened her?" asked Lewes. "Who?"

"I don't know and Mrs. Shay completely denies that it

ever happened. She keeps insisting that Cal must have misunderstood." He threw up his hands in exasperation. "Who knows? Maybe he did. In any event, his teacher says that on Wednesday Cal was okay again, said that his mother had told him she had plenty of money and for him not to give it any more thought."

Lewes frowned. "Maybe I'd better have a talk with Mrs. Shay."

"Good luck," Dwight said sourly. "She'll just start crying."

"How about I try after Jonna's friends are gone?" I offered. Even as I spoke, I was struck by a sudden thought. "Is there any chance that Pam could be hiding somewhere in the Morrow House?"

"Huh?" they both said.

"Well, think about it, Dwight. Mrs. Shay says she kept talking about Jonna being a ghost *too*, and the only other ghost we know about is the one there. Paul Radcliff's boy says that Cal told him his mother had played in the house as a child, so wouldn't Pam have played there as well? I gather they don't show any of the bedrooms on the third floor except for Elizabeth Morrow's, the one who's supposed to be the ghost."

"I don't know," Dwight said doubtfully.

"Won't hurt to turn that place inside out," Lewes said. "I get the feeling that Mayhew guy may know more than he's telling."

"And while you're there, see if you can see Mrs. Shay's bedroom window from there. It's awfully coincidental that she showed up in the wee hours just when Mrs. Shay was up and about, don't you think?"

Eleanor returned with Clark, and Dwight offered to leave me his truck keys while he rode over to the Morrow House with the two state agents, but I told him I could certainly walk the block or two.

When Lou Cannady and Jill Edwards came back downstairs, I asked Eleanor if I could make us a cup of tea.

"Of course you may," she said as she went up to see if Mrs. Shay wanted her.

Lou and Jill made noises about needing to get home, but when I said I had a few more questions, they came along to the kitchen with me. Despite their genuine sense of loss, I also sensed some of the repressed excitement I had seen before when tragedy jolts people out of their commonplace lives.

"Did Jonna talk much about her work?" I asked when we were settled around the table with steaming cups. "Any conflicts there? Anyone she didn't get along with?"

Not at all, they told me. Jonna loved being at the Morrow House. After all, it was her family. And wasn't it fitting that the last Morrow in town married the last Shay? That made Pam and Jonna the last to bear the Shay name.

"Jonna felt like it was her duty to help out over there as much as she could," said Lou. "She was very civic-minded."

"And she treated it like a real job, too," said Jill.

"A real job?" I was puzzled.

"She was conscientious about keeping regular hours and everything. She never ditched it even when it conflicted with something we wanted her to do."

"But it *was* a real job," I said. "She got paid."

They both laughed at that. "Honey, she's a Shay. Even though Mrs. Shay doesn't own Shay Furniture, whatever Jonna got paid was just pin money for her."

Still smiling, Jill pushed the swoop of hair back from her face and looped it behind her ear. "Of course, Jonna was something of a tightwad, so I'm sure she cashed every paycheck."

"Tightwad?" Their bright chatter made me feel thick-tongued as I felt my way toward an unwelcome growing comprehension.

"Not to speak ill of the dead, but she almost never picked up the check if she could help it. She wouldn't treat herself to shopping trips to New York unless one of us paid for the hotel, and even then, she would limit herself to one or two good pieces instead of buying something trendy just for the fun of it."

Trying to be fair, Lou said, "I think she was worried about Cal's future. She never talked about the terms of her trust fund, so we don't know how it was set up and whether or not it could transfer to the next generation."

She saw my blank look. "I don't mean to throw off on Dwight—and you were right: he still is one fine-looking man!—but she didn't think he'd be able to give Cal all the advantages she could. I mean, his people are just farmers, aren't they?"

That did it. It was crystal clear that they were unaware that Jonna had no huge funds at her disposal, that she treated her job at the Morrow House like a real job because it *was* a real job. I didn't like Jonna Shay Bryant very much at that point. Ashamed of her sister, ashamed to tell her oldest friends that she was living on the very edge of her finances? To let them think that Pam was an alcoholic and that she herself was a penny-pinching tightwad rather than tell the truth? Afraid she'd lose face if—

Wait a damn second here. Lose face?

"In her papers," I said. "There was something about a class gift?"

They both nodded and explained that it had all been Jonna's idea. Even though the old high school had closed eighteen years ago and was now apartments for the elderly, it still held their memories and their history and it was part of Shaysville's History on the Square. Jonna had proposed that their class rebuild the old clock tower that used to stand on the front left side of the building.

"Clock tower?"

"It was built from the same local stones, two stories high with four tall slender arches and a clock that faced the commons," said Lou. "About a year or two after they built the new high school and closed ours, a drunk driver crashed a dump truck into it and knocked it flat. Smashed the clock beyond repair and left the whole front looking unbalanced."

"So when Jonna suggested that our whole class chip in to replace it," said Jill, taking up the story, "we got estimates and it was a lot higher than we hoped even though we could get the stones at cost from another old SHS alumnus. I mean, some of our classmates still work in the furniture factory and Jonna was afraid it would be too much of a hardship."

"But then Jill and I suggested that the three of us chip in five thousand each for the clock and that would make the tower itself more affordable."

"Plus," Jill said candidly, "we'd get to put our names on the brass plaque for donating the clock separately."

"Jonna was afraid the others might think we were being too pushy, but the rest of the committee said that nobody would object to memorializing the Three Musketeers that way. We put it to a class vote, and they were right."

"I could have told Jonna that," said Jill, her huge emerald flashing as she straightened her collar. "If we gave the clock, it would mean fifteen thousand less that they'd have to contribute, so of course they agreed to it."

CHAPTER
25

How like a winter hath my absence been.

—Shakespeare

"Jonna wasn't worried that someone would smash her face," I told Dwight and the two agents when I caught up with them at the Morrow House. "She cried because she was going to *lose* face if she didn't come up with the money. Cal really did misunderstand."

I repeated what Jonna's friends had told me about their ambitious plan for a class gift and how it had mushroomed out of her control.

"All these years and she never let them know that she didn't have any money of her own." That was the part that was hardest for me to understand. "When I put it to Mrs. Shay, she broke down and admitted it."

"Did she cry?" Dwight asked cynically.

"Buckets. She's on a complete guilt trip right now, wondering if Jonna would still be alive if she had agreed to advance her the money." I looked up at the three men. "Would she?"

The other two shrugged and Dwight said, "Be a pretty big coincidence if the money's not connected somehow or other, but coincidences do happen. That's why they're called coincidences."

"She tried to rationalize it by pleading poverty herself— that the house eats up so much of her income, she had to keep up her own appearances, and of course, all the doctor visits and the different medications they prescribe. She's so torn up over it, though, that she's going to donate the money in Jonna's name. And speaking of medicines," I said to Lewes and Clark, "did Jonna's doctor have a suggestion as to what Pam took from her medicine cabinet?"

Clark started to put me off, but Lewes answered candidly. "Her doctor didn't, but the boy's doctor prescribed some codeine-laced cough syrup a couple of weeks ago and that bottle doesn't seem to be in the house."

"Jonna probably threw it out," said Dwight. "Mrs. Shay said it made Cal so groggy that Jonna quit giving it to him."

While we stood there talking in the doorway of the office Jonna and Frederick Mayhew had shared, five or six people arrived at the front entrance. I glanced at my watch. One o'clock. Opening time for the house, but these people, mostly women, seemed more like friends than casual tourists. Belatedly, I remembered that Mayhew had said that today was the monthly meeting of the Shaysville Historical and Genealogical Society at four o'clock, with a reception at three. The women headed through to the kitchen with boxes of canapés and the makings of punch.

Frederick Mayhew was everywhere, urging people to sign the register, suggesting that some of the men might begin setting up folding chairs in the double parlors, and giving us anxious looks every time he passed as if fearful we might rain on his parade before he could find the umbrellas.

"Any luck here in the house?"

"Nada," said Dwight, "and we were from the attic to the basement. Looked under all the furniture, all the closets, in every storage chest. Not that there's much of that upstairs. Like you thought, it's just those two bedrooms that are furnished, Peter Morrow's room on the second floor and Elizabeth's on the third."

"Smell any gardenias?"

"Actually, we did, so we turned that room inside out, but there's no sign of Pam or Cal anywhere."

"What's next?" I asked.

"Radcliff's got his people canvassing the area around the junkyard, but so far, ain't nobody seen nothing," said Agent Clark.

"We're going to drive up into the hills and interview the cousins that the sister stayed with earlier this week," said Lewes.

"I guess I'll stay here and keep going through Jonna's records, see if I can spot anything out of the ordinary," Dwight said.

I saw the strain in his face, heard the frustration in his voice.

"I'm starved," I said, trying to sound plaintive. "Could we go get something to eat first?"

He wasn't terribly enthusiastic about finding a restaurant, so once I'd freshened up and we were in the truck, I suggested that we swing by a grocery store, grab some deli stuff, and take it back to the house.

That sounded better to him. "We probably ought to let Bandit out, too."

Twenty minutes later, as we waited in the checkout lane at the local supermarket with sliced turkey, lettuce, sandwich rolls, and broccoli salad, Dwight reached for his wallet and a slip of paper fell out of his pocket. It was the little map Eleanor Prentice had drawn for him just before I showed them the parka I'd found.

"Damn!" said Dwight. "Dix Lunsford. I forgot all about him."

"Who's he?"

"Cleaning man for the Morrow House. He and his wife used to be the live-in help when the Shays had that bigger house before Jonna's father killed himself. I think he still does some yard work for her once in a while, and his wife comes in once a week. According to Mayhew and Mrs. Shay both, they're devoted to the family."

Yeah, right. White employers always want to think that their black employees are devoted.

As soon as Dwight had paid for our food, he hurried me out to the truck. "If he's known Jonna since she was a baby, then he knows Pam, too. Maybe he can tell us where she'd go to earth."

Because Eleanor had combined the drawn map with oral instructions, I drove while he navigated.

Every little town in the South has its black section on the so-called wrong side of the railroad tracks or main highway, and Shaysville was no exception. A block of trashy unpainted shacks will butt up against blocks of modest but well-maintained bungalows. Most middle-

class, white-collar blacks live in integrated neighbor-
hoods these days, but the poor and working class still
cling to the old familiar haunts.

"Take the next right," Dwight said as I drove slowly
down a street wreathed in the quiet of a cold Sunday
afternoon. "It'll be the third house on the right, brick
house with green shutters. There it is. Pull in here."

I waited in the warmth of the truck while he went up
to the door and knocked. Then knocked again.

My disappointment almost matched his after it became
clear that no one was home.

"Maybe they're just having Sunday dinner with someone," I said when he came back to the truck.

"Yeah, and maybe they've gone to Florida for the winter," he said gloomily. "I'll see if any of the neighbors
know."

I watched him trudge up the walk next door and ring
the bell. An older man came to the door, they spoke
briefly, then Dwight returned with a happier look on his
face.

"They've gone to visit one of her sisters and should be
back before dark," he reported.

———

Back at the house, Dwight let Bandit out and went
over to talk to Mr. Carlton while I put together a couple
of sandwiches. He returned the little dog to its crate so
that we could eat in peace. Although Bandit was too well
trained to actually beg, he would sit on his haunches to
watch with hope-filled eyes and would instantly pounce
on any stray crumb that fell to the floor.

Dwight was still on edge, but there had been a slight

easing of tension. We were both frantic to find Cal, but knowing that it was Jonna's sister who had taken him and not some faceless child molester helped a little.

As we ate, Dwight glanced at his watch, then did a double take. "Today's the twenty-third," he said, as if both surprised and chagrined.

I looked at him inquiringly, my mind a blank.

"As of yesterday, we've been married a whole month."

"Awww, and I didn't get you a present."

"Yes, you did." He reached for my hand. "You came."

The instant our hands touched, it was as if every hormone that had been quiescent those last three days flared into action.

As of one mind, we left our half-eaten sandwiches on our plates and pushed back from the table. When we kissed, it took all the willpower we could muster not to start undressing each other then and there. Somehow we made it from the kitchen to the couch, but just barely. He unzipped my sweater while I struggled with his belt buckle. It seemed to take forever. We were like two lost and half-frozen hikers who suddenly stumble upon a steaming hot spring in the middle of an ice field. We dived in, sinking down, down, down into the liquid warmth, then coming up for air just long enough to take a breath before the waters closed over us again.

Afterwards, we lay entwined and the most relaxed since Cal disappeared. Dwight pulled the blanket up over my bare shoulder and murmured, "Happy anniversary."

I yawned and snuggled closer. "Wake me in an hour, okay?"

"Ummm," he said with a yawn of his own.

———

It was closer to two hours before we awoke, and the sun was heading for the horizon in a blaze of red and gold against the western sky.

We took a quick shower and decided to split up for a while. Dwight would check in with Mayleen Richards or Bo Poole, see what was happening back home, then go question the Lunsfords. I would drive my car back to the Morrow House and try to catch Betty Ramos before the end of the HSGS's monthly meeting. If she was helping with the inventory, maybe Jonna had let something slip.

As I headed out, Dwight took pity on Bandit. "Poor little guy's not getting the attention he's used to. I think I'll let him ride along with me this evening."

He snagged Bandit's retractable leash from a nearby hook and the terrier ricocheted off the sides of his wire crate in excited anticipation.

"You're a kind man, Dwight Bryant," I told him. "Y'all have fun. I've got my phone turned on, so call me if you hear anything."

CHAPTER
26

The lion on your old stone gates
Is not more cold to you than I.

—*Alfred, Lord Tennyson*

SUNDAY AFTERNOON, 23 JANUARY

Down in Colleton County, Detectives Jack Jamison and
Raeford McLamb once again found themselves going
door-to-door. Television might sensationalize police
standoffs and car chases, but a lawman's day-to-day routine was much less exciting, and that was perfectly fine
with McLamb. After yesterday, he was more than happy
to be back in the mundane world of knocking on doors,
ringing doorbells, and questioning residents in the Rideout Road area as to whether they had noticed Sergeant
Overholt or his black Subaru sedan around sunset on
Thursday. As far as he was concerned, the less sensa-
tional the better. Getting shot at was for TV actors and
nothing he wanted to make a habit of.

The two deputies began their inquiries at the Diaz y Garcia compound, where they pulled out pictures they had taken from the Overholt trailer. "When y'all were working in that new development that backs up against Rideout Road, anybody see this man?"

The two brothers-in-law recognized Overholt's pictures from last night's newscasts; and the name of the dead woman, Darla Overholt, had not gone unnoticed by J. D. Rouse's wife. Nita Rouse was now blaming herself for her husband's death. No, she had not told Overholt about the affair. Not really. But she had friends, friends who were hotly indignant on her behalf. Maybe one of them? No, she could not, would not, name names. Naming names had left three people dead.

"On the news, they say someone else was shot," said Miguel Diaz. "The woman who came with you before— Mrs. Richards?"

"Detective Richards," said McLamb. "She's not married."

"Is she hurt bad?"

"Bad enough," Jamison said with a stern look toward the weeping Nita Rouse.

"It was only a flesh wound," McLamb told him, touching his side to indicate the place where the bullet had grazed Richards.

"She is in the hospital?"

"No, she's able to come in to work as long as she takes it easy. Now, about Overholt. Did y'all see him hanging around the Orchard Range area Thursday? Maybe he parked his Subaru back there?"

Diaz translated for his brother-in-law, who shook his head.

"But I will ask our men," said Diaz, "and I will tell you if they saw him."

———

From the Diaz y Garcia compound, they looked in on Mrs. Harper and her dog, Dixie, in the Holly Ridge development off Rideout Road. She, too, shook her head when shown Overholt's picture.

"Like I told you and Detective Richards yesterday, I don't remember any cars other than that pickup truck. And now *she* gets shot? I couldn't believe my eyes when I saw the news last night. Here she was sitting in my living room one minute and the next minute she's down there in Makely getting shot at. That man was a disgrace to his uniform. Good riddance to bad cess!"

She saw the deputies exchange glances and gave a sheepish smile. "The Colonel used to say that my temper rides my tongue. All the same, I'm really sorry to hear she got shot. Please give her my best."

———

There were fifteen houses in the Holly Ridge development, which was not on a ridge nor possessed of any holly trees. On this cool Sunday afternoon, most people seemed to be home. All had heard about the shooting even though none of them admitted to knowing Rouse. They were familiar with Mrs. Harper's dedication to keeping the road free of litter; and at one house, two preteen black sisters said they occasionally went along to help. "Dixie's cute and Mrs. Harper always gives us hot chocolate with marshmallows afterwards."

To their extreme disappointment, they had not been.

outside on Thursday afternoon when the shooting actually occurred. They had heard about it almost immediately afterwards and, although forbidden to leave their
street, they were watching at the intersection when Mrs.
Harper came back.

"She was so shook, that we pulled the wagon the rest
of the way for her," one girl said virtuously, "even though
she didn't want to let us do it."

"I didn't know white folks could turn that green," said
her sister.

———

Near the end of Rideout Road itself, they came across
a homeowner who had known Rouse casually for years.
"His mama might've loved him and maybe his little girls,
but he's not much loss to the rest of the world."

"Why, Thomas Conners!" his scandalized wife scolded.
"What a thing to say. And on the Lord's day, too."

"Tell the truth and shame the devil," he retorted. "Besides, if you can't tell the truth on Sunday, when can you?
He never cared for anything or anybody 'cepting hisself,
far as I ever saw. Too bad that poor woman had to be the
one to see it happen."

"You know her?" his wife asked. "You never told me
you knew her."

"Not to say *know*," her husband protested. "But you
see somebody enough, you get to thinking you do, you
hear what I'm saying? She's out at least once a week
when I'm coming home."

But when Conners walked out to the drive with the
deputies, he grinned and described how Mrs. Harper had
read him the riot act once.

"See, the wife, she's real religious. Doesn't hold with alcohol of any kind. Me, I like a beer once in a while. Especially in the summer, you hear what I'm saying? I'll stop off after work once in a while, get me a cold one and nurse it all the way home. Sometimes, I'd be almost home, so I'd stop along Rideout Road, finish it off and toss the can, then use a mouth spray so the wife wouldn't know. Well! I hadn't paid much mind to her before then. I mean, yeah, I knew she was out picking up stuff, but it didn't really sink in what a slob I was being till she came up outta that ditch and lit into me. I thought for a minute there she was going to sic her little dog on me! Well, I apologized for my beer can and she cooled off, but you better believe I've never so much as tossed a peanut shell since. In fact, it makes me right mad myself now when I see somebody dumping their ashtrays or cleaning out their cars by trashing up our roads, you hear what I'm saying?"

———

Detective Mayleen Richards was not a happy camper. Part of it was coming down off of yesterday's adrenaline high, part of it was the painful throb in her side whenever she forgot and lifted her arm too quickly, but mostly it was having to sit here and cool her heels while waiting for a lab report on the guns they had taken from Sergeant Michael Overholt's shattered trailer.

She had given Special Agent Terry Wilson all her contact numbers and he had promised to pass them on to the lab techs. He had also promised to move this matter to the front of the line back at SBI headquarters so that Major Bryant could stay focused on events in Virginia.

Sheriff Bo Poole had told her to take the day off, give

her gunshot wound time to start healing, but she knew she would only be calling in every five minutes to ask the guys if they had heard anything. Better to be here catching up on paperwork than to stay home pacing the floor like an anxious teenager waiting for some boy to call and ask her for a date.

Of the two handguns in Overholt's trailer, one was a .45, so how long could it take to match the slug from Rouse's head? Unless they were also waiting till they could tell her whether the soldier had killed himself or been taken out by his neighbor across the street?

Richards sighed and entered another report in her computer.

There were footsteps in the hall and she looked up through the glass wall to see a uniformed officer followed by what seemed like a large hanging basket covered in pink flowers.

"Someone to see you, Detective," said the officer. He stepped aside and the plant entered the squad room.

The man carrying it set it on the floor and there was a faint jingle as he stood up. It was Miguel Diaz.

"Okay?" asked the officer.

"Fine," she said faintly, and he returned to the front desk.

"Señorita Richards," said Diaz. "They said you were hurt. The man that shot my *cuñado*'s *cuñado* shot you, too."

"Yes."

"Yet you are here, not at home?"

"Yes." She gave herself a mental shake. Who was the interrogator here anyhow? "Why are *you* here, Mr. Diaz?"

"Your friends came to ask if we had seen the soldier who shot you and J.D. I said I would speak to my men, and I did. Now I am here to say that none of them saw him."

She looked at the plant, an extremely exuberant pink geranium. "And that?"

"When people are hurt or sick, it's the custom to bring flowers, *sí*?"

His tone was innocent, but there was mischief in his dark eyes.

"That's very kind of you," she said formally. "But I cannot accept it."

"It's only a flower." Diaz pulled a decorative hook and chain from his pocket. "Where should I hang it?"

"Don't be silly. You can't hang it here."

He glanced around the room. "You're right. No window. No sunlight."

"I appreciate the thought, but I'm afraid you'll have to take it back with you."

"No problem. It'll be better at your house anyhow, *sí*? What time do you get off work?"

"Mr. Diaz—"

"Miguel. Or Mike, if you prefer. And you are Mayleen."

"No!" she said firmly. "I mean, I'm Detective Richards."

"Why so formal? Unless . . . perhaps there is already someone special for you, Detective Richards?"

"This is crazy. Are you propositioning me? I'm a law officer."

"Is it against the law to give you flowers?"

"Look, you're part of a murder investigation. I can't take your flowers."

"But your killer is dead. The investigation's over."

"Not until we get the ballistics report."

He shrugged. "A formality, surely?"

"All the same."

Diaz picked up the plant by its hanger and swung it onto a bare spot on her desk so that she had to look over the huge pink blossoms. "I was right," he said, looking from the geraniums to her face. "With your beautiful hair, you should always wear pink."

Pink? She felt herself going brick red.

She stood abruptly, but before she could order him to leave, her phone rang and she grabbed it up eagerly. "Richards here."

It was Terry Wilson and he delivered the bad news quickly, like ripping a piece of adhesive tape from a tender wound. "The bullets that killed Overholt and his wife came from his rifle, but the forty-five isn't the same forty-five that killed Rouse. Sorry, Richards. We searched that trailer pretty thoroughly."

"Maybe he ditched it. Or what about a locker at the base?"

"We'll check, but it's not likely he'd have two forty-fives, is it?"

"Guys like Overholt, the bigger the better."

Wilson gave a sour laugh. "You got a point there."

"This Overholt. He didn't shoot J.D.?" asked Diaz as Richards closed her phone.

She glared at him. "Would you please take those stupid flowers and get the hell out?"

He looked at her a long moment. Then, with a half-smile at whatever he saw in her face, he picked up the plant and left.

Flustered and angry, she called Jamison and McLamb and gave them the bad news.

Pink geraniums indeed!

CHAPTER
27

*When the winds change, the clouds also change
and take a contrary direction.*

—Theophrastus

I was almost too late getting to the Morrow House. The
only ones left were Frederick Mayhew and three of the
trustees: Nathan Benton, Betty Coates Ramos, and
Suzanne D. Angelo.

Mrs. Ramos I had met earlier that day when we both
wound up in the restroom together before Dwight and I
left for lunch. She was late fifties, early sixties, with short
curly blond hair and wore a bright red wool suit that lit up
the late afternoon.

Suzanne D. Angelo looked to be my age, dark-haired
and vivacious in a white tweed pantsuit and heavy
gold jewelry. When we were introduced, I nodded and
said, "Mrs. D'Angelo," and she corrected me with a
smile.

"I'm afraid it's D. for Dupree. No, don't apologize.

Everyone makes that mistake. I married a Yankee and brought him home with me."

"And we're so lucky she came back." Mayhew stopped just short of abject fawning. "The Duprees are one of our oldest families and Mrs. Angelo has given us some wonderful family treasures."

Dwight had described Nathan Benton in such detail that it kept me from blurting out, "You look so familiar. Have we met before?" because he really did look like a British commander in some old World War Two movie, right down to his neat little mustache. He even wore an old battered tweed jacket with leather patches on the elbow and a striped regimental tie.

"We're all so sorry about Jonna's son," he said. "Jonna, too, of course. Bad show."

The others murmured in agreement and I thanked them for their concern, but couldn't resist asking Mr. Benton, "Are you English?"

He beamed. "My mother. My roots are here in Shaysville, but she was a war bride and I'm afraid she infected the whole family with her accent. I keep thinking I've lost every trace and then someone like you will come along and remind me that I haven't."

Behind his back, I saw Mrs. Angelo roll her eyes at Mrs. Ramos and knew that Mr. Benton probably cultivated that accent.

The four of them were sitting around a tea table in the front parlor when I arrived, and Mayhew immediately pulled up another chair in his most courtly manner while Mrs. Angelo brought me a cup of punch and gestured to the plate of canapés on the tea table. Evidently they were enjoying that pleasant afterglow when something tricky has gone off well.

"You were right about Erdman," Benton told Mrs. Ramos. "He seems quite sound on small arms and I rather regret that he didn't get to see the derringer."

Mayhew sniffed. "He may know guns but he was off by eighty years on my cut-glass syrup pitcher. Pressed glass, indeed!"

Now it was Benton and Ramos who exchanged amused glances.

"I take it your meeting was a success?" I asked.

"Almost sixty people came!" Mayhew exulted, pushing his rimless glasses up on his nose. "We enrolled four new members for the Historical and Genealogical Society."

"And one new Friend of the Morrow House," Betty Ramos added complacently.

"Are you the new president now?"

She shook her head and Suzanne Angelo said with a sigh, "No, that would be me. I was elected first vice president last month and thought I'd have a year to learn the job. Poor Jonna."

"Rest assured, we'll do everything to help you," Nathan Benton promised.

With a few casual questions, I soon learned that while Mayhew, Suzanne Angelo, and Betty Ramos were born and bred in Shaysville, Nathan Benton had been here less than four years. He had taken early retirement from a successful business in Norfolk in order to return to the town his ancestors had helped found nearly two hundred years earlier. A Benton Street just off the square and Benton Baptist Church at the edge of town were both named for his people, Mayhew told me.

Benton and Ramos were Civil War buffs, while Angelo, as befitted someone whose husband was the current CEO of Shay Furniture, was more interested in the historical changes wrought by industrialization in the years following Reconstruction. She was lobbying to return the bathrooms that had last been updated in the 1940s to something more appropriate for 1900.

Benton, on the other hand, cared little about architecture. His goal was to successfully outfit the mannequin that stood on the upper landing in the clothes that Peter Morrow's son George would have worn as a first lieutenant in a company drawn from this part of western Virginia. Not replicas, I was given to understand, but the actual period pieces. He had already given a sword and the outer uniform, but had not yet located a proper pair of boots. "Most of the things are out there in antiques stores for a price," he said, "but for me, it's the thrill of the hunt. Can you guess what's the hardest to locate?"

"A Virginia canteen?" I had seen the rarity of such an object discussed on *Antiques Roadshow*, one of my favorite programs even though I'm no collector of antiques.

"Very good," he said. "But I meant in the line of clothing."

I shook my head.

"Period underpants. I fear young George's nether regions are presently covered only by his breeches."

Betty Ramos had begun to transcribe the extensive collection of letters archived here, a task made more difficult by Peter Morrow's almost unreadable handwriting and by the way letters had to be written to conserve both paper and ink when both were difficult to come by near the war's end. She pulled from her capacious purse a photocopy of the letter she was currently trying to decipher. Even enlarged I could barely follow it. First it was written in the usual manner. Then the paper had been given a half-turn so that the original lines were now vertical and new horizontal lines crossed them. Finally, a third set of lines ran diagonally across the page. Despite the fine nib of the pen, when newly dipped, it had often formed fatter letters that obscured the letters beneath.

"And I thought briefs were hard to read," I said as I handed the copy back to her.

Amusingly, although Mayhew and Benton were both keenly interested in reading the letters as she transcribed them, both disapproved of her reasons for doing it, because she was hoping to prove that Peter Morrow had been a secret Union sympathizer.

"A traitor," said Mayhew.

"A turncoat," said Benton.

"A pragmatist," Ramos said cheerfully. "Anyone with half a brain could see that the South was bound to lose in the end. You said yourself, Frederick, that he never burned his bridges to the North."

" 'Pragmatist,' I'll give you," Mayhew conceded, "but I prefer 'politician.' "

"Too bad the North's 'copperhead' doesn't have a Southern equivalent," said Ramos.

Evidently this was an old jibe, because he merely frowned at her over the top of his rimless glasses, but Benton took her words literally and said, "That's because there were too few here as to need such an equivalent."

"We'll see," Ramos said with a serene smile as she tugged at the hem of her red skirt that tried to ride up over her knees.

"What did Jonna think?" I asked.

"I'm afraid Jonna wasn't a scholar," said Mayhew.

"No, but he was her ancestor. Surely family stories must have come down?"

Betty Ramos tilted her blond head toward me. "Interesting that you should say that. She said she thought I might find something in the letters that would prove my point, and that if I did, she would show me something that might substantiate it."

"Really? What?" asked Mayhew. As he frowned, his glasses slid almost down to the tip of his nose and balanced there precariously.

"Something in the inventory that we've overlooked?" asked Benton.

"She wouldn't elaborate other than to say it was something only a Morrow would know. Jonna always kept her own counsel, but I wonder if it was something she was saving for when she became president of SHGS."

"You all knew her well, right?" I asked.

There were nods and affirmative murmurs.

"Whoever killed her had to have had access to this house and the gun." I was abruptly aware that Jonna's killer might even be one of them, yet they all looked back at me with bland expressions of interest.

"Well, of course," said Mayhew, pushing his glasses up. "The house is open to the public. Anybody could have taken the guns."

"Would just anybody have access to the keys to the case, though?"

"True," Mayhew agreed. "But who's to say Jonna didn't take them herself as she took the bullets and the jewelry?"

This appeared to be news to the others, and Frederick Mayhew quickly described how Dwight had found a listing of the gun's bullets in the inventory and how, when the safe where they were stored had been opened, the jewelry that was supposed to be there was missing as well. "And Peter Morrow's signet ring was found in her purse."

The three trustees were shocked. As might be expected, Benton wanted to know about the bullets while the two women questioned the jewelry. Betty Ramos said, "But surely Jonna wouldn't—? I mean, that parure was a gift from her own mother."

"I know I'm showing my ignorance," Suzanne Angelo said, "but what's a parure?"

Once again, I heard Frederick Mayhew explain about a matched set, only this time Betty Ramos elaborated. "The hairwork is absolutely fabulous. Elizabeth had dark brown hair when she died at sixteen, but as a toddler it had been quite long and golden yellow. Her mother had saved several strands from babyhood, so that when the light and dark were braided together, the result was really striking. I had almost forgotten we have it. Is someone keeping an eye on eBay?"

Mayhew's brow wrinkled. "eBay?"

"To make sure they aren't being sold online. The pieces were photographed, weren't they?"

"Well . . ."

"We don't have photographic documentation of all our holdings?" asked Benton. "That's outrageous!"

"I have a digital camera," Angelo said briskly. "I'll be here first thing in the morning if anyone wants to help. I'm no professional, but at least we could get everything onto the computer and start keying the pictures to the inventory list."

"The police don't know that Jonna took those things," I said, trying to herd them back to the question of her death. "Her killer could have planted the ring. And where are the rest of the bullets? They aren't at her house, they weren't in the car."

"Did anyone check her desk?" asked Benton.

"The police were quite thorough," Mayhew assured him.

"Was she worried the last time you saw her?" I asked. "In fact, who *did* see her last? You, Mr. Mayhew?"

He frowned as he removed his glasses and began polishing them with a napkin from the tea table. Without them, he looked younger and less sure of himself. "It was last Monday, a week ago tomorrow, and she did seem a bit distracted. I had to ask her twice for last year's attendance records."

"We spoke on the phone on Wednesday," Benton said crisply. "She wanted to know how to list the perfume bottle I presented to the house today. Its provenance and maker. From the marks, I am quite certain that it's jasperware. Wedgwood, pre-1820. Unfortunately, there's no provenance because I bought it in a flea market in Winston-Salem from a seller who rather thought it might be an Avon bottle from the 1970s. I had no desire to disabuse him and even bartered him down from ten dollars to eight."

It was a story that gave him obvious satisfaction to tell, but I moved on to the two women.

Suzanne Angelo had also spoken to her on Wednesday about today's installation of officers and they had discussed food and drink for the public reception. "She sounded perfectly fine to me."

Betty Ramos was looking troubled. "Was I the last, then? I was supposed to help with the inventory on Thursday, but that morning an elderly relative slipped and broke her hip and I had to drive up to Roanoke to see about her. I stopped by here around ten on my way out of town to run off a few more of the letters and to tell her I'd definitely be here the next day. I warmed up the copier while she found the letters I wanted, then we ran them off and I left."

"What did you talk about?" I asked.

"The weather mostly. It had snowed the night before and I was a little worried about the roads. And we talked about today." She gave a self-conscious smile. "She and Dix had already hung the drapes in the Rose Bedroom but she wanted me to wait about putting the coverlet on the bed until we'd shown it to our members. Some of them can't climb steps anymore."

"You really must go up and see the room," Mayhew told me, "only I'm afraid you'll have to wait until tomorrow. Closing time was at five."

"I was hoping to stay and check out Jonna's papers and her computer," I said. "I can't help feeling there must be something that the men have overlooked. Besides, my husband's meeting me here after he interviews Dix Lunsford."

Mayhew's eyes narrowed behind his polished glasses. "Major Bryant's interviewing Lunsford? Whatever for?"

"Didn't you tell him that Lunsford was devoted to Jonna?"

"*Was*, Judge. They had quite an argument on Monday and he huffed around the rest of the day."

"Argument? What about?"

"I'm sure I can't say. They were on the third floor hanging Betty's drapes. I could hear their voices all the way down here, but I couldn't make out what they were saying. When Jonna came down and I asked her what all that was about, she said that Dix was being stubborn about following her orders and that maybe it was time we looked for someone else to clean here."

He paused as if struck by what he was saying. "Heavens! You don't suppose that Dix—? I mean, he does know his way around this house. He knows where the keys are and I wouldn't be surprised if he knows how to disarm the alarm and where the safe combination is written."

"Don't be silly," said Betty Ramos. "Dix has known Jonna since she was a baby. He may take advantage of his status as an old family retainer, but he would never hurt a Shay."

Nathan Benton looked skeptical and Suzanne D. Angelo looked at her watch. "I'm sorry to rush you, Frederick, but the Schmerners expect us for cocktails at six."

Benton glanced at his own watch and stood. "I have a dinner engagement as well."

"Well, I don't," said Betty Ramos, "so why don't I stay a while, put away the rest of the food and punch, copy off some more letters, and keep Judge Knott company while she looks at the computer? I have my key and I'll lock up when we leave."

Mayhew wasn't thrilled by her suggestion, but who was he to argue with a wealthy trustee who had just given the house a gift worth several hundreds? "You do remember how to set the alarm, don't you?"

They went off together for a refresher course on the

proper setting of the system while Benton and Angelo gathered up their coats to follow and said that they hoped we would have word of Cal by morning.

When Betty Ramos returned to the parlor alone, she said, "Before you get started, want to come upstairs? I'm dying to see how the coverlet looks on the bed."

I hadn't yet seen the Rose Bedroom myself, so I quickly agreed.

We climbed the curved stairs to the second floor, passed the mannequin that represented Elizabeth Morrow's brother, then took the surprisingly narrow flight of stairs to the third floor. There were discreet light switches and concealed lights along the way. "The house was actually wired around 1920," she explained, "but when my husband and I donated the new heating and cooling system, we upgraded the wiring as well. The electrician told us that we were probably just one power surge away from a major fire."

"Sounds like a very generous gesture."

She shrugged. "Well, it's not as showy as swords and guns, perhaps . . ."

"Not that it's a contest or anything," I said wickedly.

"Oh dear, is that what it sounded like?" She saw my smile and gave a sheepish smile of her own. "I'm afraid Nathan Benton brings out the worst in me. He's always finding these perfect little treasures at yard sales and flea markets and makes a big show of how clever he's been to pay so little. As if "—her voice slipped into a clipped British accent that perfectly mimicked Benton's—" 'I say, chappies, anyone can slosh money around, but spotting authentic pieces dead on takes a discriminating eye, what?' I mean, he's just so bloody proud of everything he finds. And poor Frederick. It humiliates him to death that he can't match Nathan's generosity. He's found a couple of nice things over in Tennessee himself, but I'm afraid his pockets aren't as deep as he'd like.

"Now, Catherine Schmerner—did you meet her? Short, white-haired woman? I think she was wearing a purple coat?"

I shook my head.

"Well, she and Suzanne have given the house quite a few items, too. In fact Catherine gave us an ebony-and-silver hand mirror just last month that could easily have belonged to Peter Morrow's wife, but she would never brag about it. I was so pleased when Suzanne held it up this afternoon and Catherine got to take a bow, too. Jonna found a picture of one just like it on an English antiques site. They were asking a hundred pounds for theirs."

Up on the third floor, the Rose Bedroom was the one nearest the landing and it was quite charming. So named for the rose silk that lined the walls, its only furniture was a bed, a chest of drawers, a couple of chairs, and a bed table that held a hobnail milkglass lamp. I was surprised to realize that the reason the bedroom doors were recessed so deeply in from the hallway was because they all contained proper closets. The one in this room was at least five feet deep and of course there was no light inside. Even with the door open, it must have been hard for Elizabeth Morrow to find her favorite dress, but it certainly beat the old freestanding wardrobes so prevalent when the house was built.

"Peter Morrow was a very practical man," Mrs. Ramos agreed. "There's an amazing amount of storage space in this house. Did you notice that he added closets under the main staircase? It was originally freestanding, but he decided it could be more useful to close it in and use it for storage."

I sniffed when I turned back from the empty closet to the room itself. Dwight said they had smelled the ghost's faint gardenia perfume earlier today, but all I smelled was the sizing on the new fabric. The drapes picked up the pink of the walls for a background that was overlaid with greenery and deeper shades of pink roses. The same material was used for the coverlet, and I helped Mrs. Ramos fit it on the bed.

"It's so pretty," I said. "Really warms up the room."

She seemed pleased by my praise. "I do love giving things to this house and watching it come back to life. It's almost like a dollhouse for adults, isn't it?"

By the time we returned to the main hall, we were on a first-name basis. As we circled the staircase to get back to the office, she pointed out how Peter Morrow had put the wasted space beneath the stairs to practical use. I had walked past this area several times without noticing because the wainscoting and decorative molding matched the rest of the house so perfectly that even when you knew the doors were there, it was hard to see them. Betty pressed on one of the rosettes and a door swung open to reveal a space crammed with cardboard boxes marked "C'mas decorations." Another held the folding chairs and yet another the usual odds and ends. Although the staircase was quite wide, the closets seemed comparatively shallow.

"That's because there's a matching set on the other side," said Betty. "My husband thought we should've run the new ductwork through the cupboards under the stairs here, but Jonna pitched a fit. Said it would be criminal to put vents in this molding. It cost a little more to run it between the floor joists and up the outside walls, but she was probably right."

We walked around and she opened a couple of the closets to show me spaces lined with shelves that held boxes of stemware and the punch bowl set.

"I hope Morrow's wife appreciated him," I said.

Betty closed the doors. "I'm afraid there were times when she didn't. One of his letters to his Philadelphia cousins said she was most 'grievously unhappy' at the changes he had made to her grand hall, but that he hoped she would come to agree with his decision."

While Betty tidied away the food and dishes from the reception, I fired up Jonna's computer and went looking. I'm no expert, but it's like driving a car. I don't care about what's under the hood, I just want to turn the key and drive to Dobbs. I know how to do what I need to do—to look up case law and precedents, I can navigate around the Internet for the things that interest me, and for everything else, there's Google. I was happy to see that Jonna had used the same word-processing program as mine, and soon I was flashing through her files and directories. Nothing jumped out at me, but then I didn't expect it to since Agents Lewes and Clark had already checked it.

Everything seemed open to view and none of the files were password protected, which wasn't surprising since there didn't seem to be much of the personal or confidential. One folder was marked "Miscellaneous/Housekeeping/Personal," but the only halfway personal thing I saw was a file containing Cal's school reports and comments from his teachers that she had scanned in, along with a record of his immunizations and the dates of his physicals. There were recipes for making enough party food to serve fifty people. Recipes for summer punches and winter mulled cider. Addresses of various rental places in town from tents to folding chairs. I looked at the spreadsheets for the budget, skimmed through the monthly minutes of the board and the director's reports that Mayhew had delivered, etc. etc.

She had methodically entered about half of the inventory that was detailed in a thick sheaf of paper, including "*Bullets*—.36 caliber. Original box of 12. Seven missing. Judge M's safe." She seemed to have assigned it a number that corresponded to items kept in the judge's office so that the list could be sorted alphabetically, by code numbers or by actual rooms.

Nevertheless, if there was anything in this computer to explain why Jonna had been killed, I wasn't seeing it.

In the meantime, Betty Ramos kept passing back and forth as she tidied the parlor and kitchen. It was after six before she switched off most of the lights and came into the office. "Any luck?"

"Not yet."

She went over to the files that held the Morrow family papers, pulled open a file drawer, and immediately gave a small *tch* of annoyance.

"Something wrong?"

"I just realized that I left my notes on my desk at home and now I can't remember where I left off. I think I'll just run home and get them. I'm only a few blocks away. You don't mind if I leave you alone for a few minutes, do you?"

"Of course not," I said. "Anyhow, Dwight'll probably be here anytime now. I'm surprised he hasn't called yet."

"I won't bother to lock the door, then," she said, "so he can come right on in."

"Fine." The desk was against the side of the front wall, and from where I sat, I could watch as she passed down the dimly lit hall and disappeared beyond the staircase. I heard the front door close and then turned back to the desk. Again, there was nothing of a personal nature in any of the drawers that I could see and I even lifted them out one by one and checked for false bottoms or something taped to the undersides.

Nothing.

CHAPTER
28

The blackest month in all the year
Is the month of Janiveer.

—*Anonymous*

SUNDAY AFTERNOON, 23 JANUARY

As Dwight was snapping the leash onto Bandit's collar, his phone rang. Agent Lewes.

"Was she there? Do her cousins know where she is?" he asked eagerly.

"Sorry, Bryant. They think she left here early Monday morning. And I hate to load any more on your plate, but they're saying she really does need to be institutionalized this time, that she's getting more and more detached from reality. They blame her sister and her mother for not stepping in and doing what needs to be done before now. They don't think she'd intentionally hurt your son, but if she's the one who did your ex-wife—"

Dwight did not let Lewes finish that thought. "Did

they have any suggestions about where she'd go? What she'd do?"

"They said the Shays own a place on a nearby lake?"

"Yeah. Cal and I go fishing out there with Radcliff and his kids, but the house burned down at least fifty years ago. Nothing there but trees and bushes now."

"What about a boathouse? Anson says that's where they found Pam a couple of summers ago."

"Boathouse? It's nothing but a caved-in roof and some old siding."

"All the same, they say that's where she was."

"That's crazy," said Dwight and realized that, well, yes, this was exactly how everyone characterized Pam's mental state. So what else was new? "Thanks, Lewes. It's only about six or eight miles out of town. I'll swing over there right now while it's still light."

He started to leave Bandit at the house, then decided that the little dog might prove useful if Pam had taken Cal there. He had half convinced himself that if Bandit got anywhere within sniffing distance of Cal, he would home in on him like one of those bloodhounds that had entrenched themselves in Pam's delusional mind.

The lake was less than fifteen minutes away, but it took another ten minutes to hike in from the rutted lane where he had parked the truck. Patches of snow still dotted the landscape on the north side of the bushes. Today's sun had helped melt the worst, but the sun was rapidly setting and the wind bit at his face and stung his eyes. Bandit was on a retractable leash and Dwight kept it fairly short so as not to get tangled in the scrub. There had been no sign of tire tracks in the lane, and so far they hadn't crossed any trail marks either. Eventually, they came to the rotting pile of lumber that had once been a boathouse for the rustic lakeside lodge. Part of the roof had come down in one section and had landed on a couple of uprights, so that it now resembled a rough lean-to. He supposed that in the summer, Pam could have sheltered under it from the sun and rain. Here in dead winter, though? With the sides open to chilling winds and icy sleet? He saw some faded fast-food cartons and an empty plastic water bottle but nothing recent.

Even though he was now almost positive Pam and Cal could not be here, he called several times, then let Bandit off the lead. "Where's Cal?" he said. "Find Cal!"

The dog raced around the area from the shoreline to the collapsed boathouse and back again without noticeable interest in any one spot until he suddenly lunged toward a bush that overhung the water, barking excitedly. Dwight hurried over just in time to watch a pair of startled wood ducks take flight across the lake in the darkening twilight. The bleak landscape mirrored the bleakness he felt as yet another possibility came to nothing.

"That's it," he told the dog. "Let's go."

———

On his way back to town, Dwight phoned the Colleton County Sheriff's Department and got Detective Richards, who gave him a negative update. The discouraged note he heard in her voice sounded like an echo of his own feelings. They had both been chasing down dead-end roads all weekend and she had even taken a bullet for her troubles. Nevertheless, she was probably closer to winding up the Rouse shooting than he was to finding Cal. And at least she'd found a solid motive for that murder, while Jonna's was still a mystery.

"Just because no one's come forward to say they saw Overholt doesn't mean he wasn't the shooter," he told Richards. "The Army that taught him how to use a hand-gun with that much accuracy also trained him how to ambush an enemy, so don't worry about the gun. If it's there, Wilson will find it. There's bound to be a buddy or someone who'll know what guns he had. Give the investigation time to play itself out."

"Yessir. But what about your son? Any news? Agent Wilson was asking."

"Nothing concrete, but we still have a few people to interview. I'll call if anything breaks. And for right now, go home, Richards. You've got nothing to prove to me or Sheriff Poole, okay?"

He called Deborah to tell her that he might be a little longer getting there than he'd intended.

"Have you talked to Dix Lunsford yet?" she asked.

"Just turning down their street," he said. "Why?"

"Mayhew said he heard Jonna quarreling with him on Monday. He doesn't know what it was about, but she was angry enough to tell Mayhew they ought to think about firing him."

"I'll ask him," Dwight said. "See you in a half hour or so."

With that, he parked his truck in front of the Lunsford house. Bandit begged to come in with him, but Dwight figured he would be back out before the cab of the truck became too cold for the little dog.

CHAPTER
29

When a wolf approaches or enters cultivated
ground in the season of winter, it indicates that
a storm will come immediately.

—*Theophrastus*

Dwight called to say he was running late. I told him about
the fight Mayhew said Jonna and Lunsford had on Monday and returned to my fruitless search.

I had forgotten to ask if Mrs. Shay's house could be
seen from the third floor of this one, and yes, I could have
run upstairs to see for myself, but the house was dark and
I didn't know where the light switches were. I told myself
that it certainly wasn't because I was nervous here alone.

Besides, all old houses creaked and groaned.

Nevertheless, I found myself tensing at every tiny
sound.

To distract myself while waiting for Betty Ramos to
return, I contemplated the six four-drawer filing cabinets
that lined one wall of this office that Jonna and Mayhew
had shared. Twenty-four drawers packed tightly with

hanging files. If one of them held the reason Jonna had been killed or a clue as to where Pam had taken Cal, finding that specific piece of paper would be sheer luck. As I thumbed aimlessly through the inventory, it struck me how very peaceful Shaysville was on a Sunday evening. Two blocks off of Main Street and I heard no cars. Of course, that might be because the house was so well built. I hadn't heard Betty's car leave the parking lot either.

Not that I sat in complete and utter silence. Following an afternoon with sixty extra people walking around here, the old house snapped and clicked as the floorboards readjusted themselves. All the same, it was so quiet that I jumped when the grandfather clock out in the hall struck the quarter hour.

Deciding that I might as well print out Cal's records as long as they were on the hard drive, I pulled up the document again, set the printer for fast draft, pressed print, and sat back to wait for the pages.

The printer coughed into life and quickly began to turn out sheets. It was set so that the last sheet printed first.

To my surprise, instead of printing the last page of Cal's records, it printed a picture and the page was numbered twenty-six.

Huh?

I quickly scrolled down the computer's screen. Pages five to twenty-two were blank. The second picture was emerging from the printer when I hit page twenty-three.

Why, Jonna, I thought. *You sneaky little devil.*

I instantly flashed on the testimony of a woman in a divorce action that had come before me. She and her husband shared a home computer and she had discovered the whole e-mail correspondence between him and his mistress. He had tucked it away at the bottom of their tax records, figuring she would never bother to look there. Unfortunately for him, printing out a copy of one's joint tax return is one of the first things a wife is advised to do when her marriage is coming apart. Divorce attorneys know that cheating husbands may lie to their wives, but that they seldom tell significant lies to the IRS.

The pictures puzzled me. From what was said earlier, I didn't think any of the Morrow House treasures had been photographed, yet here were the digital prints for four of them. I looked closer and realized that these had been saved from the Internet. One bore the name of an unfamiliar town in Tennessee and read "ca. 1853. Missing since 2003." Another was labeled "Faison House, Roanoke, Virginia. Disappeared May 1999."

The printer finished with Cal's records and went silent. I closed the file on Jonna's computer, lifted the sheets from the printer tray, and after discarding the superfluous blank pages, leaned back in her chair to contemplate the significance of what I was seeing. Unless I was very mistaken, this was why Jonna had been so willing to work overtime on the inventory when the house was usually closed and she could search the Internet unobserved. This must also be why she was killed.

Was it blackmail? Did she say, "Give me five thousand and I'll let you steal back the things you gave, so that you can return them to their rightful owners?"

Dwight was so sure of her honesty, but if this wasn't evidence of blackmail, why hadn't she taken these pictures straight to the board?

Or was I misreading the situation? Had she kept quiet out of compassion? Because she recognized someone whose needy pride was so similar to her own? Another case of—

My eyes were focused on the pictures, yet I was abruptly aware of a faint sound in the hall and my peripheral vision registered a movement that had been so fleeting, I could almost think I'd imagined it.

"Betty?" I called. "Dwight?"

Cold air swirled through the room and sent chill bumps down my spine. I slid the pictures under Cal's records and laid them down beside the computer, then walked over to the doorway. "Hello? Somebody there?"

"Hello?" I called again.

No answer.

An outside light was on, but Betty had turned off the main lights before she left and I didn't know where that switch was either. I moved cautiously out into the shadowy hall and found the source of my chill bumps. She hadn't closed the front door properly, and it was the icy air blowing in around the crack that had creeped me out. I shut it firmly and started back to the office, jeering at myself for letting the house unnerve me.

That's when I noticed that the end closet door was also slightly ajar. It suddenly dawned on me that maybe it wasn't Betty who had left the door unlatched. Had someone been hiding in the closet, thinking that everyone had left and that it was now safe to sneak out and escape? The thief that had stolen the guns and the jewelry from the safe? Jonna's killer?

Holding my breath, I opened the door wider and peered in. All was dark, and yet, despite the darkness, there was something odd here. For a moment, I couldn't think what it was until it hit me that the closet was now deeper than it had seemed when Betty first showed it to me. I needed better light, though. Where were the damn switches? I remembered moving a flashlight in one of the drawers of Jonna's desk and I quickly retrieved it, then played the light over the interior of the closet, past the stacked chairs, and into an empty space behind them that had definitely not been there before. There was just enough room between the stacks for me to slide through. The whole back panel had been pushed aside, and when I stuck the flashlight inside, I was dumbfounded to see that steep, narrow steps had been sandwiched between the back-to-back closets, steps that were only wide enough for one person.

One short person. If I went up, I'd have to stoop.

Not that I had any intention of going up. Not without someone to watch my back. I'm no gothic heroine to go flitting around a castle's ominous dark turrets in a wispy nightgown.

Besides, I'd left all my wispy nightgowns at home.

As I turned to go find my phone and call Dwight, I heard the one thing that could make me forget common sense—somewhere a child began to cry.

Cal?

I flashed the light up the steps that seemed to dead-end at a blank wall.

"Cal? Is that you?"

Crouching, I hurried up the steps, which were nothing more than sloped boards with horizontal strips of wood to offer a foothold. When I got to the top, there was a turn and a proper set of narrow steps. The ceiling here was tall enough to walk upright and I realized that they paralleled the staircase I'd walked up earlier with Betty. Indeed, these steps seemed to be part of the original treads with only a thin wall between them. Part of my mind was having an *Aha!* moment of realization as to why those other stairs had struck me as less spacious than expected. The rest was focused on the heartbroken sobs of the child up above me.

At the top of this flight, a shallow landing made a sharp turn to the left and ended about four feet away. There, the flashlight revealed a simple latch, and when I lifted it and pushed, the panel slid smoothly to one side with no squeaks or scrapes and I was in a space that measured roughly five by fifteen feet. A battery-powered lantern cast a dim glow over the secret room. Painted on the walls in lurid colors was a vision of the peaceable kingdom, where black lions lay down with snow-white lambs in green pastures and a black Jesus shepherded them all. I saw empty soft drink cans and some cups from the kitchen downstairs. I smelled urine and an overly ripe banana, but what tore at my heart was the soft, hopeless crying that came from the small form curled up on a rough pallet in the corner with a teddy bear beside him.

"Oh, Cal!"

I rushed over, set my flashlight on the floor, and knelt down to gather him up in my arms. He seemed groggy and only half-alert, but he began to wail louder as he recognized me and put his arms around my neck. "Miss Deborah! Is Daddy with you? I want my daddy! Please?"

"He's coming, sweetheart," I promised, stroking his small head and making automatic soothing noises.

I no sooner registered the smell of gardenias than he stiffened and tried to jerk back. I heard him cry, "No!" then someone dropped a piano on my head.

CHAPTER
30

A whole is that which has beginning, middle, and end.

—*Aristotle*

SUNDAY EVENING, 23 JANUARY

Dwight knocked on the door and the black man who opened it was just under six feet, with short curly hair that was more salt than pepper. If he and his wife had been working for Mrs. Shay at the time of Eustace Shay's death, then Lunsford had to be at least sixty, yet his erect frame showed no signs of coming frailty. He wore a long-sleeved white shirt that was open at the neck, no tie, and black dress pants; and he had answered the door in his stocking feet. Ordinary Sunday night comfort.

"Mr. Lunsford? Dix Lunsford?"

"Yes?"

The wary caution in the man's face was familiar to

Dwight. He knew he had cop stamped all over him. There was nothing he could do about his looks. All the same, at times like this, he could wish that strangers did not see flashing blue lights the moment they met him.

"I'm Dwight Bryant."

"Yes?"

"Jonna's ex-husband."

Nothing in his expression changed. "Yes?"

"May I come in and ask you a few questions about Jonna and Pam?"

That did get a reaction. "*Pam*? What you asking about Pam for?"

A querulous voice from inside said, "If you'd let the poor man in, Dix, maybe he'd tell you."

Lunsford stepped back and gestured for Dwight to enter.

The house was warm and cozy after the biting wind outside. Two recliners faced a flat-screen television set. Golfers walked across perfect greens under golden sunshine. A sturdily built woman, Mrs. Lunsford had her coarse gray hair pulled back in a neat bun. She wore gold-rimmed glasses and a wine red pantsuit; and as Dwight entered the room, she brought her recliner to its upright position and muted the sound on the television.

"You find your boy yet?"

"No, ma'am. That's why I'm here. I was hoping y'all could help me. Mrs. Prentice—you know her?"

Mrs. Lunsford nodded.

"She says you two have known Jonna and Pam since they were babies."

Again the affirmative nod.

"We think Pam's the one that took Cal Friday afternoon."

She shot an inquiring look at her husband, who shook his head. "Every time I've seen her, she was by herself."

"But you've seen her?" asked Dwight. "Where? When?"

"At the Morrow House. She showed up Monday while I was working."

"You didn't tell me that," said his wife.

"'Cause you always take Jonna's part and Jonna didn't want her there, but where was she gonna go? Her husband didn't want her, Miss Laura didn't want her, Jonna didn't want her. It was coming on for cold weather and that big house all empty upstairs? What did it hurt?"

"Is that what you and Jonna fought about on Monday?" Dwight asked.

A mulish look came into the older man's face, one that must have been familiar to his wife, for she said sharply, "Dixon Lunsford, Jonna's laying dead in her coffin, her little boy's missing, and his daddy's a policeman. You don't tell him where Pam is, he's gonna think you got something to do with it."

"All I did was bring her some of our old blankets so she could make a pallet and sleep up in one of them empty rooms for a couple of nights. Poor little thing's not herself right now."

"Where is she now?"

"Still at the house, I reckon. Leastways that's where she was Thursday morning."

"You were at the house that day?"

"Didn't think it'd hurt to stop by on my way to the schoolhouse, maybe take her a sandwich."

Mrs. Lunsford rolled her eyes in exasperation and explained that one of her husband's odd jobs was to buff and polish the floor tiles of the main lobby of the high school once a week.

"The old school across from the Morrow House?"

They both nodded. "Only now it's a retirement home."

"Wait a minute," Dwight said. "Let me get this straight. You were in the Morrow House with Pam Thursday morning?"

"Jonna, too."

"What time was that?"

"Well, I usually do the floors about ten-thirty, so it was before that. I didn't stay but long enough to give Pam the food because she and Jonna were getting into it pretty heavy. Jonna wanted to take her to the hospital and Pam didn't want to go, so she ran off upstairs."

"You didn't follow her?"

"Wasn't any use to. Ever since they were two smarty-pants little girls, they knew how to hide so nobody could find them. You'd swear they were on the third floor, and next time you turned around, they were all the way downstairs. They used to say Elizabeth Morrow's ghost taught them how to disappear. Anyhow, Jonna told me to go on. That she'd take care of Pam and—"

Dwight's phone began to ring. "Excuse me a minute."

It was Paul Radcliff. "Hey, bo, where are you?"

"I'm here talking to Mr. and Mrs. Lunsford, why?"

"Well, get your ass over to the old high school. One of my men just found Pam Shay's car parked around back with the residents' cars. I called Lewes. He and Clark are going to meet us there."

———

The white Honda Accord with Tennessee plates was surrounded by several prowl cars and officers. Residents of the converted school peered down from their windows, curious and alarmed by the flashing blue lights. Radcliff already had officers going door-to-door inside, questioning them as to what they had seen and to ask if any were harboring Pamela Shay Morgan and her nephew.

The state agents had sent for their evidence truck to come and process the car, and while they waited Dwight told them of his fruitless trip out to the lake and of his interview with the Lunsfords. They were interested to hear that Pam and Jonna knew of places to hide in the Morrow House, and when he drove around to it, Paul Radcliff and Nick Lewes followed.

"We never checked the attic," Dwight said. "Are there stairs?"

Radcliff shrugged. "Bound to be, wouldn't you think?"

"Usually are," Lewes agreed.

As they came up the front walk, they saw someone peering out at them with anxiety evident in every syllable of her body language.

"Oh, Chief Radcliff, Major Bryant!" said Betty Ramos. "Is Judge Knott with you?"

"No," said Dwight. "Isn't she here?"

Mrs. Ramos shook her head. "I was wondering if she had to leave for some reason."

"Her car's still here. Why?"

"Well, I'm sure I don't know. She was going through the files on Jonna's computer when I left. I was only away a few minutes, and when I came back she was gone. Her

purse is still there on the desk and so is her phone, but—"
She shook her blond head in bewilderment. "I've looked
all over the house and there's no sign of her, so I thought
maybe she had to leave in a hurry, but then why would
she leave her things?"

"She wouldn't," Dwight said decisively. The sight of
Deborah's red car coat on the back of the office chair
chilled him with its implications.

"Are there steps to the attic?" Lewes asked. "We didn't
see any this afternoon."

"That's because they're concealed up on the third
floor," said Mrs. Ramos. "I'll show you."

As she led the way upstairs, she described how she and
Judge Knott had come up earlier to put the new coverlet
on the bed in the Rose Room. "And when we went back
downstairs, I cleared away the rest of the food and tidied
up the kitchen while she got started with the computer."

At the top of the second flight of stairs, she paused to
catch her breath and explained how she had gone home to
fetch some notes she had forgotten. "I wasn't gone more
than fifteen minutes."

Dwight glanced at his watch. "And I talked to her myself about twenty-five minutes ago."

Mrs. Ramos continued down the hall. Halfway to the
end, she paused in front of a blank wall. Like the rest of
the walls of this house, it was embellished with elegant
carved garlands and swags and other details of the Federalist period. She pushed one of the rosettes and a flush
door swung open to reveal a staircase.

"Does Dix Lunsford know about this door?" Dwight
asked.

"I should think so," she said, "but I really don't know.

We haven't needed to store things up there yet with so many empty rooms available down here."

Cold dead air met them as they climbed, and soon they were up in a cavernous space that appeared to be completely empty. There were no electric lights up here but their pocket flashes showed nothing of interest. Nothing to hide behind, no dormer alcoves to crouch in, only a low hip roof that almost touched their heads when they stood.

They spread out over the house then, from the basement back to the third floor and down again, opening every door into every room, closet, or cupboard.

When Lewes tried to suggest that Deborah might have left for a perfectly logical reason, Dwight cut him off in midsentence. "Without her coat? Without her phone and purse? If she's not here, then someone took her. There's no sign of a struggle, no—oh *shit*! Where's my goddamned head?"

"What?" said Radcliff.

"Bandit!"

"Huh?"

"Cal's dog. Maybe he can find her."

He hurried out to the truck and returned moments later with the little terrier trotting along in front of him. Once inside, Dwight turned toward the office to let Bandit sniff Deborah's coat, but the dog immediately strained for the stairs, whining with excitement. Dwight let the leash out to its full sixteen feet and ran to keep up with him, the others following.

With absolutely no hesitation, Bandit rounded the landing and headed up to the third floor. He scratched at the door of the Rose Room and Dwight felt a moment of despair. He himself had already searched this room thoroughly. Nevertheless, he opened the door before Bandit could take all the paint off the bottom, and the dog bounded through and over to the closet where he repeated his anxious scratching, the stub of his small tail wagging like a flag on the Fourth of July.

Once that door was opened, he threw himself against the far closet wall, barking and whining and looking back as if to beg Dwight to open yet another door.

With the help of Lewes's penlight, Dwight soon found the inconspicuous latch that looked almost like just another clothes hook. When he pulled on it, a low door opened outward.

There was only darkness beyond, but Bandit charged in, yipping happily. Dwight stooped to follow.

As he flashed the light around the small room with its vivid wall paintings, he first saw Deborah sprawled on the floor almost at his feet. Beyond, a woman was huddled in the corner. Her short dark hair swirled wildly around her face as she squinted from the sudden light and tried to push the dog away.

"Bloodhounds!" she shrieked. "No! You can't take him!"

In her arms was the limp body of his son.

CHAPTER
31

Love, unconquerable . . .
Keeper of warm lights and all-night vigil . . .

—Sophocles

When I came to, I could not at first remember where I was nor how I had come to be in this shadowy space full of loud male voices while a woman's shrieks faded away in the distance.

"Don't get up," someone said as I attempted to push myself into a sitting position. I felt a hand on my shoulder, holding me down. "There's an ambulance coming."

"Dwight?"

"I'm here, shug. Lie still."

My head hurt like hell, and when I touched it, I felt a knob the size of Grandfather Mountain. "Cal!" I said, as memory returned.

Gingerly, I turned my head and pain shot through every nerve. Dwight was sitting on the floor beside me with Cal cradled in one arm while his other hand cupped my face. Bandit was curled up between us with his head resting soulfully on Cal's leg.

"Is he—? He's not—?"

"He's been drugged. We found a bottle of cough syrup. That's what Pam took from the medicine cabinet Friday night. She must have given it to him to keep him quiet."

"Was that her screaming?"

"Yeah. They're taking her to the hospital. She thought we were slave-catchers."

"Slave-catchers?"

"Yeah. Know what this room is?"

I tried to shake my head and flinched with the pain.

"Mrs. Ramos thinks it was a station on the Underground Railroad."

I lay motionless and let my mind connect the dots. "That's what Pam was raving about? The trains to freedom? Bloodhounds?"

"You got it."

"And these pictures of Jesus?"

"Yeah."

The ambulance arrived and, despite my protests, I was lifted onto a gurney, strapped in, and wheeled out through a closet into the Rose Bedroom.

"This isn't the way I came in," I said. "There are secret stairs under the real stairs."

"We know that now. How did you find them?" asked Dwight, who walked beside me, still carrying Cal.

"She left the closet door open, and when I looked in, I heard Cal crying and—Ouch!"

The rescue team carried my gurney down as carefully as they could, but pain arced through my head with every little bounce. As they lifted me into the ambulance and

Dwight crawled in with Cal, I suddenly remembered his records! "I left them on the desk."

"Everything's fine," Dwight soothed. "Just lie still."

"No!" I said, struggling to sit up and held by the straps. "Where's Paul? Where are those explorers?"

"We're here," an amused voice said from outside the ambulance.

"Look on the desk beside the computer," I called. "There are pictures beneath Cal's records. Make Betty Ramos talk to you."

"Here we go," someone said, then the doors closed and we were moving.

I shut my eyes as the tires hit a pothole.

"Stay with us, ma'am," said the nurse or whoever she was, lifting one of my eyelids and shining a light into my pupil.

"I'm fine," I said, swatting the light away. "I'm not going to pass out again, so would you please undo these damn straps?"

"Ma'am—"

"Do it," said Dwight and a moment later I was free again.

"Thanks," I said. "How's Cal?"

I was speaking to Dwight, but the nurse answered. "His blood pressure's a little low but not in the danger zone."

I reached for Dwight's hand. "How did you find us?"

"Bandit. He caught Cal's scent as soon as I brought him inside and went straight up the stairs to that hidden door in the closet."

"He's going to do just fine down on the farm, isn't he?"

He squeezed my hand tightly. "Soon as we get home,

I'm buying him the biggest steak I can find. God, Deborah! When you disappeared on me, too—"

He broke off as Cal stirred. "Daddy?"

"Right here, buddy."

"Good," he murmured and snuggled deeper into Dwight's arms.

———

As I expected, the emergency room doctor took a good look at the lump on my head, looked into my eyes with his light, asked lots of questions about whether I was confused or dizzy, then told me to take aspirin for my headache and call him in the morning. He grinned when he said it, so I figured there was no permanent damage.

Cal's doctor ordered an IV drip to help flush his bloodstream of the codeine-laced cough syrup and wanted to keep him at the hospital overnight for observation. Dwight and I could have gone back to Jonna's house for the night, but no way were we going to let him out of our sight. There was a recliner in the room and they rolled in a cot so that we could take turns stretching out if we wanted. Extra pillows and blankets were ours for the asking.

We dimmed the lights and moved away from the bed to the window that looked out over the town. The moon was three nights from full and it starkly silhouetted the skeletal limbs of the oaks that would shade the building in summer. We stood with our arms interlaced and talked quietly.

"Where's Bandit?" I asked.

"Paul said he'd take care of him tonight."

"Can we go home now?"

"Soon as the funeral's over."

Funeral. It wasn't that I had forgotten that Jonna was dead or who probably killed her and why, but I *had* forgotten that there would be a ceremony to get through. The rituals of death.

"When?"

"Probably Tuesday morning. I called Mrs. Shay while they were checking out your head."

I looked at the sleeping child. "You'll have to tell him."

He nodded.

"And help him talk about all of it, including this nightmare with Pam. We can't let him bottle it up."

"I know."

"And your mother! I promised we'd call her this evening."

"I already did. She'll pass the word on to Mr. Kezzie and Minnie. She said to tell you that Kate and the baby will come home tomorrow."

"A new baby." One life ended, another begun. "Another first cousin for Cal."

"This is going to be so damn hard on him," he said.

I nodded.

"On you, too."

"Oh, Dwight—"

"We've both read the magazine articles, seen the pop psychologists on all those talk shows. Hell, we've seen it in your courtroom and my jail."

"Yes."

"He's going to be sad and angry and he'll probably take it out on you more than me."

"Like Andrew," I said.

"Andrew?"

"Didn't you ever hear about that? When Daddy's first wife died, they say it was a neighborhood scandal how quickly he married Mother. The younger boys were too young to hold on to Annie Ruth's memory, and Robert and Frank were old enough to be reasoned with, but Andrew was old enough to remember and too young to understand. He resented the hell out of her for years."

"But he loved Miss Sue," Dwight protested.

"Took him till he was twenty-five to come around's what I always heard. I just hope it won't take Cal that long."

He held me closer. "We'll work it out. I promise you we'll work it out."

I laid my head against his chest and was comforted by the strong steady beat of his heart. We stood there in the moonlight for several long moments until Paul Radcliff discreetly cleared his throat from the doorway. He carried my coat and purse and Cal's teddy bear and he also came bearing news of an arrest.

"Those pictures you found let us get a search warrant for Nathan Benton's house," he said. "Soon as Betty Ramos saw them, she recognized that every one of those items were things Benton had given the Morrow House. She's one pissed-off lady right now. Kept saying, 'Well, no wonder he found treasures every time he turned around. I could find treasures, too, if I shopped in museums and used a five-finger discount.' Turns out he has his own private museum down in his basement."

"Does he say why he killed Jonna?" I asked.

"Swears he had nothing to do with her death and is

admitting nothing. Claims he bought everything at flea markets or antiques stores. Knows nothing about the pictures on Jonna's computer and was shocked—absolutely *shocked*, I tell you—to hear that they were stolen. In fact, he's claiming that it's all a bunch of coincidences because none of the items are one-of-a-kind. He says they were manufactured by the thousands. Once we find the guns we'll nail him on them if nothing else, though, because they'll have serial numbers. And Lewes thinks that when the lab goes over the stuff microscopically, they'll find ID marks from some of the true owners. Clark did a quick computer search for reported thefts, and in a couple of cases, a man who fits Benton's description was the last visitor before the things went missing. There are places like the Morrow House all over the country with non-existent security and display cases that wouldn't stop a two-year-old."

"But Jonna?"

"I'm afraid it's all going to be circumstantial if we can't find some eyewitnesses besides Pam."

Dwight frowned. "Pam?"

"We tried to question her, but it's hard to separate reality from delusion. Best we can tell, she was watching from the upper landing of the Morrow House Thursday morning when Benton came out of the library with a gun and forced Jonna from the house. She heard him threaten to find Cal and kill him if Jonna didn't come quietly. Somehow all this got mixed up in her head that Benton was a slave-catcher, so when Jonna didn't come back by next day, she thought she had to save Cal from being sent back into slavery, too. I don't have to tell y'all what a defense lawyer would do with her testimony, right? For right now, the only thing he's charged with is theft."

He gave a fatalistic shrug of his shoulders.

———

Dwight insisted that I take the cot and I didn't fight him. After swallowing more aspirins, I drifted into restless sleep. Sometime after midnight, I became aware of low voices and lay motionless as I heard Dwight say, "—it's to help you get all that cough syrup out of your system. The codeine's what's made you so groggy."

"But I quit taking that last week. Mother said it was too strong."

"Aunt Pam gave you a drink, though, didn't she?"

"She put it in my Pepsi?"

"Probably."

"So *that's* why she kept telling me I had to drink plenty of fluids. Every time I woke up she made me drink more. She could've killed me," he said indignantly. "That stuff's like poison if you take too much."

"I don't think she meant to hurt you, Cal. I think she just wanted to make sure you'd stay quiet."

I almost smiled at his skeptical "Humpf!" but then his voice came small and tentative.

"Dad?"

"Yeah, buddy?"

"Aunt Pam said a lot of awful crazy stuff while we were hiding."

"Like what?"

But Cal wasn't quite ready to go there. "Is Miss Deborah okay? Aunt Pam hit her really hard."

"She's got a big lump on her head, but nothing serious."

"Good. I was afraid Aunt Pam killed her. When we were looking for Mother . . ."

"Yes?"

"Aunt Pam said Mother was in trouble. I wanted to go back and get you, only she said Mother said for me to go with her and not to let anybody know or she'd be hurt, but then she kept driving around and around till it was almost dark because she said somebody was following us, then we sneaked in the Morrow House while Mr. Mayhew was back in the office. I thought Mother was going to be there, but she wasn't. We went upstairs to that secret room with the Jesus pictures and she said we'd be safe there. She said a bad guy took Mother and wanted to take me, too, and we'd have to stay there for a while. I kept telling her you'd take care of any bad men, but she wouldn't listen. She said they had bloodhounds and could track us down."

"Sounds scary," said Dwight.

"Well actually, it was a little bit," Cal admitted. "Especially when I woke up and Aunt Pam was gone, but then she came back and everything she said was just flat-out crazy because she said Mother was dead and I'd have to stay really quiet or they'd get me, too. I tried to make her tell me what happened to Mother, but she didn't make any sense and then I kept being so sleepy I couldn't stay awake."

There was a long silence, then Cal said, "Dad? Is Mother actually dead like Aunt Pam said?"

"I'm afraid so, son."

Cal began to cry and I opened my eyes a narrow slit to see Dwight lie down beside his son and hold him till we both fell asleep again.

CHAPTER
32

It is a bad plan that admits of no modification.

—*Publius*

Night's dark sky was a dirty gray when the three of us were awakened by a nurse with strawberry blond hair who came in to check Cal's vitals and to remove the IV needle from his wrist. We could hear the clatter of the stainless steel food cart working its way down the hall.

"Looks like this room's going to be empty real soon," she said cheerfully.

I could never deal with the life-and-death traumas of medicine, so whenever I come across someone like—I looked at her nametag—like Stephanye Sanderson, RN, I am always grateful that such women are there for the rest of us.

"How is he?" I asked.

She smiled at me, but addressed Cal with a formality that left him gravely pleased. "Your blood pressure's back in the normal range, Mr. Bryant, and your breakfast tray will be here in a little bit. What about you, Judge Knott? How's your head?"

"Much better," I told her. "It's still tender, but I don't have a headache anymore."

"Good. The doctor usually makes rounds by eight, so this young man can probably get dressed as soon as he's been examined."

I had caught a whiff of Cal's clothes in the ambulance last night and knew he'd be embarrassed to realize that he'd wet himself during one of the long sleeps of his captivity.

"Tell you what," I said, after I'd splashed water on my face, combed my hair, and put on lipstick. "How about I go pick up our toothbrushes and bring you some fresh clothes?"

"I can do that," said Dwight.

Cal put out an involuntary hand to hold him there, but I didn't take it as a slight. After what he'd been through, of course he wanted his dad there.

"No, you stay with Cal." I picked up the plastic bag with Cal's dirty clothes and slung my purse over my shoulder. "I won't be long."

"Okay. I'll walk you out." He handed Cal the TV remote. "Be right back, buddy."

As we walked down to the elevator, he thumbed his phone and called Paul's office. It was too early for the chief to be there, but when one of his officers answered, Dwight identified himself. "Any chance of getting a car over to the hospital to take my wife to the Morrow House?"

By the time we walked outside, a patrol car had pulled up to the curb. It was freezing cold and I was glad for my coat and gloves. Dwight gave me the key to the house and I promised to be back within the hour with coffee.

"No chasing up any more secret staircases," he told me as he opened the car door.

"You got it," I said, sliding in next to a young patrol officer.

Our lips touched, then Dwight closed the door.

"I appreciate the ride," I told the officer as we drove down the hill to the center of town.

"No problem, ma'am. Things are usually pretty quiet on a Monday morning." He looked barely old enough to drive, much less carry a gun. I can't decide if I'm getting older or recruits are getting younger. "Heard y'all had a lot of excitement last night."

"We did," I agreed. "Were you there?"

"No, ma'am. I'm pulling eleven-to-sevens this month, but man! I must've been in that Morrow House a half-dozen times since I was a little kid in the Cub Scouts and nobody ever said a word about secret passages and hidden rooms. That's awesome."

"Sounds like something out of a movie, doesn't it?"

"Yeah. I can't wait to see it. You reckon they'll open it to the public?"

"Probably," I said, thinking they'd be dumb not to. It would be a terrific drawing card and surely Betty Ramos had to be happy to see her suspicions confirmed. This was going to make everyone reevaluate old Peter Morrow and his reputation for playing both ends against the middle. No wonder his wife protested the closets under the main staircase. Had they been caught, the house would have been torched and he would have been shot or lynched as a traitor to the cause. Blood ran hot out in these hills during the Civil War. And not just during, but long after. Even now, I was willing to bet there would be plenty who would feel he had slimed the Morrow name.

On the other hand, he might have been genuinely conflicted—hating slavery, but loving the South? After all, he'd lost a son to that war. A daughter, too, if the romantic tales of a young girl's broken heart were true.

At the Morrow House, I thanked my driver again. Chivalry is not totally dead. Before driving off, he waited until I'd cranked my car and had actually backed out of the parking space.

A state trooper's car sat in front of the house and I saw lights on inside, but I had promised to get back to the hospital quickly, so I didn't stop to see if there were any new developments.

By the time I got to Jonna's house, the eastern sky was a bright pink and gold as the sun edged up to the horizon.

Once inside, I realized that the bag Dwight had packed for Cal on Friday probably held everything he would need this morning.

Friday. Only three days ago.

A weekend.

Normally, I would be walking into the courthouse this Monday morning, greeting clerks and attorneys—

"So, hey, how was your weekend?"

"Get much done this weekend?"

"Y'all go away for the weekend?"

—the casual chatter as another workweek begins.

Three days ago, I was a bride of one month, still adjusting to a husband, still learning not to say, "Oh, sure, I'll be there, sounds like fun" before I checked to see if his idea of a fun weekend was the same as mine.

From now on, there would be a child to consider as well. And not just any child, but one whose mother had been brutally murdered, who would be grieving, who would probably resent the hell out of me because I was alive and she wasn't.

"Two days ago, you stood in this very house and promised that if Cal was safely returned, you'd do whatever needed doing," my internal preacher reminded me.

"Your mother took on eight sons when she married their daddy," said his pragmatic roommate. *"Are you eight times less the woman?"*

I straightened my shoulders, put my makeup kit in a tote bag, and added Dwight's toiletry bag and a complete change of clothes for Cal.

As I locked the door and started down the walk, I saw Jonna's neighbor peering from the window and went over to tell him that we'd found Cal.

"Now, I'm glad to hear that," he said. "It's real bad about his mother, though. I reckon the funeral will be tomorrow?"

I told him we'd let him know as soon as we knew for sure.

———

On the way back to the hospital, I swung past a fast-food window to pick up two cups of steaming hot coffee and some sausage biscuits and was back in Cal's room before he'd finished his breakfast.

His eyes were red and I knew he'd been crying again. When he went into the bathroom to brush his teeth, Dwight uncapped his coffee and drank deeply. "I needed that."

"Is everything okay?"

"He wanted to know exactly how Jonna died and I told him. Not about the note or how she must have known what was going to happen, just that she couldn't have felt any pain or—"

He broke off as Cal stuck his head out of the bathroom. "Is it okay if I take a shower? I feel dirty."

"Sure," Dwight told him. "But you can't get dressed till after the doctor's seen you, okay?"

"Okay."

I unwrapped a biscuit and handed it to him. It was still warm and fragrant, the sausage nicely flavored with sage. As he took a bite, I said, "What's on the agenda today?"

"Cal wants to see her. What do you think?"

I shook my head. "That's a tough call. Has he ever seen a death?"

"Just dogs or cats." He took another bite. "No, I take that back. One of his classmates was in a bad car wreck right after school started. The whole class went to the funeral, but I don't know if the casket was open."

"If he really wants to see her, then I think you ought to take him. But go this afternoon or tomorrow morning when the two of you can be there alone."

"What if he wants to touch her?"

I remembered standing in front of Mother's coffin. Intellectually, I knew she was dead, but it wasn't till I touched the hands lying neatly folded that the permanence of her death sank in. From my earliest memories, her hands had danced across the piano keys when Daddy played his fiddle. They had shelled peas and butter beans, patted out biscuit dough, scrubbed bathtubs, plucked chickens, spanked disobedient sons and a willful daughter, cupped a flame to her cigarette, dealt out poker hands, and helped me hold the hymnal on Sunday morning so that I could follow the words. And always, always those hands had flashed in the air before her as she talked, enhancing her conversation and vividly depicting her emotions.

Daddy used to say, "Cut off your mama's hands and she couldn't talk," and to tease her, he'd catch her hands in his and hold them motionless till she laughed and pulled away.

But there in that casket, those hands had been cold and forever stilled.

"Deb'rah?" Dwight looked at me worriedly. "Shug?"

"Sorry." I shook my head and blinked away the tears. "I was thinking about Mother. You have to let Cal do what he wants, Dwight. Just give him enough time to do it. Don't hurry him."

We finished eating and Cal came out of the bathroom with a towel wrapped around him. His brown hair was damp and tousled and drops of water clung to his shoulder blades. At eight, his sense of modesty was in its most rudimentary stage of development, and when his towel slipped as he crawled back onto the bed, he didn't seem to notice or care.

The doctor, Cal's regular pediatrician, came in soon after, looked at his chart, and gave it as his opinion that Cal had not been seriously harmed by the cough syrup. "He had taken three or four doses by the time Mrs. Bryant called to report his sensitivity to the codeine. There couldn't have been all that much left in the bottle."

"So can I go home now?" asked Cal.

"Well, if it was me, cold as it is, I believe I'd put on a

coat and some shoes first," the doctor said and Cal laughed.

I handed Dwight the tote bag and followed the doctor out to the nurses' station to get his address and phone number so that we could send for Cal's records once we'd found a pediatrician down in Raleigh.

"Nice kid," said the doctor as he scribbled his e-mail address on a prescription pad.

"Any advice for his new stepmom?" I asked.

"Treat him kindly and respect what he's going through," he said promptly, "but don't let him use it to con you. Set the rules and hold him to them. Eight-year-olds are resilient and Cal's absolutely normal, so he's going to laugh and you'll think he's over it, then he's going to cry and you'll know he's not. Just relax and enjoy him. One good thing—you've got a couple or three years before he hits puberty. I suggest you make the most of them. Once the hormones kick in, all bets are off till he hits twenty."

"Yeah, I know," I said dryly.

"That's right. I heard you were a judge."

"I'm also the aunt of several teenagers," I told him.

He laughed. "Even better."

As we said good-bye, the elevator pinged and Paul Radcliff stepped off, carrying a Thermos of coffee that Sandy had sent over.

"We've both had the hospital's coffee," he said, following me into Cal's room. "Thought y'all might could use something stronger to get a jump-start on the day."

A second cup was welcome to both of us.

"Hey, Cal," he said. "How's it going?"

"Okay," the boy said. He was fully dressed now except for tying his sneakers.

"Everybody's real sorry about your mother, son."

Cal concentrated on his shoelaces.

"Jimmy's gonna skip school today and Miss Sandy wants you stay with them this morning."

Cal raised stricken eyes to his father. "Dad?"

"I'm sorry, buddy, but there are things I need to see to."

"Okay," he said in a small voice, but then he looked at me.

Hoping that I wasn't misinterpreting that look, I said, "That's awfully kind of Sandy, but I thought maybe Cal could help me this morning. We need to figure out what to take back to North Carolina with us tomorrow. Is that all right with you, Cal?"

"Yes, ma'am," he said gratefully.

CHAPTER
33

Perhaps my name, too, will be joined to theirs.

—Ovid

The grocery store was open as Cal and I drove down the hill, so we turned in and I picked up some empty cardboard boxes and a roll of strapping tape.

"Could we go and get Bandit now, too?" he asked.

"Good idea," I said. "He'll be really happy to see you. Did your dad tell you how he was the one who found us last night? That was pretty amazing."

"He's the smartest dog *I* ever knew," Cal said complacently.

———

Our stop at the Radcliff house was brief. Sandy was just back from dropping Jimmy off at school and she was deliberately matter-of-fact when she spoke with Cal about how well-behaved Bandit had been. When we were leaving, though, there were tears in her eyes as she hugged him.

With the dog in the car as our buffer, it was easier to talk to each other, and once we were at the house, it became easier still.

Cal already had a room of his own at the farm and he had stayed on after the wedding to spend Christmas with us, so he knew what was there and what he wanted to take with him. By the time Dwight arrived around noon, we had filled several boxes with his books and toys and most of his clothes. We left out his Sunday suit and the leather shoes that were almost too tight. "Mother said we could probably get one more month out of them," he said, "but I don't know about that."

I made sandwiches for lunch, then while they went to the funeral home, I cleaned out the refrigerator and started a load of laundry.

It was nearly two hours before they returned and Cal's freckled face was so pinched and drained that he didn't argue when I suggested he take a book and go lie down with Bandit for a while.

Once we were alone, Dwight told me that it had been a little rough. "He cried when he touched her face and he told her he was sorry she got killed, but I think he's handling it pretty good, overall."

"It was awful that Pam took him and scared the hell out of him and us, too, but in a weird way, going in and out of sleep for two days might have had one benefit," I said. "Don't you think it might have given his subconscious time to get used to the idea in a less traumatic way than if he'd been awake and scared the whole time?"

"Maybe. We stopped back by Mrs. Shay's so she could see for herself that he's all right."

"How's she doing?"

He shrugged. "It's still all about her. She can't deal with Pam, but she wanted me to know that the family portraits and most of the antiques here in the house were just loans to Jonna, and she wants them back. Thank God for Eleanor. She got there as we were leaving. Said for us not to worry about anything. She and her daughters will come over and take care of things over the next few months, dispose of the clothes and empty out the refrigerator and cupboards. There's no furniture here we want, is there?"

I shook my head. "You might want to sign an informal note that will allow Eleanor to act as your limited agent for now, then you and Cal can come back in the spring after he's settled at the farm. If it turns out that there's something he's really attached to, we'll find space for it down there. There are photo albums in Jonna's room that will mean a lot to him someday, so we should take those with us tomorrow."

He went up to check on Cal and came back to report that he was sound asleep.

"Any news about Benton?"

Dwight yawned and said, "He's got an attorney that's going to try to get him a first appearance today or tomorrow in the hopes of getting out on bail. Unless the guns and jewelry are found before he gets out, though, we can kiss a murder conviction good-bye. He'll deep-six any incriminating stuff as soon as he has a chance."

He yawned again and I said, "Why don't you lie down a while, too? You can't have slept much last night."

"What about you?"

"I had the cot, remember? Besides I thought I'd go over and pick up my phone unless you brought it back?"

"Sorry, shug. Didn't know it was there." He yawned a

third time and gave me a sheepish grin. "Well, maybe I will stretch out a few minutes till Cal wakes up."

———

The Morrow house was still swarming with police when I got there, and according to Agent Lewes, there were more officers going over Benton's house with a metal detector to try and locate the guns they presumed he'd hidden.

The trustees were also out in full force and so were members of the Shaysville Historical and Genealogical Society. Having decided that Nathan Benton was a thief and a murderer, they were now on the trail of something even larger in their eyes.

"That little company he was supposed to have sold before he retired here?" said Suzanne Angelo. "My husband made a few phone calls. He was the manager, not the owner."

"*And* we think he falsified his ancestry papers," Frederick Mayhew said darkly. "We don't think he's related to Bartholomew Benton at all."

"Now why would he lie about something like that?" I asked.

"For the same reason he stole things to give to the house," said Betty Ramos, who seemed to have a kind heart. "He's such a Civil War buff, I think he wanted to claim a part of that history as his own. He probably came across Bartholomew Benton's name when he was researching his family tree and decided that sounded like a more interesting background than his own Bentons. Or maybe he couldn't trace his own line very far back and since there were no more Bentons over here in

Shaysville, thought he could get away with saying our Bentons were his. Certainly today is the first time anyone's questioned the lineage he presented. Why would we? Unless someone claims to be related to Robert E. Lee or Washington or Lincoln, who would bother to go look up all the deeds and wills and census records he cited?"

I've never quite understood why some people brag about their family being here since the Revolution. I mean, so have mine, so have a ton of others. The way Americans intermarry, almost anybody who's been here three or four generations has at least one line that goes back that far. Maybe if I had more statesmen and officers perched in my family tree, I'd brag, too, but with so many bootleggers and dirt farmers and ancestors who did their best to avoid becoming cannon fodder no matter who was issuing the call to arms, it's hard for me to work up much pride about it.

Pride.

Pride kept Mrs. Shay from getting Pam the help she needed.

Pride had probably spurred Jonna to blackmail because she couldn't bring herself to tell her friends she didn't have five thousand for a class gift.

And then there was the dangerous pride of Nathan Benton, who had fashioned himself into a blue-blooded big fish in a very small pond.

Not that anyone connected with the Morrow House suspected blackmail. No, their assumptions made Jonna an innocent victim.

"It's too bad she didn't turn him in as soon as she realized what he'd done," said Suzanne Angelo. "She was probably going to let him withdraw his donations and return them to their rightful owners."

"Or else she caught him stealing the guns, too," said one of the other trustees. "Remember how he didn't want to invite Hamilton Erdman to come and address Sunday's meeting? We thought he was jealous of Erdman's reputation as a small arms expert, but I bet he took all three guns because he was afraid that the two he'd donated might be recognized."

In the office, a state police officer was going through Jonna's computer files one by one to see if there was anything else to incriminate Benton, but she obligingly printed out another copy of Cal's records for me as I found my phone and tucked it in my coat pocket.

"Glad to see you're okay today, Judge," said Agent Lewes, who was in the main hall when I came out to leave. Dwight and I agreed that he reminded us both of one of Daddy's droopy-faced hounds, and today more than ever when he admitted that it didn't look as if they were going to be able to charge Benton with Jonna's murder. But while we stood talking in the entry hall, his phone buzzed and a big smile lit up those baggy eyes.

"Got him!" he said when the call ended. "There was a second spare in the trunk of his car—so old and beat up, it looked like something he was taking to the dump, but when Clark took it out to lift up the mat, he felt something rattle. There's a slit in the tread just long enough to let him pull it apart and slide stuff inside. Long as they were just shifting the tire from one side of the trunk to the other, nobody noticed. We've got the guns, the cartridges, and the jewelry, too. Let's see the bastard talk his way out of this!"

CHAPTER
34

*So far as it goes, a small thing may give analogy
of great things.*

—*Lucretius*

Jonna's funeral was at ten o'clock Tuesday morning. Pam was still too out of it to attend, even though Dwight had spoken privately with Paul and the state agents and asked that she not be charged for abducting Cal. Dwight and Cal entered and sat with the family. I sat inconspicuously at the back of the church and watched as Lou Cannady and Jill Edwards, both elegant in black designer suits, spoke of their grief at losing their third musketeer. There was a huge wreath from her classmates.

Mrs. Shay wanted Cal to come back to the house afterwards, but Dwight stood firm and, to Cal's barely concealed relief (not to mention mine), told her that we needed to get on the road.

While I went by Cal's school to get his records and turn in his books, he and Dwight picked up some plastic sheeting at the hardware store to wrap the boxes we'd packed in case the weather turned messy again. They wedged them in the back of Dwight's truck, alongside Cal's bike and Bandit's wire crate, then covered everything with a well-secured tarp. Bandit rode in the cab of the truck with Dwight and Cal. There were more boxes in the backseat of my car, and our bags were in my trunk.

I led the way as we caravanned south. I agreed to keep my cruise control set smack on the speed limit and not a single mile over. Dwight agreed to keep up. Even stopping for lunch in Greensboro, we were home by mid-afternoon.

While I helped Cal unpack and settle in, Dwight checked in at the office.

He had kept me up to date on the investigation of J.D. Rouse's murder and I heard him call Terry Wilson and razz him about not finding the .45 that Sergeant Overholt used to shoot J.D. Nevertheless, Bo Poole was ready to close it out as a cleared case even though they would not have been able to convict Overholt for J.D.'s death without the gun.

"Don't you find one thing a little odd?" I asked as I finished unpacking our clothes and hung Dwight's suit back in his side of our walk-in closet.

"You mean something odder than Overholt knowing J.D. would be driving down that road? Or for that matter, how he even knew what J.D. drove, much less what he looked like when he just got back from overseas?"

"Well, I hadn't thought about those two points, but yes."

"What else?"

"Overholt had several handguns, right?"

"That's what Richards and Terry say."

"Yet he used a rifle to shoot his wife at fairly close range and a handgun to shoot a target that's moving away from him?"

Dwight frowned. "Good point. Maybe I'll ask Bo to hold off on closing the file right now. Give Richards another day on it, see if she can turn up new suspects."

"The wife's brother is definitely cleared?"

"Not definitely, but he seems unlikely. The crew all vouch for him, but even more, the developer saw him about ten or fifteen minutes before the shooting. He would have had to rush to the back of the property, through the woods, and get in position just as Rouse came driving past."

He showered and shaved while I wrapped the gift we were giving Kate and Rob's infant son—a jumper swing that clamps on a doorframe.

"Isn't he too little for that?" Cal asked dubiously as he watched me.

"He is right now, but in just a few months he should get a kick out of it. Want to sign the card?"

"What's his name again?"

"They haven't decided whether to call him Bobby or R.W., but his full name is Robert Wallace Bryant Junior, which now makes your Uncle Rob Robert Wallace Bryant Senior. You know what the Wallace is for, don't you?"

Cal shook his head.

"Before she married your grandfather, your grandma's name was Emily Wallace."

"And Dad is Dwight Avery Bryant because his grandmother was an Avery, right?"

"Right."

"And I'm Calvin for Dad's father and Shay for Mother."

"That's right," I said as I tied the package with a big blue bow. "And if I'm not mistaken, her Anson grandfather might have been a John."

I kept my voice as casual as possible because I wanted Cal to feel comfortable talking about Jonna with us.

"Who were you named for?"

"Well, my mother used to say she just thought it was a nice name. There aren't any Deborahs on either side of our family, though, and she did like family names. My middle name is Stephenson because that was *her* family name, so I've always had the feeling that there was a mystery about why she named me that."

"Does Mr. Kezzie know?"

"If he does, he's never said. If he tells you, let me know, okay?"

"Okay." He read through the welcome-baby card and said, "I think I'm gonna call him R.W." Beneath where I'd signed my name and Dwight's, he carefully wrote in newly acquired cursive, "For R.W., love, your cousin Calvin Shay Bryant."

———

The baby was adorable but he looked more like Dwight than Rob, who has Miss Emily's red hair and slender build.

"Takes after the good-looking side of the family," Dwight said with a grin for Cal.

When Kate read our card, she said to Cal, "Did Jake and Mary Pat put you up to this?"

"Up to what?" he asked.

"They want to call him R.W., too." She gave a mock sigh of regret. "Looks like I'm outvoted."

"Yay!" said Mary Pat, who was six months older than Cal. Her cheer was echoed by four-year-old Jake.

They had been a little stiff with Cal at first in deference to his new half-orphan status, but since both of Mary Pat's parents had died before she was three, she had no memory of losing a mother, and of course, Jake couldn't conceive of losing Kate, so they were quickly reverting to normal. By the time we were ready to go have supper with Miss Emily so that Kate could rest, they were back to teasing and shoving one another.

As the three children followed Dwight out to the car, Kate and Rob asked for the condensed version of what had happened in Virginia.

"We were hoping to see more of Cal as he got older, but not like this," Rob said, shaking his red head.

"Anything we can do to help," Kate said, "let us know."

"If it gets rough, I'll come borrow Jake and Mary Pat," I told them.

———

Because it was a school night, we cut the evening short. Cal was apprehensive about what his new teacher and classmates would be like, but Miss Emily had used her position as a principal in the school system to ensure that Cal would be in the same classroom as Mary Pat.

"You'll really like Mrs. Ferncliff," she promised Cal.

"She's going to be my teacher when I get to third grade," said Jake, who wasn't even in kindergarten yet.

When we turned onto our road that night, the headlights picked up the green-and-white sign on the shoulder that announced that it had been adopted by the Kezzie Knott family.

As Cal read it aloud, I spotted a fast-food cup lying at the base of the sign.

"Better stop and let me get it up before Reese sees it and wants you to process it for fingerprints," I told Dwight.

"Why?" asked Cal when I was back in the car with the cup.

I explained what adopting a road meant and how we'd picked up all the debris on Saturday morning. "But when we were coming back from lunch, I was riding with my nephew Reese and we saw somebody throw trash out their car window. Well, Reese went absolutely ballistic and chased down the car and—oh!"

"What?" asked Dwight.

"He went ballistic," I said again. "Only he didn't have a gun."

"Oh," said Dwight.

"What's ballistic?" Cal asked from the backseat.

"Means lose your temper," Dwight said slowly. "Do crazy things."

"So what did Reese do when y'all caught him?" Cal asked me.

I explained that the he was a she and that Reese had shamed her into going back and picking up the trash she'd tossed, but all the time, I was watching Dwight play with the possibilities.

———

Back at the house, while Cal went on into his room to brush his teeth and get ready for bed, I said, "Is it possible?"

"She had a bunch of her father's marksmanship medals framed on the wall," Dwight said. "He might have hung on to his service revolver and maybe he taught her to shoot, too. She certainly was devoted to him. And Richards says she reamed a guy out for dumping an occasional beer can. The cab of J.D.'s truck had no trash in it and we know he'd drunk at least one beer."

"And didn't you say his right-hand window was halfway down? What if he flung a can out right there in front of her every evening?"

Littering seemed like a bizarre reason to shoot someone, but I remembered Reese's rage. He's such an impulsive hothead that I could see him try to shoot out that girl's taillight if he'd been on foot.

And if he'd had a gun.

Dwight called Mayleen Richards from the kitchen phone, and when he came back, he gave a shrug to my lifted eyebrow. "She doesn't think it's so crazy. Wanted to know if you'd sign a search warrant or if she should ask someone else."

"I hope you told her someone else."

"I did."

Our separation of powers treaty was back in place.

But both of us went in to say good night to Cal. He was snuggled down under the covers and Bandit nestled at his feet as if he'd been sleeping there for years.

I dropped a light kiss on Cal's forehead and left so that Dwight could have a few quiet minutes alone with him. He was looking a little weepy-eyed and I had caught a glimpse of Carson's plush ear sticking out from under the pillow.

Made me feel a little weepy-eyed, too.

CHAPTER
35

*It is now clear, from what has been said, how
many are the causes of death.*

—*Theophrastus*

TUESDAY NIGHT, 25 JANUARY

At nine-thirty that evening, Deputies Mayleen Richards,
Raeford McLamb, and Jack Jamison rang the bell at the
small neat house in Holly Ridge. Immediately, they heard
the sharp bark of the little corgi. A moment later, Mrs.
Lydia Harper opened the door and blinked as she saw the
three standing there.

"Yes?"

"I'm sorry, Mrs. Harper," said Richards, "but we have
a warrant to search your house for a forty-five-caliber
revolver."

The older woman put her hand to her throat. "A
warrant?"

"Yes, ma'am." She held it out.

"It's so late. I was about to get ready for bed. Can't you come back in the morning?"

"I'm afraid not, ma'am."

"But you can't just come in here and stomp around my house and go through my things," she said, her temper flaring. "This is America. What gives you the right?"

"This search warrant," Richards said, offering it to her again.

Mrs. Harper snatched it from her hand and read it through from first sentence to last signature while the deputies waited outside in the chilled night air. It had begun to rain and the rain was predicted to turn into sleet by morning.

"I want to call an attorney," said Mrs. Harper.

"Fine," said Richards, "but we're going to start our search now. You can make this easy or you can make it hard. It's up to you." Struck by sudden inspiration, she added, "Besides, what would the Colonel say? It was his gun, wasn't it?"

Mrs. Harper stiffened, and then, in another of the sudden mood swings they had seen before, she crumbled. Tears flooded her eyes. "I didn't mean to kill him. I just wanted to scare him. Make him stop throwing his beer cans on the Colonel's road. Every day, another Bud Light can. I yelled at him once and he just gave me the finger and kept on going like he was king of the world and everybody else could clean up his mess. It got to the point that he'd wait till he saw me to toss a can because some days, if I went early, there might not be any Bud Lights. But if I was there, he'd slow down and throw out three or four cans at a time, like he'd saved them up just to spit on the Colonel's good name. But I never meant to kill him. I just wanted to shoot out his window. Let *him* clean up a mess for once."

Mayleen Richards shook her head. Not marksmanship, after all. Just an unlucky shot. And here they'd been figuring trajectories and angles, trying to work out how Overholt or Miguel Diaz's brother-in-law could have known when and where to be, when all along it was just a little old lady with a bee in her bonnet about honoring her father's memory.

The gun was in Colonel Frampton's dresser drawer. It appeared to have been cleaned and oiled since its last firing, but that was not too surprising for a woman who was so obsessively neat that even her coffee-table magazines were stacked in a graduated pile with the edges precisely aligned to the edge of the table.

As they came back down the hallway with the gun, McLamb stopped to look at the medals and commendations that were framed and hung on the wall alongside certificates for proficiency and meritorious service. Richards started to pass by and then her eye was snagged by the name on one of the marksmanship certificates: it was signed by a Captain John Forlines and it had been issued to Lydia Frampton Harper for scoring a 98% at a Fort Benning target range. The certificate was dated fifteen years earlier.

———

They had gone to bed early themselves and were almost asleep when the call came through. Deborah gave a sleepy protest, but she rolled over to listen to Dwight's end of the conversation. When Dwight snapped his phone back into the charger on the nightstand and said, "Can you believe it?" she replied, "Believe that Mrs. Harper shot J.D.? Sure."

"Not that she shot him, but that she kept her marksmanship certificate hanging on the wall."

"Rack another one up for pride," Deborah murmured as she fitted herself back into the curve of his arms.

"Pride? I'd call it arrogance."

"Close enough," she said and her lips found his while the cold winter rain beat against their windows.

ABOUT THE AUTHOR

MARGARET MARON grew up on a farm near Raleigh, North Carolina, but for many years lived in Brooklyn, New York. When she returned to her North Carolina roots with her artist-husband, Joe, she began a series based on her own background. The first book, *Bootlegger's Daughter*, became a *Washington Post* bestseller that swept the top mystery awards for its year and is among the 100 Favorite Mysteries of the Century as selected by the Independent Mystery Booksellers Association. Later Deborah Knott novels *Up Jumps the Devil* and *Storm Track* won the Agatha Award for Best Novel. To find out more about the author, you can visit www.margaretmaron.com.

When a family farm becomes nothing
more than a link in an agribusiness chain,
Deborah Knott discovers that greed
can lead to heartbreak and violence . . .

~

Please turn this page
for a preview of

Hard Row

by Margaret Maron

available in hardcover.

JANUARY

El Toro Negro sits next to an abandoned tobacco warehouse a few feet inside the Dobbs city limits. Back when the club catered to the country-western crowd, a mechanical bull used to be one of the attractions; but, after a disgruntled customer took a sledgehammer to its motor, the bull was left behind when the club changed hands. Now it stands atop the flat roof and someone with more verve than talent has painted a picture of it on the windowless front wall of the warehouse. As visibly masculine as his three-dimensional counterpart overhead, the painted bull is additionally endowed with long sharp horns. He seems to snort and paw at hot desert sands although it is a frigid night and more than a thousand miles north of the border. It is two weeks into January, and yet a white plastic banner that reads *"Feliz Navidad y Próspero Año Nuevo"* still hangs over the entrance. A chill wind sweeps across the gravel parking lot and sends beer cups and empty cigarette packs scudding like tumbleweeds until they catch in the bushes that line the sidewalk.

Every Saturday night, the parking lot is jammed with work vehicles of all descriptions and tonight is no exception. Pickup trucks with extended crew cabs predominate. Pulled up close to the club's side entrance is a refurbished school bus, its windows and body both painted a dark purple that looks black under the lone security light. A rainbow of racing stripes surrounds the elaborate lettering of the band's name. Los Cuatro Reyes del Hidalgo are playing here tonight and whenever the door opens, live music with a strong Texicano beat swirls out on gusts of warm air.

Like most of the Latinos clustered beneath the colored lights around the doorway, the muscular Anglo who passes them is without a woman on his arm. He has clearly been drinking and the bouncers at the door glance at each other, silently conferring if they should let him in; but he has already handed over his fifteen-dollar cover charge. They sweep him thoroughly with their metal detector and make him empty his pockets when the wand beeps for a handful of coins, then stamp the back of his hand and let him pass.

Inside, he heads straight to the far end of the long bar that stretches down the whole length of one wall. Even though dark faces beneath wide cowboy hats line the bar three and four deep, they move aside to let him prop a foot on the wooden rail and order a Corona. In addition to the hats, most of the other men are wearing tooled cowboy boots, fleece-lined jackets, and belt buckles as big as tamales. The Anglo is tall enough to see over the hats and when his beer comes, he takes a deep swig and scans the rest of the room.

On a low stage at the back, the Hidalgo Kings are belting it out on keyboard, drum, and guitars to an enthusiastic audience. Colored lights play across the dancers' bodies as their feet keep time to the pulsating rhythm. Between songs, the click of balls can be heard from the pool tables in a side room.

The bouncers keep an eye on the Anglo, but the sprawling club is crowded, men outnumber women at least four to one, and tempers can flare with little provocation. A Colombian accuses a Salvadoran of taking his drink when his back was turned and the bouncers move in to break it up.

At the bar, the Anglo orders another *cerveza*, and after a while, the bouncers relax their surveillance of him.

Shortly before midnight, he leaves his third beer on the counter and moves through the crowd toward the restroom just as a woman bundled in a bulky jacket and knitted hat urgently approaches a knot of men still nursing their beers.

"¿Donde Ernesto?" she asks.

With a tilt of his head, one of the men gestures toward one of the side rooms and the woman hurries over to the pool table. *"¡Ernesto! ¡Prisa!"* she says to the man who looks up when she speaks. *"Es Maria. El bebé está viniendo."*

He immediately throws down his cue and follows her through the crowd. His friends call after him, *"¡Buena suerte, amigo!"*

Inside the bathroom at the far end of the club, the big Anglo quickly grabs a man waiting his turn at a urinal. The man is smaller and shorter, and before he can defend himself, his white hat goes flying and the Anglo has his bolo tie in a stranglehold with his left hand while his right fist delivers a punishing blow to the victim's chin.

A second blow opens a gash over his eye. Gasping for

breath as his bolo tightens around his neck, the Latino fumbles frantically for a beer bottle lying atop others in the trash bin and in one sweeping motion smashes the end against the sink.

Several men reach to pull the two apart. Others open the door and cry out to the bouncers as the bottle gleams in the dull light.

Blood suddenly spurts across the white cowboy hat now trampled beneath their feet and the big Anglo crashes to the floor, writhing in pain.

CHAPTER

1

*If a man goes at his work with his fists he is not
so successful as if he goes at it with his head.*

—*Profitable Farming in the Southern States,*
1890

DEBORAH KNOTT
FRIDAY, FEBRUARY 24

A cold February morning and the first thing on my calendar was the *State of North Carolina* versus *James
Braswell and Hector Macedo.*

Misdemeanor assault inflicting serious bodily injury.

I vaguely remembered doing first appearances on them
both two or three weeks earlier although I would have
heard only enough facts to set an appropriate bond and
appoint attorneys if they couldn't afford their own. According to the papers now before me, Braswell was a
lineman for the local power company and could not only
afford an attorney, but had also made bail immediately.
His co-defendant, here on a legal visa, had needed an appointed lawyer and had sat in the Colleton County jail for
eleven days until someone posted his bail. Each was

charged with assaulting the other, and while it might have been better to try them separately, Doug Woodall's office had decided to join the two cases and prosecute them together since the charges rose out of the same brawl. Despite a broken bottle, our DA had not gone for the more serious charge of felony assault because keeping them both as misdemeanors would save his office time and the county money, something he was more conscious of now that he'd decided to run for governor.

Neither attorney had objected even though it meant they had to put themselves between the two men scowling at each other from opposite ends of the defendants' table.

Braswell's left hand and wrist had been bandaged last month. Today, a scabby red line ran diagonally across the back of his hand and continued down along the outer edge of his wrist until it disappeared under the cuff of his jacket. The stitches had been removed, but the puncture marks on either side were still visible. I'm no doctor, but it looked as if the jagged glass had barely missed the veins on the underside of Braswell's wrist.

The cut over Macedo's right eye was mostly hidden by his thick dark eyebrow.

I listened as Julie Walsh finished reading the charges. Doug's newest ADA was a recent graduate of Campbell University's law school over in Buies Creek. Small-boned, with light brown hair and blue-green eyes, she dressed like the perfectly conservative product of a conservative school except that a delicate tracery of tattooed flowers circled one thin white wrist and was almost unnoticeable beneath the leather band of her watch. Rumor said there was a Japanese symbol for trust at the nape of her neck but because she favored turtleneck sweaters and wore her long hair down, I couldn't swear to that.

"How do you plead?" I asked the defendants.

"Not guilty," said Braswell.

"Guilty with extenuating circumstances," said Macedo through his attorney.

While Walsh laid out the State's case, I thought about the club where the incident had taken place.

El Toro Negro. The name brought back a rush of mental images. I had been there twice myself. Last spring, back when I still thought of Sheriff Bo Poole's chief deputy as a sort of twelfth brother and a handy escort if both of us were at loose ends, a couple of court translators had invited me to a Cinco de Mayo fiesta at the club. My latest romance had gone sour the month before so I'd asked Dwight if he wanted to join us.

"Yeah, wouldn't hurt for me to take a look at that place," he'd said. "Maybe keep you out of trouble while I'm at it."

Knowing that he likes to dance just as much as I do, I didn't rise to the bait.

The club was so jammed that the party had spilled out into the cordoned-off parking lot. It felt as if every Hispanic in Colleton County had turned out. I hadn't realized till then just how many there were—all those mostly ignored people who had filtered in around the fringes of our lives. Normally, the Latinos wear faded shirts and mud-stained jeans while working long hours in our fields or on construction jobs. That night they sported big white cowboy hats with silver conchos and shiny belt buckles. The women who stake our tomatoes or pick up our sweet potatoes alongside their men in the fields or who wear the drab uniforms of fast-food chains as they wipe down tables or take our orders? They came in colorful swirling skirts and white scoop-neck blouses bright with embroidery.

We danced to the infectious music, drank Mexican beer from long-necked bottles, danced some more, then stuffed ourselves at the fast-food *taquerias* that lined the parking lot. I bought *piñatas* for an upcoming family birthday party, and Dwight bought a hammered silver belt buckle for his young son.

It was such a festive, fun evening that he and I went back again after we were engaged. The club was crowded and the music was okay, but it felt like ten men for every woman and when they began to hit on me, I had to get Dwight out of there before he arrested somebody.

So I could picture the club's interior as Walsh called her first witness to the stand.

"*Habla inglés?*" she asked.

Despite his prompt "*Sí,*" Macedo's attorney asked that I allow a translator because his own client's English was shaky.

I agreed and Elena Smith took a seat directly behind Macedo, where she kept up a low-pitched, steady *obligato* to all that was said.

"State your name and address."

The middle-aged witness twisted a billed cap in his callused hands as he gave his name and an address on the outskirts of Cotton Grove. His nails were as ragged and stained as his jeans. In English that was adequate, if heavily accented, he described how he'd entered the restroom immediately after Hector Macedo.

"Then that man"—here he pointed at Braswell—"he push me away and grab him—"

"Mr. Macedo?" the ADA prompted.

"*Sí*. And he hit him and hit him. Many times."

"Did Mr. Macedo hit him back?"

"He try to get away, but that one too big. Too strong."

"Then what happened?"

"Hector, he break a bottle and cut that one. Then he let go and there is much blood. Then the bouncers come. And the *policía*."

"No further questions, Your Honor," said the ADA.

Braswell's attorney declined to cross-examine the witness, but Macedo's had him flesh out the narrative so as to make it clear to me that the smaller man had acted in self-defense when Braswell left him with no other options.

A second witness took the stand and his account echoed the first. When Walsh started to call a third witness, Braswell's attorney stood up. "We're willing to stipulate as to the sequence of events, Your Honor," whereupon the State rested.

Macedo, a subcontractor for a drywall service, went first for the defense. Speaking through the interpreter, he swore to tell the truth, the whole truth and nothing but the truth. According to his testimony, he had been minding his own business when Braswell attacked him for no good reason. He did not even know who Braswell was until after they were both arrested.

Under questioning by Braswell's lawyer, he admitted that he was at the club that night with one Karen Braswell. Yes, that would be the other defendant's ex-wife although he had not known it at the time. Besides, it wasn't a real date. She worked with his sister at the Bojangles' in Dobbs and the two women had made up a casual foursome with himself and a friend. He'd had no clue that she had a husband who was still in the picture until the man began choking and pounding him. Macedo's attorney called the sister, who sat in the first row behind her brother and strained to hear the translator, but Braswell's attorney objected and I sustained.

"Defense rests."

"Call your first witness," I told Braswell's attorney.

"No witnesses, Your Honor."

"Mr. Braswell," I said as his attorney nudged him to stand. "I find you guilty as charged."

"Your Honor," said his attorney, "I would ask you to take into consideration my client's natural distress at seeing his wife out with another man while he was still trying to save their marriage."

"I thought they were divorced," I said.

"In his mind they're still married, Your Honor."

"Ms. Walsh?"

"Your Honor, I think it's relevant that you should know Mr. Braswell was under a restraining order not to contact Mrs. Braswell or go near her."

"Is this true?" I asked the man, who was now standing with his attorney.

He gave a noncommittal shrug and there was a faint sneer on his lips.

"Was a warrant issued for this violation?"

"Yes, Your Honor, but he made bail. He's due in court next week. Judge Parker."

"What was the bail?"

"Five thousand."

I could have increased the bail, but it was moot. He wasn't going to have an opportunity to hassle his ex before Luther Parker saw him next week. Not if I had anything to say about it.

"Ten-days active time," I told Braswell. "Bailiff, you will take the prisoner in custody."

"Now, wait just a damn minute here!" he cried; but before he could resist, the bailiff and a uniformed officer had him in a strong-arm grip and marched him out the door that would lead to the jail.

Macedo stood beside his attorney and his face was impassive as he waited for me to pass judgment. I found him guilty of misdemeanor assault and because he'd already sat in jail for eleven days, I reduced his sentence to time served.

He showed no emotion as the translator repeated my remarks in Spanish, but his sister's smile was radiant. "*Gracias,*" she whispered to me as they headed out to the back hall to pay the clerk.

"*De nada,*" I told her.

"*State* versus *Rasheed King,*" said Julie Walsh, calling her next case. "Misdemeanor assault with a vehicle."

A pugnacious young black man came to stand next to his lawyer at the defendant's table.

"How do you plead?"

"Hey, his truck bumped me first, Judge."

"Sorry, Your Honor," said his attorney.

"You'll get a chance to tell your story, Mr. King," I said, "but for our records, are you pleading guilty or not guilty?"

"Not guilty, ma'am."

It was going to be one of those days.